LOREN HUXLEY

PARADISE ENTOMBED

SEAS OF PARADISE BOOK ONE

Paradise Entombed
Copyright © 2023 Loren Huxley
Twisted Heart Publications, LLC
All rights reserved.

All rights reserved. No part of this publication may be reproduced, distributed, or transmitted in any form or by any electronic or mechanical means, including information storage and retrieval systems, photocopying, and recording, without written permission from the author, except as permitted by U.S. copyright law. For permission requests, contact Twisted Heart Publications, LLC, or the author at contact@lorenhuxley.com.

This is a work of fiction. All names, characters, places, and events are of the author's imaginations. Any resemblances to historical events, locations, and people both living and dead is purely coincidental.

© Cover Design by Etheric Tales
Internal Artwork by Etheric Tales
Editing by Norma Gambini at Norma's Nook Proofreading

ISBN: 978-1-962508-00-1

DEDICATION

To my friends and family members, thank you for supporting me, but I hope you never read this.

To everyone else, if you know me in real life, no you don't. Now turn that page and STFUATTDLAGG.

AUTHOR'S NOTE

Paradise Entombed is an adult, dark fantasy romance that contains mature and graphic content not suitable for all audiences. The main character is a villain. If you're looking for a redemption arc or a bad guy turned good, you won't find it here. This is a fictionalized work of literature, and I in no way condone any situations or actions that may take place between the main characters.

This is **NOT** a safe read. If you have never read a dark romance before, please do not start with this one.

If you wish to go in blind, please skip ahead to *Chapter One.* For a complete list of content warnings, you can find them by scanning the QR code on the following page, by visiting Loren Huxley's website www.lorenhuxley.com, or by emailing her at contact@lorenhuxley.com.

Reader Discretion is Advised.

CONTENT ADVISORY

Paradise Entombed is a dark romance that includes the following content ...

If any of these situations are triggering for you, please do not read this book. Self care is best care.

Paradise Entombed is the first book in the *Seas of Paradise* series. While it's primarily an m/f romance, the main character is building her harem as the series goes, so sharing is a common theme.

BONUS CONTENT INSIDE

Keep reading after the final chapter for an exclusive look at *Seas of Malice,* the second installment in the *Seas of Paradise* series.

CARTHINIA

PRESENT DAY

PRINCESS EZRAH VARREN

FORTRESS HEDRA, CENTRAL CARTHINIA

I stand on the gilded balcony, dressed in nothing but dark underlace and a matching tiara. Sweat slicks my palms, my nape. Icy wind whips at my long golden hair, flinging it into my burning eyes and tear-soaked cheeks. Everything aches. The force of the cold is almost crippling as I swing one leg over the side of the metal railing and prepare to jump.

A flurry of snowfall bombards the world below, covering everything—the pines, the hills, the glittering castle walls. It's bright against the night sky. Obtrusive. The only thing that hasn't been consumed by it is the pond underneath my balcony, but even without the ice or snow on top, I know the water's deadly. The drop alone might kill me. But then again, that's kind of the point.

You can do this, Ezrah. Just let go.

It hurts to breathe, like there's a boulder crushing my chest. My heart roars as I reach for the black tiara stuck to my braided coronet and yank it free. Golden threads come with it—not hair anymore, but solid metal. I fling the crown into the pond. It splashes as it lands, but the noise gets lost over the whistling wind, the howling wolves from the forest surrounding Fortress Hedra. Black waters consume the metal band in an instant, ripples fading as quickly as they appear.

Me next. My numb fingers tighten on the gilded rail, refusing to cooperate. *Fucking do it already.*

"Ezrah, what in Daliah's name are you doing out there?" My husband's smug and callous voice comes from the open doorway. He steps onto the balcony, wearing nothing but a black towel around his hips.

Water drips from Malin's curly undercut, the dark strands turning stiff as the wind hits him. He doesn't shiver or wrap his arms around himself. Instead, he leans against the palace walls and assesses my own scantily clad figure.

A cruel smile twists his lips, his eyes landing on my breasts. "Mmmm. Black's a good color on you."

My cheeks heat at the words. At how cheap they make me feel. At the way my body responds when it's been made to feel that way. Years of training got me to this point, transformed me into the perfect plaything for a man like Malin Varuz.

My nipples brush against the underlace that he's forced me to wear, forming stiff peaks through the sad excuse for a nightgown. It's the push I need to swing my other leg over the railing.

Spitting the hair from my mouth, I grip the palisade so hard, my knuckles turn white.

"I'm a necromancer, Ezrah," he says. "If you jump, I'll bring you back as a construct and you'll have no choice but to obey me. It's better you submit now by choice rather than later by force."

It's not a matter of *can he do that*. I know he can. Malin is one of the greatest mages in Ranada, his talents *almost* on par with my father's. If he weren't, I wouldn't be here right now, his hand-picked prize for sparing our kingdom from his skeletal hordes.

"If I jump, you might be able to resurrect my body, but you can't bring back my mind," I say.

"And that's where you're wrong." He rakes a hand through his stiff hair and swaggers to me. "If you jump, the only thing I lose is the ability to sire a child with you, but you'll lose a great deal more."

He slowly traces his index finger up the length of my arm then leans in close. Warm, wine-scented breath caresses my ear, my neck, and an involuntary shiver runs down my spine. "So, what'll it be? Would you rather be my construct or my wife? I'll take either."

"Please," I whisper. "I just want to go home."

"You are home. Now, give me your hand and I'll help you off this balcony."

Tears burn the backs of my eyes. I don't know why this is happening to me—why Malin attacked our kingdom last year or why he chose me over my sisters—but my whole body trembles at the idea of having to submit to him. Of having to consummate this new marriage. He doesn't look like a monster, but not all monsters are made from fur and teeth. In my kingdom, it's the mermaids you have to watch out for, the ones with pretty words and even prettier faces. They'll lure you to your death in a heartbeat.

I have no doubt that Malin will be the death of me . . . except I'll never die. I'll live in this nightmare forever as his prize.

As I reach for my husband's hand, my numb fingers shake from fear and cold. White puffs of air spill from my frozen, burning lips. I'm not meant for this weather. I'm meant for the hot sand and ocean breezes half a world away.

"Good girl," Malin says.

He pulls me over the railing, and I stumble into his chest. Thick, muscular arms wrap around me, but only long enough for him to wipe the hair from my face and throw his towel around my shoulders. Naked, he guides me into our bedroom and shuts the door behind him.

The lock latches.

He nudges me toward the roaring fireplace then pushes down on my shoulder. Hard. Wincing, I collapse onto my knees and land in a pile of soft animal furs. Pain blooms where he's touched me, a ruby welt forming over my glittering, gem-infused skin.

"I like you better on your knees," Malin says. He runs his fingers through my hair then fists the locks in his palm. I whimper as he yanks my head back, and our gazes meet.

"Malin," I plead.

He clicks his tongue, and his black irises fill with shadows. "That name isn't meant for dirty sluts like you."

My mouth falls open, cheeks burning with anger.

"There's no point in denying it, Ezrah. That's why I picked you. I've heard all about your conquests—in the shooting tourneys *and* in bed. Prince Remi, Prince Leon, Princess Marri, General Oren . . . Should I go on?"

Shit.

A lead ball drops into my stomach. Outside, the whistling wind whips against the glass balcony doors, and garden furniture slams into the railing. It would be better to be out there, to be anywhere other than in this room.

My throat turns bone dry. Pins and needles prick the tips of my fingers and toes. Scorching heat exits the fireplace in waves, but I barely feel it. "You knew?" I ask.

"Of course, I knew. Everyone in Ranada knows you'll let anyone between your legs."

The words sting.

I try not to stare at Malin's nakedness, but with his erect cock just inches from my face, it's impossible not to. When he sees me looking, a sly half-smirk spreads across his cheeks. "You look so innocent," he whispers. "So well behaved."

He runs his thumb across my trembling bottom lip then pulls it down. The gaze in Malin's eyes is pure lust—hotter than the roaring fire at my back—as he slips his thumb between my teeth. "Why don't you show me what that pretty little mouth of yours can do?"

My pulse pounds between my thighs, and I clench them together, shifting uncomfortably on the fur rugs. The pain in my shoulder barely registers as I twirl my tongue around Malin's thumb and cast a sidelong glance at his growing erection. It will be a challenge to fit the whole thing in my mouth. Somehow, I doubt there's going to be much choice.

"Spread your legs," Malin says, pulling his thumb away.

For a second, I hesitate.

"Now, slut." He grinds his fingers into my shoulder and I fall forward, tears blurring my vision.

The pounding between my legs is now a steady, embarrassing ache that I don't want him to see. Wincing, I push myself off the floor, back into a kneeling position, and do as he says. The underlace offers no privacy, no protection, as he cups his hand over my cunt and squeezes. Hard.

I yelp then whimper when he slides his hand away.

"Wet already?" Malin asks. He lets out a satisfied chuckle then pushes against my chest so that I fall backward into the animal furs. Without wasting any time, he leans over me, slips his thumb beneath the underlace, and presses against my clit.

"A piercing? How scandalous." He tugs on the ring and I scream, the pain white-hot. "I wonder what your father would think of this."

My ears ring. Swallowing, I tear my gaze away from him and stare into the fire, but his fingers keep tugging on the piercing, keep tracing slow circles around my clit. Within seconds, the pain is replaced by pleasure, and I squirm beneath him, moaning against the sensation.

So close. I'm so close.

Seconds before I climax, Malin pulls his hand away and withdraws it from the underlace.

"Please, Mal—" One look at him and I know better than to finish that word. "Your Majesty, don't stop."

I hate the words. Hate him. Hate that I'm begging this monster to touch me, but he's reduced me to a heaping pile of need on the floor, and I doubt he'll let me finish the job myself. Sweat clings to my aching body, my breaths come in ragged gasps. I touch the edges of my one-piece and debate dipping my hand inside.

"You really are something." He returns his fingers to my cunt and whispers a low incantation under his breath. It sounds like gibberish. When the words are over, the tips of his fingers glow dark purple. "It's fun to see you beg, though. I think we'll make this a permanent arrangement."

"What do you mean?"

Malin smirks. "Come for me and you'll find out."

His thumb is back on my clit, tracing slow circles with his glowing fingertips. Panting, I fist the furs in my palms and close my eyes. "I'm close."

"Beg me to let you finish."

I bite my bottom lip.

"Beg me."

I can feel it building, so I throw my head back and thrust my hips against him. My muscles tense and untense, but nothing happens; it's as if I'm being held in a state of near release. Tears fill my eyes, frustration and desperation bubbling to the surface. "What did you do to me?" I cry.

"From now on, when you want to come, you'll

have to ask permission first." His thumb keeps moving in slow, agonizing circles, each one so painful, it makes my entire body ache.

"You can't do this!"

He chuckles at that. "Beg. I want to hear how desperate you are."

I can't breathe. I can't think. The only thing I can feel is the throbbing between my legs. A full minute passes like this. Then two. Shame burns bright hot as I say the words he's been waiting to hear. "Please, may I come?"

"Good girl. That wasn't so hard, was it? Go ahead and come for me."

I unravel underneath his thumb into the most explosive orgasm I've ever had. Legs shaking, I scream until tears roll down my cheeks and my mind seems to detach from my body. Malin pulls his hand away and shoves his glistening thumb between my teeth.

"Lick it clean."

I obey, cleaning myself off him through half-lidded eyes. It's all I can do to keep from falling asleep right then and there, especially with the warm fire heating my aching skin. His eyes look gentler now and for a second, he reminds me of someone I know—or rather, someone I used to know, but that person is long gone and never coming back. Still, the memory is enough to make my heart clench.

Without thinking, I reach out, brush the black hairs from his face, and let myself pretend it's him.

Malin sighs. I think he's going to lean into the touch, but then I blink and the softness is gone, replaced by a sneer. "You're not done yet. Not even close."

He flips me over, pulls my underlace aside, and sheaths himself inside me in one sharp thrust. Fuck. I've never felt so full before. Panting, I lift my head and try to relax around him, take his length in stride. Malin wants none of that. He grabs a fistful of my hair and pushes my face into the floor.

His cock slides out of me then back in, all the way to the hilt. The sound of my scream is muffled by the furs in my open mouth. "That's it, Ezrah. Scream louder." Again, he pulls all the way out before slamming home.

Letting go of my hair, Malin grabs my hips and digs his nails in. Pain blooms. Black dots flicker across my vision. I moan against the intrusion. The fullness of him inside me is too much, and my cunt clenches around his cock as he pumps into me hard and fast.

"I can feel you getting tighter. Why don't you reach between your legs and play with your clit? I want to feel you come on my cock."

I swallow but don't move. It's too embarrassing. I can't let him watch me—

"I don't like to repeat myself."

Hands trembling, heart racing, I do as he says. My strokes start slow then turn frantic like his, and within minutes, I'm practically writhing against him. I'm so close, and then I remember I have to beg for it.

"Please let me come."

His thrusting is more than I can bear.

"Please, Your Majesty," I say between gritted teeth.

Whack!

He slaps his palm against my ass, and my pleasure reaches a fever pitch. "Gods, the noises you make are so fucking pathetic. Go ahead. Come on my cock like a good little slut."

He doesn't need to tell me twice. I squeeze his cock with my cunt and back my ass into him, driving him deeper. The tension explodes, and I shudder around him, the woman I was before tonight, before this marriage, shattering to dust. Too bad Malin isn't the kind of man who'll pick up the pieces, fix what's broken.

His release follows mine. The second he finishes spilling himself inside me, he shoves me off and rolls onto his back, breathing deeply. Orange light casts strange shadows on his scarred chest, and the urge to run my fingers across it hits me out of nowhere. Instead, I curl up beside him but keep my fingers to myself, my mouth shut.

"Next time I catch you out on that railing," Malin says, rolling so that we're face-to-face. "There better be a damn good reason for it. I won't pull you back a second time."

And with that, he leans over and runs his thumbs under my tear-stained eyes. "Clean yourself up. You look like shit."

VARREN

EARLIER...

PRINCESS EZRAH VARREN

THE GOLDEN COAST, CAPITAL OF VARREN

A thread of amethyst light shoots into the sky then bursts—a million fireworks exploding across the horizon. And then they're gone, the light replaced by a flickering oil lantern in my periphery.

White seafoam laps against the sand, tickling the edges of my bare feet. A shiver runs through me, the water so much colder than I expected it would be. As dawn crests the horizon, I scoot my butt farther into the sand and lean back against Tristan, watching pinks and oranges bloom across the blue-tinted sky. The moon is still visible, the stars glittering beacons overhead.

"Tristan," I whisper, staring out into the wide expanse of sapphire ocean. His black ship bobs in the harbor, and I watch it with tears in my eyes. Soon, he'll be going on wild adventures and I'll be trapped here, in a kingdom I never wanted and didn't ask for.

A ball wedges in my throat. I try to swallow it down but can't. My home is on that ship, on the open ocean with him. "Take me with you," I whisper, not bothering to look away from the skyline.

Tristan slips his arms around me and pulls me tight against his chest. "We both know your father would never let that happen. You're Varren, Ezzy, and I'm a privateer. There are rules."

"I can run away. I can—"

He scoots aside my long golden hair and plants a trail of kisses up the column of my throat. Normally, that would make my breathing hitch, my pulse quicken, but not today. Seagulls call overhead, and tiny rowboats bounce across the waves, approaching the ship that will take Tristian away . . . again.

"Arrovin pays for that ship," Tristan says. "The crew is loyal to him, not me. One look at you and they'll know who I've taken. We wouldn't even make it out of port."

Blinking back tears, I turn my cheek from him when he tries to kiss me. Emotions make my throat too thick to talk so I stare instead, focusing on anything but him. The clouds break, lighting the waves in brilliant flashes of gold. A wall of rocks surrounds us, hides us from the world, but I can hear the city thrumming to life. Footsteps shuffle against creaking wooden planks. Loud men shout profanities as they haggle for fair to Alta, the nearest port city, which is a week's journey away.

One week. I would give anything for Tristan's voyage to be that short.

"I hate it here," I say.

He squeezes my waist. "I know."

"I belong out there, not cooped up in a castle hosting dinner parties, waiting for my parents to marry me off to the highest bidder. I want more than that."

Silence thickens the air.

The sun rises, heating my cheeks, my skin, igniting me in rays of gold. Light bounces off my glittering flesh, transforming it into a beacon. Tristan is right. Even if he wanted to take me, I couldn't go. Not with skin that sparkles like crushed gemstones or hair that turns to gold when it's pulled from the scalp. My body is as much a prison as Daddy's palace.

"When will you be back?" I ask, twisting the golden strands around my index finger. Maybe if I yanked them all out and flayed the skin from my bones, they'd finally leave me be.

"I'm not coming back, Ezzy." Tristan's voice is barely a whisper. "Your father placed my ship under Governor Harquin's command. I'm to port in Alta until further notice."

I grind my molars together and shake my head. "No, he can't—"

"He can and he did." Tristan kisses my shoulder, nuzzles his nose against it, but I can't bring myself to look at him.

"Ezzy, no suitor is going to marry you if they think you've been ruined by some lowlife privateer."

"But you're not . . . We haven't . . ."

"Arrovin found out about us."

My stomach drops to my butt. My ears buzz, garbling the sound of his next words.

"He saw us kissing last night. Someone must've told him where we'd be." Tristan squeezes me again, and a water droplet rolls down my shoulder. When I glance back at him, his eyes are red-rimmed, his messy blond hair covering blotchy cheeks.

"I can change Daddy's mind," I say.

Tristan releases a dry chuckle. "He watched me act untoward with his youngest daughter. I don't think—"

"It's not untoward if you tell him your intentions are to marry me."

Tristan shakes his head. "I come from a long line of criminals, Ezzy. I have no money, no lands, no titles. Hells, even my ship belongs to your father. What right do I have to be with someone like you? Or to ruin you for someone else?"

"So, this is it? You're just going to leave me

behind and never look back?" I ball my hands into tight fists and bury them in the thick, slushy sand. It's all I can do to keep from screaming.

"I don't want this, Ezzy."

"What do you want, Tristan?"

"You know what I want." Sighing, Tristan lets go of my waist and pushes the pale locks from his seagreen eyes.

"No, I don't," I say. I mean it. I've been sneaking away with this man for almost three years now and he still hasn't claimed me, hasn't proposed, hasn't made promises of grandeur or offered to whisk me away from my spoiled life of tedium.

"I want you in that damned ship." The words are unusually forceful. "I want you in my bed, laid bare in front of the open ocean, where I can take you wherever and whenever I want."

Heat curls in my gut. The image of it has me looking anywhere but at him.

"I want to ruin you like you've ruined me." His hand lands on my thigh, inching up the pink silk dress that covers it. Gasping, I close my eyes and lean my head against his thickly muscled chest.

"You're all I think about. Gods, Ezzy, you have no idea how hard it is not to rip you out of that dress and take you right here, right now, where anyone could spot us."

Something like a mewl escapes my lips as I

imagine that very scene playing out. What would people say to see their king's favorite daughter taken by the captain of the *Black Death*? Ruined so publicly that no one else could barter for her hand?

Wetness pools between my thighs, and my heart roars in my chest.

"Then do it," I whisper.

"You sure?" Tristan slides his hand between my legs and cups me through the layered dress.

Moaning my approval, I part my legs for better access. On the other side of the rocky cove, the shipyard is in full swing. People are laughing and swearing, no idea we're tucked away only a few feet past the docks. "I'm sure, Tristan."

His hand brushes against my clit, teasing me through the soft fabric. "I can't. The guards would pull me off you in two seconds flat. Besides, you deserve better than a quick fuck in the sand." He bites my earlobe, and I shudder out a breath.

"I don't want my first time to be with a man I hate," I say. The words don't matter. I can tell by the way Tristan pulls his hand away that he's made up his mind. Still, I continue, determined to make him hear me. "I don't want some cruel man to marry me for the political alliances my family can offer them. Please, if you won't take me with you, then at least make it so no one else will want me."

The waves reach my ankles now, washing the

sand away from my closed fists. Already, the humid air tastes like salt and sweat and stale beer.

"I'm sorry."

The abrasive sand scrapes my knees, turning them an angry shade of ruby red as I crawl away from him. I wipe at my eyes then brush the dirt from the front of my dress, staring at it rather than him as the sand granules fall into the ocean. With a groan, Tristan wobbles to his feet and reaches for my hand. I jerk it away and take a step back. Sharp rocks dig into my skin, trapping me between Tristan and the cliffside.

"Ezzy..."

"Goodbye, Tristan." I tuck a loose strand of hair behind my ear and stand up straighter. "I hope you have a very happy life in Alta."

"Don't be like that. This is hard enough already." He squeezes my shoulders, and I stare at the sand and squish it between my toes, unwilling to let him see me cry.

"Don't touch me." I press my hands against his bare chest, feeling his heart hammer beneath my palm. The only thing covering his body is a pair of loose-fitting breeches with a dagger fitted to them—a dagger I made for him on his twenty-fifth birthday out of sea glass and white shells. Scars line his sun-kissed skin, blade wounds from too many fights gone wrong.

"I wish I'd never met you, Tristan Fontaine."

I shove him, but he doesn't budge. His body is a looming presence over mine. "Let me go."

"Ezzy, I love you."

"Fuck you, Tristan. I hope your ship sinks at sea." I duck underneath his arms, which have me pinned to the rocks. Snatching my shawl off a pile of sand, I wrap it around myself then step over the cliff and never look back. It's the hardest thing I've ever had to do.

I love you too, you fucking asshole.

CARTHINIA

PRESENT DAY

PRINCESS EZRAH VARREN

FORTRESS HEDRA, CENTRAL CARTHINIA

There are tears in my eyes, on my cheeks and chin. I'm practically drowning in them. Swallowing, I bury my face into the soft furs that envelop me, breathing in the scent of wood ash and tanned leathers. I wait for Tristan's arms to surround me, to soothe me the way they used to whenever I had a bad dream, but they don't.

Of course, they don't. He's gone.

It's too much to think about Tristan right now, given everything that's happened. So, I push those memories aside and wipe the sticky tears from my face.

Wallowing isn't a good look on me. I'm a woman of action, and when action doesn't work, a woman of avoidance. With Malin, that means jumping off balconies and not thinking about the consequences.

With Tristan . . . With Tristan, that means never looking back.

As the dream fades, my heart rate steadies. And the reality of my newest hell comes crashing down.

Malin.

Bitterness seeps from the center of my chest to the marrow of my bones. I'm trapped in a situation I've spent my whole life avoiding. Sold to the highest bidder. Forced into a loveless marriage to a cruel man whose only use for me lies in the space between my legs. Every part of me rebels at being here, in a landlocked country surrounded by forest and ice, so far from everything and everyone I've ever known and loved. The balcony would have been a mercy.

Rolling to my side, I curl into a ball and run my hands along the soft furs that encompass me. They're so warm, it almost feels like home. Light shines from overhead, and I open my eyes a sliver, prepared to take it in. It's white and bright—the color of snowfall.

Pins prick the sides of my temples. Sweat slicks my skin. Wincing, I grope around for the blankets and slide the furs up my legs, over my head. Darkness. An escape. Part of me knows that staying like this isn't an option—I need a tincture for my head and an escape from the warmth—but the other part of me, the one that doesn't care about pain, is content to let me hide in here until the world crumbles to dust.

"I'll be in meetings all day today," a smooth voice whispers.

My breath catches, and I hug the blankets a little tighter. If I ignore him, maybe he'll go away, forget I'm here.

"The guards will show you around, take you wherever you want to go." The mattress sinks and dips where Malin sits on the corner. "Unless, of course, you plan on staying in bed all day."

Better to face him now rather than later.

With trembling fingers, I peel back the edges of the blankets and am met by stinging brightness and crisp winter's air. Shivering, I pull the furs down just enough to catch a glimpse of Malin as he laces his leather boots and buttons the top of his silk tunic. He doesn't look any less frightening in the daylight. Dark black hair hangs over his pale face in messy half-curls. Black veins line the underside of his glossy, obsidian eyes—no pupils or irises, just a void-like darkness that shakes me to my core.

Say something.

"Did you carry me to bed last night?"

Not that.

Malin doesn't look at me. His fingers are too busy threading shirt buttons. "You'll want to familiarize yourself with the layout of the palace. I've been told it can be difficult to navigate."

"So, I'm not your prisoner then?" I ask, inching the rest of my head from its protective cocoon. The balcony doors are open and snowfall trickles in, the color a bright contrast to the black tiles in Malin's bedchambers.

"Do you want to be my prisoner? I can chain you to the bed if you'd like, but I won't have time to play until nightfall."

The words make my stomach curl. Heat spreads between my thighs and I quickly snap them together as I imagine myself splayed across the massive four-poster bed.

What's wrong with you, Ezrah?

Smoothing back my messy hair, I sit up just as Malin stands. "If I'm not your prisoner, what am I?" I ask.

"My wife." He shrugs and places an obsidian diadem on his head. It blends almost perfectly into the black locks. "My slut. My queen, too, once you've earned the title." Straightening the crown over his curls, Malin strides toward the door and leans against it, crossing his arms.

And then the sunlight hits him.

The glossy crown shimmers, little diamonds twinkling within it like it's made of stardust. He offers up a sly half-smirk, and flecks of silver swirl inside his abyssal eyes. "I came to the conclusion a while ago that it's easier to turn a slut into a queen than a queen into a slut. Eventually, you'll learn the inner workings of our kingdom, but I don't have time to coddle you today."

He gives me a long once-over then clicks his tongue. "Try not to fall into the lake while I'm gone. It'll be hard enough to fish your crown out of it. Don't want to deal with your corpse as well." And with that, Malin pushes off the wall and leaves, shutting the door behind him.

What just happened?

Brows furrowed, I climb out of bed and shiver when the winter wind slaps my tanned flesh. No underlace. Malin must've stripped me bare in my sleep. Crossing my arms, I scurry to the balcony doors and slam them shut, twisting the latch behind me. Goosebumps cover my arms, and my nipples tighten into peaks.

Clothes. Where to find clothes?

A quick scan of the room reveals a gown draped over the front of Malin's mahogany desk. It's long and black, with slits high up the sides, no doubt intended for easy access to my cunt. When I hold it up to the sunlight, all the air whooshes from my lungs. Tossing it back onto the desk, I shake my head and scan the room again, searching for something else—anything else—all to no avail.

The dress is completely sheer, meant to expose every inch of my naked body—my nipples, navel, the golden curls between my legs. There's no underlace in sight, nothing at all that might help me cover up.

"No."

The Varren are known for their bodies—golden hair, golden eyes, and golden blood. Sun-kissed skin that glimmers like it's been crafted from goldstone. The legends say we're descendants of Eliah, the goddess of sunlight and joy, and while I don't know if that's true, I do know that people come from all over Ranada to catch glimpses of our bodies. It's supposed to be a prize, hidden and intimate. I'm used to exposing more skin than my sisters, but this . . . This is something altogether different.

Malin aims to show me off, to parade me around like the bought and paid-for whore that I am so that he can humiliate me and my family. I choke back a sob and sink to the floor. The tiles are ice against my back, but it doesn't matter. I'd rather freeze to death than put on that damned dress.

Is this really my life now?

Time passes. Sunlight fades to orange and purple then, finally, to midnight blue. Still, I lie there, staring up at the black ceiling, numb and cold and more alone than I've ever felt in my entire life.

Like with Malin's crown, diamonds have been crushed into the paint above me. It reminds me of the night's sky, and for just a minute, I allow myself to pretend that I'm on the *Black Death*, that the floor is rocking beneath me, that Tristan is beside me, teaching me to read the stars.

And then the world breaks.

OCEAN WAVES CREST and fall beneath me. The shore is a small speck on the horizon, too far to swim to but too close to escape. For a second, I'm caught between worlds, and then the currents come, dragging me down, down, down.

Kicking my feet, I break the surface of the water and gasp, coughing up salt and seafoam. My lungs ache. The water burns my throat and ravages my nostrils.

"Please! I need help," I cry, scanning the waves that wash over me. Tiny chunks of wooden debris bob along the surface—planks from a cerulean-blue mezzanine deck. A half-full bottle of rum grazes my arm.

Above me, electricity crackles and thunder booms. Puffy gray clouds pelt my face with rain, forming a million tiny ripples on the water's surface, making it impossible to see into the depths below.

"Ezrah, come home," whisper a dozen female voices.

Something pink and iridescent splashes in front of me then sinks. Heart pounding, I dive for it until cold blue water ensnares me from all sides. Another flash. Red this time.

Please! You have to help me. I'll do anything.

"Join us, Ezrah. Come home."

THE BEDROOM DOOR SLAMS OPEN, jolting me to alertness. Malin swaggers in, his boots tracking mud and snow onto the polished marble. "Have you been lying there all day?"

I don't answer. My throat is sore and scratchy. What started as pinpricks in my temples feel like hammers pounding against my skull.

"Ezrah?" He nudges my shoulder with the front of his muddy boot, not enough to hurt but enough to make me look at him.

"Have you drunk any water?"

I lick my chapped and peeling lips then shake my head. The slight motion sends a pang directly into my brainstem, and I stave off a whimper. Malin bends and extends his hand to me, but I don't take it.

I'd rather lie here forever than go anywhere with him.

Sighing, he scoops me off the floor and throws me to the bed. It bounces underneath me, forcing my stiff body to bend in all the wrong ways.

"Is there a reason you've spent the entire day on the floor?"

I moan and roll onto my belly, giving my tender back a break for the first time since this morning. "I'm not wearing that dress," I hiss. The soft pillows muffle the sound, but I don't have the strength to say it again. Talking, moving, it's all more than I can stomach.

"We're having dinner with my inner council tonight. You have five minutes to get dressed." Malin leaves the bedside and disappears into the adjoining bathroom.

I don't move.

"Ezrah?" Malin asks.

I clear my scorching throat and turn to face him. His arms are crossed, his lips pursed into a hard frown. I'm not sure how long he's been standing at the foot of the bed.

"I'm not wearing that dress," I say, puffing out my chest.

"Fine. You don't have to." Malin wraps his arms around my waist and throws me over his shoulder like a sack of rice. Everything sways. The ceiling becomes floor and the floor becomes ceiling, and I can't do anything but grope around for something to latch onto. My gut drops. Black dots flicker across my field of vision. Silk fabric crumples beneath my tightly closed fists as I hold onto the back of Malin's shirt for dear life.

"Let me go," I snarl.

The door slides open. We slip out into a wide hallway lit by purple fire in shining silver sconces. The light bounces across black tile, making the whole section sparkle like diamond-infused obsidian. "Where are you taking me?"

"I already told you. We're having dinner with my inner council."

I freeze against him. He wouldn't.

"I'm not wearing any clothes."

"And whose fault is that?" He readjusts me on his shoulder and carries me down a flight of winding stairs.

"Malin, please don't do this."

"Next time, do as I say and I won't have to."

We descend another flight of stairs, which opens into the grand foyer. It's a large, dark space full of violet tapestries and matching cashmere rugs. A chandelier hangs overhead—the size of two people standing side by side. Amethyst gems and black diamonds glitter in the metalwork, and rows of black candles cast an eerie light across the tiled walls. It's so similar to the pomp inside my father's palace, a different color but a similar design.

It figures Malin would be no different from any other king—he must love to show off his wealth and power. His toys.

I hang my head and ease the grip on his tunic. There's no use fighting. I can't escape this fortress, and even if I could, where would I go? Who could hide a Varren with my golden hair, golden eyes, and sparkling skin? Who would interfere in an alliance between my kingdom and his? I'm Malin's prize. His property. This hell is where my father wants me, and it's where I belong.

"Good girl," Malin says. "Don't worry. No one but me will be touching you tonight."

The way he says tonight makes my whole body stiffen. I've participated in group sex before, but I've always been the one in control in those situations. This is different, and I don't know whether to be terrified or excited, anxious or disgusted, that the possibility of sharing me has crossed Malin's mind. Maybe I'm all of the above.

Thankfully, I don't have to decide that right now. I don't have to do anything—just what he says.

PRINCESS EZRAH VARREN

FORTRESS HEDRA, CENTRAL CARTHINIA

Boisterous laughter comes from a hallway at the opposite end of the grand foyer, and I shift my attention toward it.

"Malin, please don't make me meet them like this."

"It's Your Majesty, and you'll meet them in whatever pleases me. Complain again and I'll bend you over the table and fuck you in front of them. Maybe give them a go at that pretty little ass of yours."

That shuts me up. Turns my blood cold.

"That's what I thought," Malin says, possessively squeezing my thigh. "Behave yourself tonight and maybe I'll even let you come again."

He carries me through a labyrinthine corridor past a dozen dead ends and through an equal number of false and hidden entrances. An open doorway appears from seemingly nowhere, small enough that Malin will need to duck to pass through. Violet light and white smoke pour from the room, turning the air thick and hazy, filling the hallway with rich scents of roasted meats, honeyed wine, and a zillion other spices I've never tried before.

My stomach growls. Saliva pools in my throat.

"Good behavior means you're going to eat and drink while we're inside," Malin says. "I won't have you wasting away in my quarters out of some stupid desire to hide a body that's already been bought and paid for."

The words slice through me. I ball my hands into tight fists, grind my molars together, and force myself not to think about the truth behind them. To take my new role in stride. I'm stronger than I look. If my father couldn't break me, neither can Malin.

Multiple voices ricochet off the walls in front of us, echoing as we enter a private dining room. It's a cramped space dominated by a round obsidian table and a half-dozen black leather armchairs. The sconces on the walls are carved from silver, twisted so that kneeling naked women hold the purple flames in their raised hands. The ceiling is tall and black—I can't see the top of it—and shadows swirl around the floor, swallowing Malin's feet as he walks.

The room falls silent when we enter. Besides a cursory glance, I don't look at Malin's guests. From what I can tell, there's only four of them, and they're all lounging in armchairs, sipping from black crystal goblets filled with golden wine.

"This is my wife Ezrah," Malin says, dumping me into one of the empty chairs. As I scramble to right myself, he claims an empty seat to my left and leans back, touting a smug expression. "She decided the clothing I provided wasn't adequate."

He snatches a bottle of wine off the table and pours himself a drink. "Suits me just fine, though. I prefer her this way."

My cheeks heat as I straighten in the chair then slide my legs out from underneath me. As I press my feet to the floor, shadows wrap around them—not incorporeal anymore, but stretchy and soft. They tighten around my ankles, binding them—binding *me*—to the base of the chair. I look to Malin with pleading eyes, but his gaze is in his chalice as the shadows spread my legs apart and hold me there, exposing my cunt to the entire room.

I squirm against my bonds. They tighten.

"Relax," Malin says, setting his glass on the table. "Your cunt is so pretty. It would be selfish to keep it to myself."

The words send fire coursing through my veins. My breath hitches and my breasts tighten, even as panic bubbles up my throat. There's a million protests on my lips, but I swallow them down—in part because I'm powerless here and he knows it, but also because I'm curious to see how this scene plays out.

I don't know why I'm like this—why the thought of being exposed to a room full of strangers makes my blood sing and boil all at the same time. I'm Varren. I can't enjoy this, and yet . . . my gaze lingers on Malin's lap, on the rigid outline of his cock against the buttons on his trousers, and I lick my chapped lips.

"I think some formal introductions are in order," he says, clearing his throat.

My blush deepens when his attention shifts away from his chalice to the tips of my breasts. Golden hair spills over my shoulders and covers my nipples, but he reaches over and scoots the locks aside, draping them behind my back. I shift uncomfortably in the chair, chewing on a piece of dried skin on my bottom lip. Tasteless, golden blood floods my mouth, but I'm quick to lick it away.

"Ezrah?" Malin asks.

I can't bring myself to look at him—at them. Instead, my gaze shifts and lingers on the floor. There aren't any tiles there, just a void of empty space reminiscent of the darkness in Malin's eyes. If I stare at it long enough, maybe it'll swallow me whole, drown me like a ship in the sea. I point my toes, searching for something solid to step onto, but there's nothing there.

"Ezrah." Malin clicks his tongue. His icy fingers grab my chin and yank, turning me so that I face the man directly across the table. "Pay attention. I don't like to repeat myself. This is General Avum. He handles the human divisions of our armies."

Our armies.

Avum's smile churns my stomach, but not in a good way. His dark eyes are serpentine, his expression feral and cruel. Salt-and-pepper hair marks the man as considerably older than me, and he has more ribbons on his military jacket than any singular person in the Varren army. Still, that's not what my attention lingers on—cut through the center of his right eye is a wicked, hook-shaped scar that seems to gleam in the room's dim lighting.

"Your Highness," he says with a nod. "It's a pleasure to see you tonight."

See—not meet.

A shiver rolls down my spine at the way Avum's eyes trail over my breasts, then lower and lower still. My clit piercing isn't visible through the golden curls —thank the gods—but that doesn't make me any less interesting to the general. Disgust floods me, even as heat spreads to my core.

Please don't let him touch me, I say with pleading eyes, pouting lips.

Malin only smiles as he gestures to the person beside me. "This is Madam Lyria. She manages our imports and exports."

It's a relief to see another woman in the room, even if that woman is old enough to be my mother's mother. She's got a big, straight nose and tired gray eyes that match the color of her hair. Liver spots and worry lines accentuate Lyria's sharp features, making the gaunt angles of her cheekbones more prominent.

"She looks uncomfortable, Malin," the woman says, wrapping a black shawl around her thin, bony shoulders.

I blink. No one's ever tried to help me before, not with my parents and certainly not with Malin. My eyes flicker between the two of them, awaiting my husband's response. A slow smile spreads across his brilliant white teeth, and the muscles in my body pull tighter than a bowstring.

Don't hurt her, I want to scream, but my raw and stinging throat refuses to cooperate.

"Is that so?" Malin arches an eyebrow.

"I can see her cunt dripping from here. It's cruel to leave her sitting like that."

The blood drains from my face. Tears fill my eyes and I twist in the chair, struggling against the bonds until Malin puts a hand on my thigh. "Stop moving, Ezrah."

Shame burns through me when his fingers slip between my curls and press against my slick center.

"You're right," Malin says. His eyes are on Lyria as he plays with my cunt and thrusts a finger deep inside me. Fighting back a moan, I bite my bottom lip and focus on the pain instead. "She's absolutely soaked. I should start paying better attention to her."

He slips his finger out of me, and I can't stop the whimper that escapes my lips. "Don't worry, I'm not going anywhere," he says, wiping his finger across the top of my thigh. "But you need water before I start playing with you. Don't need you passing out on the table."

He grabs a crystalline decanter and empties it into the chalice in front of me. "Ezrah hasn't drunk anything since last night. I'm surprised she can still get this wet."

Shadowy tentacles rise from the floor and coil around my wrists, binding them to the arms of the chair. Malin leans over, brings the chalice to my lips, and orders me to drink. It's a balm against my sore and scratchy throat. I guzzle it down, ignoring the snickers that pass between the council members. Cold water runs between my lips, spilling onto my breasts, my thighs. Goosebumps spread along the surface of my skin, and my nipples tighten into peaks.

When I'm finished drinking, Malin pours a second cup, and we repeat the process.

A satisfied hiss escapes my lips as I lean back and take in ragged gasps. The headache hasn't gone away yet, and my stomach feels a little sloshy, but the worst of my discomfort has subsided.

Malin slides the chalice across the table and pets the top of my head like I'm a dog. "Good girl," he says, loud enough for the others to hear. "You're such a well-behaved slut, aren't you?"

I glare at him and imagine drowning him in the Karmaskus Sea.

"Where were we?" Malin asks. His hands return to the apex of my thighs, where he tugs on my clit piercing. Zinging pain shoots up my core in waves, building and building until I scream. "Mmmm, I love that sound." He shoves two fingers inside me, burying them to the third knuckle, and I scream again, digging sharp fingernails into the chair's armrests.

It's too much, but I can't squirm away from him, can't do anything but embrace the touch. *Fuck.*

"Don't close your eyes, Ezrah," Malin says. "I still need to introduce you to the others."

He sets a slow, leisurely pace with his movements, and I have to remind myself to breathe. To focus. To not lose myself to the touch that's lighting every nerve ending on fire. I'm so needy, despite the others watching me, maybe because of it, and it takes every last ounce of concentration to keep from moaning my approval.

"Ezrah, this is Bron..."

He keeps speaking, but I can't hear anything past the pounding in my skull. My toes curl, and sweat drips down my brows as I arch my back.

Oh, gods.

Oh, gods.

Oh, my fucking gods.

Malin adds his thumb to the mix, circling my clit as he thrusts his fingers into me, driving me closer to oblivion. *I'm going to come in front of all these people. I'm going to—*

I'm not going to do shit.

Malin's magic holds me on the edge, his touches growing more and more painful by the second. My skin is so sensitive, and his slow-moving fingers are so damn insistent. I can't bite back the whimpers that spill from my mouth, the tears that squeeze past the corners of my eyes.

Please, Malin.

I press my pouty lips together, silently begging him for release, but my husband isn't watching me; he's saying something to one of the four people seated around us. I try to listen to the words, to focus on the conversation.

". . . really outdid themselves with this one. I didn't expect a Varren girl to be so amiable. You should feel the way her cunt is clenching around my fingers right now. I'm surprised she isn't breaking them."

I pant and squirm, and another shadowy tentacle slides up the chair and wraps around my waist, constricting me in a vice grip.

"They'll expect you to honor your alliance, though," General Avum says. "You'll need to send our soldiers to the southern border to deal with their raiders. The Varronians are already getting squirmy —not as squirmy as her, but you get my point." He cocks his head toward me, and my husband lets out a throaty chuckle.

"I do. I'll send Claudia to Sera Cay to scout ahead, see the number of soldiers we're going to need."

My ears are ringing. I can't breathe, can't think. Across from me, General Avum smirks then takes a long swig of wine, ogling me over the top of his chalice. I'm thrusting my hips in tandem with Malin's hands, driving him deeper, and my entire body quivers, turning to putty in the seat.

I tear my gaze away from the general, mortified that I can't bring myself to stop rocking against my husband's fingers. "Your Majesty?" I whisper. My cheeks turn hotter than fire. I pray the others can't see my embarrassment or hear the words I'm about to say.

"What, Ezrah?" Malin snaps, swiveling his head in my direction. I don't know what I've interrupted, but it must've been important.

My cunt clenches around his fingers as I hover on the precipice of release. "Please, can I come?" The words are barely a squeak, and I hate myself almost as much as him for making me say them. For making me demean myself like this to a group of people who should be my subjects.

His fingers slow then slip from my dripping cunt. I whine in protest, thrash against the bonds as I try desperately to shift my hips so his fingers touch me again. Malin plays with the curls above my mound, his fingers glistening with arousal. I want to scream at him, claw his eyes out, and beg him on hands and knees not to leave me like this—aching and wanting and empty. The absence of his fingers is so much worse than the teasing. I crave them almost as much as I crave the ocean that's half a world away.

"She's a greedy slut." Malin pulls his hand away and raises it to my lips. Without prompting, I open my mouth and suck his fingers down, slowly licking them clean. "Interrupt me again and I'll fill your mouth with something else."

Malin withdraws his fingers and reaches for a

loaf of bread in the center of the table. It crunches as he splits it in half, then he tears it into bite-sized pieces. Clearly, he's done playing with me. I give the bonds a tentative tug, wishing I could fix the ache myself, could slip my fingers into my cunt and—

"We're a landlocked country, Avum," Malin says. "When I said we'd send troops, I thought that meant to supplement the Varren regiments. I have no interest in building ships and teaching soldiers to crew them."

Malin leans over and nudges a piece of bread toward my mouth. I open my lips obediently, chewing in silence while the council speaks. He keeps feeding me until the loaf is gone then reaches for a bushel of violet moongrapes—an import from my home city and a childhood favorite.

"If we're going to build the ships, we'll need permission to send a permanent regiment to Alta. I'm not going to drag boats across the continent," Malin says.

Alta? For the first time in a half hour, I find myself interested in the conversation.

"We shouldn't have to build any ships," Madam Lyria interjects. She dabs a napkin over her crumb-filled lips. "We agreed to supply the Varronians with lumber and to send troops. We did not agree to build them an entirely new navy."

"A new navy?" I ask.

They all stop what they're doing to stare at me as if they've suddenly remembered I'm a real person, not some room decoration designed for Malin's entertainment. A moongrape squishes between my teeth—the sound deafening in the quiet of the room—and sour honey floods my mouth. Shifting in my seat, I swallow and repeat the question, trying my best not to look at Malin, who's glaring daggers at me.

"M-my parents' navy . . . did something happen to it?"

General Avum levels his gaze at me, but before he can answer, Malin holds up his hand. "That's twice now you've interrupted us. There won't be a third."

Shadows slither up my legs, my arms, my neck, coiling around every part of me like a snake readying to consume its prey. They feel snake-like too, flexible and muscular, smooth as silk. "Malin, please—"

A tentacle crawls inside my mouth, cutting off the sentence. It spreads my lips as wide as they'll go then keeps expanding.

"*Mmmmrphh*," I cry, my pleas turning to mush against the thickness of it. The tentacle fills my cheeks then slithers deeper, toward the back of my throat. I gag. Tears blur my vision as it forces its way down another inch of my throat, then another. Lungs burning, I thrash against the bonds that pin me in place and claw at the leather armrests, scratching white lines into them.

"*Arrrrmph.*" I look to Malin then the others. Not one of them moves to help me.

Another tentacle slithers between my legs. I jerk in my seat, trying to escape it as it presses against my entrance.

"You look so fucking pathetic right now, squirming in that chair," Malin says. "I bet your cunt is soaked."

The tentacle in my mouth retreats, and I greedily suck in air, coughing and gasping as my head falls forward. Drool drips from my open mouth, spilling onto my thighs. The tentacle between my legs eases past my slick opening, filling me in one fast motion.

I moan, too tired to struggle, too sore to move my aching legs, which feel like they've been turned to lead. Malin stands from his chair and leans over me. "Next time, don't disobey orders," he says, pressing his lips to my ear.

The tentacle expands inside me, filling me until I scream, then it starts thrusting. My cunt clenches around it and I throw my head back, panting as it drives me toward climax.

"That's it, Ezrah. Show them what a good slut you are."

I try to fight the building pleasure, to deny how

good this makes me feel. *I'm Varren. I'm better than this. I'm—*

"Tell me to stop," he says.

My pleasure is climbing, climbing, climbing, crescendoing into a fever pitch. I'm shaking in the bonds, struggling for air.

"Tell me to stop," Malin says, "and I'll undo your bindings and let you participate in the discussion. Or you can beg me to let you come in front of this room full of people and keep your mouth shut like a good little slut."

Swallowing, I try to form a coherent thought, let alone a sentence.

"I'm waiting, Ezrah," Malin says. "Everyone's waiting. Make your decision so the grown-ups can talk."

"I can't—" The tentacle hits a spot inside me that chases the words from my mouth. I can't look at the others, only at Malin. My cheeks turn bright hot. "Please, let me come," I whisper so that only he will hear me.

"Louder. I want them to hear what a slutty wife I have."

I feel the heat spread from my cheeks to fill my entire face. The tentacle hits the same spot again, and I grip onto the armrests of my chair. "Please let me come."

"Good girl. Go ahead and come for us. Show them what my money's paid for."

Before he's even finished the sentence, I'm unraveling beneath him. I quiver in the chair, clench around the tentacle, and scream my release.

PRINCESS EZRAH VARREN

FORTRESS HEDRA, CENTRAL CARTHINIA

"Where were we?" Malin asks.

He reaches for a bushel of apples in the center of the dining table then snatches one off the top. The husk is crimson and black with an upper layer that resembles a drooping skull—a pair of eyes, a nose, teeth. I've seen blood apples in paintings before, but never up close. They can only be grown in Malin's kingdom—*our* kingdom—in the thick walls of thorny bramble that separates Carthinia from the rest of the continent.

Malin never allows outsiders to pass through his walls to eat his native food. If the legends are true, then the magical creatures hidden within my husband's borders are just as powerful as he is, and the food just as deadly.

Bearing a smug smile, Malin withdraws a knife

from his back pocket and flips it open. The handle is made from carved bone, the blade obsidian. With the apple in hand, he slices through its husk, and dark, viscous liquid oozes down the sides of it onto a plate below. It stains his palm a dark crimson, the color identical to blood, and the fleshy bit of fruit he bites into looks more like raw and stringy muscle.

The contents in my stomach sour as he wipes his sticky red hand on my thigh, but I don't say anything. I can't. Malin's shadows are coiled inside my mouth, locked around my head in the shape of a knotted gag. A ball of shadows presses between my teeth, prying my lips apart. The texture is slick, like glass. I run my tongue along it, trying to stop a glob of drool from spilling out.

No luck.

My thighs are wet with saliva, now with apple carnage too. My wrists and ankles are still bound to the edges of the dinner chair, my naked body still exposed. Every time I move my arms, Malin's bonds tighten and the texture shifts from fine silk to abrasive sand. Stinging red welts are all that's left of my wrists, so I've stopped struggling. There's no point to it anyway. Malin will do as he pleases, regardless of how I, or anyone else, feel about it.

"Ah, ships," Malin says, licking his gory lips. "That's what we were discussing before my wife so rudely interrupted us." He slices off another hunk of apple and crunches it between his teeth.

I glare at him, but Malin's coal-black eyes are directed to the man seated beside him—Bron, I think. His face is young and eager; he can't be much older than I am with his messy auburn hair, soft facial features, and a rail-thin body adorned in red silks. My sister Aliyah would be swooning over him if she were here.

"We'll need a road to move the timber," Malin says. "Do we have the funds to build one by the end of spring?"

Bron swipes a carving knife from the table and turns it over in his hand. "The funds? Maybe. The men?" Sighing, he pushes back a loose strand of copper hair and leans into his leather chair. "It'll be difficult to entice our workers to build in the Crynthian Wilds during wintertime. Too many monsters."

Malin cuts into his apple again, and I swear I can hear it screaming. The blood leaks down his chin and over the sides of his purple, crystalline plate, forming a puddle on the obsidian table.

"I can clear them," Malin says between bites.

Beside me, Madam Lyria snorts. "Maybe for a while, but they'll come back the second you leave. Only a fool would risk their lives building roads for the Varronians." She reaches for her own apple, and a high-pitched wailing comes from it the second her teeth pierce the skin.

"Then, I won't leave. I'll aid in the construction if that's what it takes," Malin says.

"You're needed here." General Avum's tone is bored. Across from me, he carves up a chunk of drunken pork and takes small bites from it. "Until we know who has been attacking Arrovin's men and why, it's inadvisable to leave Ezrah unsupervised."

Malin arches an eyebrow. "You think she's dangerous?"

"I think she's *in* danger." When Malin's brows furrow, Avum clanks his silverware onto the table and releases a frustrated groan. "Assassins, Malin. Not all of us have the same magical defenses as you. It's hard enough to keep a Varren safe under normal circumstances, but in the middle of a war?"

"Hmmm. I suppose you're right. I could always take her with me."

"That's out of the question. The moontouched would tear her apart," Avum says.

Malin leans forward in his chair. "I didn't realize you were the arbiter of my actions. Tell me, general, what would you have me do?"

I tune them out. My mind is whirling at a million miles an hour, trying to piece together what I've heard so far. My father's navy is gone. There are raiders on the southern border of my homeland and enemy fleets in the Karmaskus Sea. My family is fighting a two-front war on land and sea with unknown assailants.

How long has this been going on?

A pit forms in the center of my gut, a cruel realization creeping in. I don't want to think about it, but my mind won't let me push the thoughts aside.

A year ago, Malin and his skeleton horde appeared on my family's doorstep, I thought with the intent of starting a war. Now, I'm not sure. Maybe my father asked him to come. Maybe Arrovin needed Malin and his legions to fight an already existing battle—one they never told me about. Did Malin even threaten my lands, or did my father give me away as an act of good faith? For troops and timber?

Is that all I'm worth to him?

Tristan's bobbing ship dances at the edges of my memory, disappearing into the tempest seas, and I can feel my heart shattering all over again. Suddenly, it hurts to breathe. To exist. To know the world is still spinning without us in each other's arms. Chest tightening, I close my eyes and try to swallow back my emotions, but Tristan's face is there, taunting me.

"I love you, Ezzy."

My eyes burn. I dig sharp fingernails into the heel of my palm, focusing on the stinging pain rather than him.

The table rattles, and I jump as someone's chalice smacks against the obsidian slab. Golden wine spews into the air as the man seated across from me—beside General Avum—rises from his chair. I can't remember the man's name, but I'm almost certain Malin introduced us. Still, it's the first time I've really looked at him, and I'm only looking at him now because he's glaring daggers at my husband and me. With a face lined by scars and short-cropped hair, the man appears more a mercenary than the type to sit in on council meetings.

"Don't be so dramatic, Rayne," General Avum says, sipping from his chalice. His voice is cool, but his eyes dart from Malin to me, to Rayne, then back again.

What in the nine hells did I miss?

"He's right though," Bron interjects. "We need to negotiate better trade routes with Varren. If they want our supplies, they should maintain the roads and offer some compensation for our soldiers."

"You know we can't do that," Malin says. His apple is nothing more than a bone-white husk on the plate.

"Why not?" Bron asks.

"Because," Rayne says, turning his full attention on me. "Ezrah Varren *was* the compensation."

I can practically feel the disgust dripping from his voice. His steel-gray eyes scour me from head to toe—not with lust, like with Malin—but with raw hatred. Rayne's gaze finally settles on my cunt, and the left side of his face twists into a cruel sneer. "I've never seen a man pay so much for tarnished goods."

My heart stops. All the blood drains from my face and what little I've eaten today threatens to return as bile.

The man is right, of course—I spent years trying to make myself worthless—but knowing it and hearing it are two very different things. It's all I can do to keep my head held high and my mask in place. Malin, though, he doesn't have the same qualms as me.

My husband drops the bread he's holding and leans back. The black veins underneath his eyes elongate, twisting through his cheeks and down his neck. "Watch your tongue, Rayne, or I'll desiccate it."

Rayne puffs out his chest and grips the corners of the table so hard, his knuckles turn white. "Our father would be rolling in his grave right now to know you've settled for filth like her."

The shadowy tentacles release me and ensnare Rayne, snaking around his torso and neck, shoving his face into the table with a squish and a crunch. Metal plates clang to the floor. Food scraps roll beneath the table. Rayne struggles against his bonds and manages to lift his face a fraction of an inch.

Blood flows from the mutilated cartilage that used to be his nose, gushing everywhere.

My husband opens his mouth, but before he can say anything, Bron places a hand on his shoulder and squeezes. "I think it's time for us to leave now. It's been a very stressful day for everyone, and we're all prone to saying and doing things we don't mean." He flashes Rayne a look, too, then stands from his chair.

The others wait for Malin's permission. When he nods, the tension breaks and the black veins recede into the shallows of his eyes.

One by one, the shadowy bonds fall off Rayne, who spits a glob of blood onto the table then straightens. "This kingdom is my birthright," he snarls, turning to me. "And I'll be damned before I let that Varren trash sit on my mother's throne."

And with that, he storms from the room, General Avum following close behind.

For a long moment, no one says anything; they're all staring at us, waiting to see what Malin will say. His attention is on the open doorway and for a second, I think he might follow Rayne. Instead, he folds his arms over his chest and turns on Lyria. "I'll need you here first thing in the morning," he says, his voice low and sharp. "We'll need to discuss timber logistics."

She nods. "And Rayne?"

"You're dismissed," Malin hisses. Bron opens his

mouth to speak, but my husband cuts him off. "You're all dismissed."

They quickly spill from the chamber, leaving Malin and me alone. The quiet between us is deafening.

"You should eat," Malin says.

My stomach is in knots. I shake my head and curl into the armchair, tucking my arms around my knees. It's been a long day, week, a long three years, and I'm just so tired.

"Ezrah," Malin whispers, his voice oh-so-soft.

I don't look at him. My wavy hair surrounds me in a curtain of sparkling gold. My forehead is pressed to my knees, my body as small and as shielded as it can be given the circumstances. "I'm not hungry."

"You haven't eaten all day."

Besides the bread and moongrapes, I haven't eaten all week, but I'm not about to tell him that.

With an overdrawn sigh, Malin stands from his chair and stomps across the room. Plates click together then slide across the table.

Thunk. Thunk. Thunk.

What in the nine hells is he doing?

Sniffling, I tuck a strand of hair behind my ears then rest my chin on my knees. Malin is bent over the table, collecting an assortment of foods from the center: crumbly cherry tarts, cubes of soft cheeses, colorful fruits, and cut meats. They're all stacked precariously on a crystalline plate. Malin slides the mountain of food across the table—the sound of glass scraping against stone is enough to rattle my teeth. To my left, bubbling liquid trickles into a chalice I can't see.

"Eat, Ezrah. I will not ask a third time."

The food is pretty and tropical, but right now, it looks as delectable as ash. My stomach turns at the thought of eating; my eyes burn from knowing he'll punish me if I don't. Still curled into a ball, I stare into Malin's black, void-like eyes and wait.

Raking hands through his hair, my husband groans, grabs the plate of food, then returns to his seat. "Come here," he says, placing the food on his lap. "Now, Ezrah."

I flinch at his harshness and slowly uncurl myself from the ball I've made. The second my feet touch the floor, shadows float across them the texture of warm mist. I stand from the chair and approach Malin, my body weightless on the dark floor. It reminds me of water. If I close my eyes, I think I might be able to convince myself that I'm back at sea.

"Kneel," he says, spreading his legs apart.

Swallowing, I do as he says and lower myself onto the floor at his feet. The shadows engulf my legs. Off-balance, I fall forwards into Malin's lap, who merely chuckles as I right myself by gripping onto his knees.

"Don't worry, you'll get used to it," he says. Then, he grabs a cube of soft cheese and presses it to my lips.

I shake my head. "No."

"This isn't up for debate."

With men, anything is up for debate. I reach past the plate of food and fumble for Malin's belt buckle. Before I can unclasp the hook, his shadows are on me again, binding my wrists together. They've taken on a sharp edge, like steel cuffs.

"What are you doing, Ezrah?"

"What women like me do, *Malin*." I say the name and brace for impact. He's never hit me before, but Arrovin has, and for much less. I wince when Malin's hand comes down but there's no sting. No slap. The back of his knuckles graze my cheek instead, the touch softer than silk.

"My brother is a prick," he says finally.

A knot forms in the center of my throat, but I swallow it down. "He isn't wrong. I'm not the kind of girl parents want for their sons."

I don't mention how that's been my intention all along, that I tried everything in my power not to end up in a place like this, married to a man who wants something from me rather than me. What's the point? I'm royalty, and this has always been my fate no matter how hard I've tried to avoid it—if loving Tristan taught me anything, it's that.

Tears blur my vision. I stave off the encroaching memory and open my mouth, letting Malin push the cube inside. It doesn't taste like anything, but the slimy texture makes it easy to swallow.

"Do you know why I chose you?" Malin asks. His voice is unusually tender as he reaches for yet another cube and plops it into my open mouth.

"Because I'm Varren," I say between bites. "Because my father wouldn't let you have any of my older sisters."

He snorts. "Like I'd want them. You saw the way Aliyah looked at me when I removed my helmet. I thought she was going piss herself."

Aliyah did piss herself, but I have no intention of telling him that. As much as I hate my family, I'm not interested in humiliating them.

Malin traces his index finger along the contours of my jaw, scoops my hair into his palm, and pushes it over my shoulders, exposing the long column of my throat. "I picked you because you're experienced. You've seen my face. You have some idea of my appetites. I have no interest in traumatizing virginal brides or schooling them in bedplay."

A small smile tugs at the corners of my mouth as I picture Aliyah—the mousiest, prissiest woman on the continent—as Malin's bride, her face shoved into the fur rugs, her cunt exposed to a group of people. She wouldn't survive a second here.

Leaning forward, Malin places a kiss beneath my earlobe. It's the first time he's ever kissed me, and the heat of his breath sends my pulse racing.

"Rayne is old-fashioned," Malin whispers, "but I wanted a queen like you." He licks a trail down my throat and I tilt my head for better access, moaning when his teeth nip at my skin. The bonds slip from my wrists, allowing me to rest my palms on Malin's thighs.

"Everyone I've ever been with has been afraid of me," he says. "They flinch when I touch them, cower when our gazes meet. You can't imagine what it's like to look the way I do."

"Can't I?" I arch an eyebrow. "I'm Varren, Malin. The first thing anyone sees when they look at me is my skin. I may not be feared like you, but I'm judged in other ways."

If I didn't look so damn pretty, I wouldn't be here. I'd be on the open ocean with Tristan, kneeling between *his* legs, halfway to the new world by now.

Stop thinking about him.

In need of a distraction, I climb on top of Malin and straddle his hips. This time, he doesn't bind me or hold me back. The plate of food clatters to the floor, but neither of us are looking at it. We're staring each other down. Malin grips my hips with bruising force—his need for control battling with his desire to fill me. I can practically see the gears in his head spinning as I reach between us and unhook his belt buckle in one swift motion.

"Ezrah," he warns, his voice a low growl.

My stomach curls at the way his voice rumbles against my collarbone. This is what I'm used to. Power. Control. Bringing my lovers to their knees. When I'm straddling someone, I can forget how devastatingly unhappy I am. Malin is right—I'm not some virginal bride meant to be bossed around and kept; I'm a wild thing who knows all the best ways to pleasure and manipulate men, even ones like him.

"Malin," I coo, undoing the buttons on his trousers. "You said you wanted someone like me, so let me show you what I can do."

When he doesn't object, I bite my bottom lip and run a hand through his silky, curly hair. Men are so easy.

Giving his locks a tentative tug, I pull Malin's head backward and watch the black veins beneath his eyes spread to his cheeks then lower, to his neck and arms. His gaze is icy-hot, deadly, but he doesn't stop me when I wrap my hand around his cock and angle it so that he's pressed against my slick center.

"Fuck, Malin." Moaning, I close my eyes and lower myself onto him, stretching my cunt until it's so full, it hurts. "Gods, you feel so fucking good inside me."

"You've got a foul mouth," he says, running his thumb across my bottom lip. "Fitting for a slut like you."

The words send butterflies straight to my stomach, and arousal pools between my thighs. My cheeks burn bright hot as I rock my hips against him, wincing when his nails dig into flesh. I fist his hair in my palm and let Malin's hands rock my hips, guide my movements.

"Ezrah, look at me when you ride my cock," he says.

I do as he says.

Black veins cover every part of Malin's body. The whites of his eyes are gone, replaced by dark voids that don't reflect anything—not the light around us or my glittering reflection. The sight is terrifying and thrilling all at the same time.

"Are you afraid of me?" Malin asks.

I'm not going to lie to him. I think he'd be able to tell.

"Yes," I say, never once taking my eyes off his. Swallowing, I lean forward until the tip of his cock slides out of me, then I lower myself onto Malin again, this time going painstakingly slow. "But I like being afraid."

The words are like electricity between us. Malin

grabs me by the throat and pushes his thumbs against my windpipe until I'm gasping and sputtering for breath. Uncoiling my hand from his hair, I grab his wrist and try to pry it free, but he digs in tighter. My whole body is tingling— desperation and need all-consuming.

Malin eases up, and I choke in a handful of breaths.

"Did I say you could stop riding me?" he hisses.

I don't need further prompting. Bouncing on his cock, I slip my hand between my legs and rub circles into my clit, moaning with the rising pleasure.

Malin clicks his tongue. "Did I say you could touch yourself?"

"Malin, please." My body is thrumming with need, my clit an unbearable ache.

"No." His grip on my neck tightens ever so slightly, and I remove my hand, threading my fingers through his hair, twisting it until his face contorts into a scowl.

"Please," I say.

His lips curl. "Take a deep breath, Ezrah, because you're not going to breathe again until you've made me come."

My eyes widen. "No. You can't—"

"Deep breath, Ezrah."

Shaking my head, I take the deepest breath I can manage. His thumbs press against my throat and the tingling returns, my clit begging to be played with. I ride him hard and fast, tears spilling from my eyes as I try and fail to draw breath.

Shit, shit, shit, shit, shit!

I claw at his arms, his chest, scraping through layers of pale flesh. Dark blood beads the surface but he doesn't let up, doesn't even wince. Starbursts cloud my vision, and blood pounds behind my ringing ears. I twine my fingers through his curly locks, pulling as hard as I can.

It isn't hard enough.

"I'm going to come inside that pretty little cunt of yours," Malin says, thrusting in tandem with my moving hips, driving himself deeper. I scream, but all that comes out is a high-pitched whimper.

Fuck!

Each thrust gets me closer to euphoria, to blacking out, but before I'm pushed over the edge, Malin releases my neck and his tense muscles go lax. Chest heaving, I feel his cock pulse deep inside my cunt. I try to pull myself off him, but he grips my hips and pins me down, spilling himself inside me to the very last drop.

"That's a good girl," he whispers. As I pant and cough, Malin strokes my hair then uses his thumbs to wipe the tears from my face. "You're such a talented slut. Did you enjoy riding my cock?"

I nod my head, unable to meet his gaze. Shame

and desire burn through me; my cunt is still pounding with need.

"Is something wrong?" Malin asks. Shifting, he slides out of me and begins rebuttoning his trousers.

I'm so empty without him. Pouting, I keep my focus on the buttons of Malin's shirt then answer in as quiet a voice as possible. "I didn't come."

"I know," he says, threading his belt loop through the buckle. "Maybe next time, you'll rethink trying to manipulate me. You're my plaything, Ezrah, not the other way around."

"Malin, please," I say, my throat sore and dry.

"It's 'Your Majesty' and no. You'll come once I feel like you've earned it. Now, get up so we can go to bed."

I grind my molars together but do as he says, standing on shaking legs. Malin grabs an armful of fruits from the table then cocks his head, gesturing toward the door. "Will you walk, or do you need to be carried again?"

"I'll walk," I hiss, storming past him. He catches up to me and presses one of the fruits into my hand —it's blue and round, covered in a thick rind. "What's this for?" I ask, taking it.

"I said you would eat tonight. Now, you can either feed yourself or I can do it for you, but one way or another, you're going to finish a full meal."

Groaning, I peel the rind away and take a bite out

of the indigo fruit. It's bitter and sweet. The juice stains my sharp fingernails and drips down my palms. "This is horseshit," I say, padding up the staircase. I no longer care who sees me naked. I'm too damn tired.

"Tomorrow, you will get out of bed and you'll wear whatever I damn well please. Is that clear?" He's walking behind me now, so close I can smell the wine on his breath.

"Yes, Malin."

"No more sulking and no more starving yourself."

"Yes, Malin."

"And no more calling me Malin."

We'll see.

With a yawn, I open the door and collapse onto the bed, ignoring Malin when he flips me over and suggests I take a shower. Maybe I can't trick or manipulate him into doing what I want, but at least I can be difficult.

I'll make him regret choosing me if it's the last thing I do.

VARREN

EARLIER...

PRINCESS EZRAH VARREN

THE GOLDEN COAST, CAPITAL OF VARREN

Black shadows curl around an amethyst sky, darkening the horizon. A second later, they're gone, replaced by golden rays of sunlight that heat my flesh. I blink, shake my head, then resume my song.

> Come, all you blackhearts and listen to me.
> Come taste the salt and the spray of the sea.
> Hey-oh, hey, ah-ha!
> Come set the rigging; come hoist the sails.
> Escape all your problems, no taxes, no jails.
> Hey-oh, hey, ah-ha!

> The land folk are pretty, the ladies are fair.
> But nothing's more precious than Karmaskus air.
> Hey-oh, hey, ah-ha!
> There's burdens—

I stop singing and scratch my head, trying to conjure up words that'll fit the rest of the shanty. I've only heard it a handful of times, and only in bits and pieces. The sailors won't sing it around Varrens, so what little I know comes from lurking around corners and hiding my face behind cloaks and masks.

"There's burdens on . . . There's burdens in . . . *something*?" Sighing, I lean against the rock wall that surrounds me and snatch my golden spyglass from the sand. Half a dozen books are sprawled around my hidden cove along the coast, their pages open to nautical texts and world maps. Someday, somehow, I'll find my way on board one of those ships and I won't look back. Better prepare myself now while there's still time.

Gazing through the spyglass, I watch sailors climb the rigging aboard the *Black Death*. Despite being in my family's employ, the privateers look no different from pirates—they don't wear uniforms nor hoist the Varren colors. Their feet are bare, their hair either shaved, close cut, or tied back into tails and braids. Long hair like mine would be a hindrance on a deck like that. One day, it will have to go.

"Yes!"

The words come to me as I twirl a golden strand around my index finger.

> There's burdens a plenty all waiting back home.
> The high seas are freedom, a canvas to roam.
> Hey-oh, hey, ah-ha!
> No taxes, or children, or filthy disease
> No judges or zealots, or piss royalty
> Hey-oh, hey, ah-ha!
> So come, all you blackhearts. Come below deck.
> Lift up the anchors. Come grab the nets.

Sand crunches and shifts on the other side of the rocks as sloppy footfalls plod toward my favorite hiding spot. Inhaling sharply, I close my eyes and go stiff as driftwood, waiting to see what happens next. No one is supposed to be here. This is a private section of the beach at the border between the Varren property and the public access port. My family would never come so close to the common folk, and the common folk would never dare wander so close to our lands. But still . . .

Their footsteps are mere inches away.

My heart screams at me to run, tells me that a Varren shouldn't be out here on her own. Barefoot and dressed in a long gown, I doubt I'll make it very far. I'd probably make a fool of myself tripping over the rocks, snagging my skin and dress on the jagged pieces. Bracing for a thief or kidnapper, I grip the spyglass in both hands until my shimmering knuckles turn pearly white. Maybe I can't get away, but I can still give them hell.

"Why'd you stop?" A uniformed man climbs over the rocks and hops onto the ground beside me, kicking sand onto my open books. He's young for a naval officer, maybe only a few years older than me, with tousled ash-blond hair that glows in the sunlight.

"Pardon?" I ask, my posture going lax at the sight of him. Wearing the Varren colors, the biggest threat he poses is escorting me back home.

The man wipes sand off his freshly pressed breeches then smooths down the edges of the bright white and gold fabric. "Why'd you stop singing?" he asks again. His voice is deep and lilting, and it makes my stomach flip-flop in ways it probably shouldn't. "You have such a beautiful voice."

My cheeks heat at the words. Swallowing, I relax my grip on the spyglass and try to speak past the knots in my tongue. "That's awfully forward of you," I say, flashing him a toothy grin. I wipe sweaty palms onto my already damp gown and lean against the rocks, hoping to appear casual.

The man's sea-green eyes widen as he takes me in, his cheeks turning a deep shade of scarlet. I'm acutely aware of how inappropriate my dress is—how removing the gown's corset and underskirts have forced it to cling to me in a way that would make most decent men blush. I'm also acutely aware that my dress is not the reason he's looking at me like that. My golden hair, golden eyes, and sun-kissed skin—they're sparkling like a million diamonds in the afternoon light.

"You're Varren," he whispers, eyes downcast. "Excuse me, Your Highness. I didn't know."

He turns to leave, but I grab the man's wrist and pull him toward me. The second I realize what I've done, I yank my hand back faster than if I'd touched a goldstone. *What in the nine hells is wrong with you, Ezrah? You can't just go around touching strangers.*

"Please stay," I say, tucking a strand of hair behind my ear. "You're the first person I've spoken to all day."

His gaze darts between the rocks and me, and my heart squeezes.

"That's not an order," I clarify. "You're free to leave if you wish."

He folds his arms and leans against the rocks. "You shouldn't be out here unchaperoned. It isn't safe. Do you know how much a single strand of your hair would sell for at market?"

I don't answer. Instead, I grab a strand of hair, pluck it from my scalp, and offer it to him. It goes rigid in my hand, mutating from soft silk to solid gold.

"Are you insane? You can't go giving away pieces of yourself to strangers." He shoves the thread back into my hand and stares at the horizon. "What's a Varren doing out here anyway?"

"I like the ships," I say, pocketing the gold. "The ocean calls to me."

"Come home, Ezrah." The words are deep and dark, said in a hundred feminine whispers like there's a crowd of women waiting for me beneath the waves.

I lift my hand, and water droplets rise from the ocean then twirl around my outstretched fingertips. Moving it is as easy as breathing air. The naval officer's attention is hyperfocused on me, on the magic I'm doing.

"You're not using any spells," he says.

"I don't need them." I close my hand into a fist and the water falls, splashing back into the ocean in a thousand little ripples. Back where they belong.

"You belong here too."

I shake my head and blink, focusing on the officer instead of the imaginary voices in my head. Impressing someone is much easier when they don't think you're crazy. "So, are you going to introduce yourself?" I ask, twirling a strand of hair.

The man shoves both hands deep into his pockets and crosses his feet. The posture is full of arrogance, the expression something a royal might make. "First Lieutenant Tristan Fontaine," he says.

The man—Tristan—doesn't offer me his hand. Common folk aren't allowed to touch Varrens, even decorated officers like him.

Him, an officer?

I scan the lieutenant again, certain I must have guessed his age wrong, but there are no wrinkles or worry lines on his face. No beard. No sunspots. The man is . . . perfect. My attention drifts to the hard planes of his chest, the sharp angle of his jaw, that cute dimple on the left side of his cheek, and it feels like my heart might fly from my throat.

I haven't been around a lot of men—only nobles and guards, but they've always kept their distance. Tristan is much closer than they'd dare get. I can feel his breath on my skin, can smell something sweet like cologne on his silk clothes.

Swallowing, I lean back on my hands and let them squish into the soggy sand. "I'm Ezrah," I say.

Tristan bends and retrieves one of my texts from the beach, shaking out the sand before thumbing through its pages. "This isn't exactly light reading."

"I've studied ships all my life. One day, I'm going to build the fastest ship in all of Ranada."

His brows furrow as he scans me again, reassessing. "I've never met a woman who cared the slightest bit about ship work. Is it the engineering that fascinates you or the adventure?"

"It's the freedom," I say, staring at the ships as they bob along the coast. "I'm a caged bird here. Something pretty for the nobles to gawk at and barter for. I want to build a ship so fast, no one will ever catch me again."

The sand shifts behind me as Tristan lowers himself to the ground. "You don't want to be here?"

"Would you?"

"You're Varren though. You have everything you could possibly want."

"I want to be free. I'd sooner spend my entire life as a beggar on the piss-soaked alleyways than another second locked behind those walls. If I didn't look like this, I'd already be gone." I gesture to my body. My stupid, perfect body that can't be scarred or disfigured. That can't be hidden away. It's the strongest cage of all . . . one that will trap me forever.

Tristan's gaze lingers on my sea-green dress—oddly enough, it's the same color as his irises. Heat curls in my stomach when I catch those eyes falling to my breasts. The cloth there is damp and tight, the neckline too low, and it does nothing to hide my shape. When he catches me catching him, Tristan's cheeks flood again, and he returns to the text, flipping through it with renewed interest.

"Did you draw this?" he asks, unfolding a sheet of paper tucked between the book's margins.

I swallow and squish the sand between my palms. "Yes, it's just an early blueprint though. Not ready to be built yet."

"It's quite good."

My heart hammers, pride burgeoning in my chest. "You really think so?"

"The shape is small and streamlined. Could easily outmaneuver a frigate like the *Black Death*."

"It only needs fifteen people to sail it too," I say. "Half the crew of a carrack. Of course, finding that many men would still be tricky, since sailing with me means committing treason against the Varren."

"Not an easy ask. Your parents have the strongest navy in Ranada. Even with the wind in your favor, you can't outsail an entire fleet." Tristan continues analyzing the prints, perhaps doing calculations in his head.

I try not to let his words get to me. He's only voicing aloud what I already know to be true. "I've done some research on camouflage as well, " I tell him. "There's a dye in Kamaran that turns light blue in the sunlight, midnight blue in the evenings."

"Huh. Is that why you've named your ship the *Midnight Sun?*" He shuts the text with a thud then leans against the rocks, his full focus on me.

I lie in the sand and watch tufts of white clouds float across the baby-blue sky. "Yes. The *Midnight Sun* will be the fastest, most well-hidden ship in the Karmaskus Sea, and I'll be its captain."

Tristan snorted. "Do you even know how to sail?"

"I've read about it," I snap.

"Reading about it and doing it are two very different things, Your Highness."

"Don't call me that. And don't act so condescending. I'm not a silly child with her head in the clouds, lieutenant. When I want something, I take it. Obstacles be damned."

Tristan rolls toward me, stopping only when our arms brush. "Ezrah," he purrs.

Fire licks across my skin, and there's an ache between my thighs that I've never felt before. Swallowing, I swat a strand of hair out of my face and try very, very hard not to look at the lieutenant.

"I can teach you how to sail." He grabs my hand and threads our fingers together.

Part of me knows this is wrong, that I should push him away or, at the very least, voice an objection. The other part of me craves this small bit of human connection. The Varren aren't allowed to be touched. It's been years since I've felt skin brush against mine, and the thought of losing it so soon is unbearable. So, I don't object. I squeeze instead and pray we can stay like this forever.

"I can teach you how to chart the stars at night," Tristan says. He and his sea-green eyes are staring at me, his lips so close, I can smell citrus on them. "And I can even help you build your ship."

"But?" I ask, trying very hard not to imagine those lips pressed to mine.

"But I want something in return."

Everyone wants something in return.

"Gold?" I reach to pluck another strand of hair from my head, but Tristan rolls onto his side and stops me.

Placing a hand atop mine, he leans over and casts my face in shadow. I lick my lips and take a deep breath. The scent of his cologne is cloying. Spicy like peppers, sweet like honey.

"Not gold, Ezrah." He moves his free hand away from my scalp and traces my bottom lip with the pad of his thumb. The skin tingles where he touches me, and the ache between my thighs becomes an unbearable pounding that matches the rhythm in my chest.

"Then what?" I ask, breathless now.

"I want to hear you sing."

My brows lower. "What?"

"Every day that I'm at port, I want you to sing for me."

I scoff. "You're joking, right?"

His expression is deadly serious, his lips a firm line. "No. That's what I want."

"Then, you have a deal," I say.

For a second, I think Tristan might kiss me, but instead, he rolls onto his back and squeezes my hand. Together, we watch the clouds float by, and I sing to him. Not a shanty this time, but an old lullaby my mother taught me. As he starts to drift, I let myself memorize the angles of his face, the way his sloppy hair falls in front of his eyes. This man ... I don't know him and yet, being beside him feels like being home.

"Tristan Fontaine." I say the name slowly, letting it roll off my tongue. "I'm going to marry you one day."

I kiss his forehead and let the waves lull me to sleep.

CARTHINIA

PRESENT DAY

PRINCESS EZRAH VARREN

FORTRESS HEDRA, CENTRAL CARTHINIA

Malin's wedding band is a heavy weight on my finger. Smooth and black. Cold as ice. I twist it in circles, wishing I could be rid of it entirely as I traverse the musty stacks of Malin's private library.

Turning the corner, I pass beneath a series of grand arches that extend all the way to the back of the room where my husband keeps his ancient texts. Sleek and polished darkwood creaks beneath my bare feet, but the noise gets lost under Madam Lyria's ragged breaths, under the *tap tap tap* of her bone-carved cane against the wooden boards. Behind me, she walks at a snail's pace, which I'm forced to endure—the pungent stench of her old-lady perfume making the already unpleasant experience even worse.

I'm still twisting the ring, still contemplating why I didn't toss it into the pond alongside my crown, when we reach the back wall. Shelves of colorful books tower over us, each protected by a thick glass panel with a locking mechanism at the bottom. My reflection glimmers in the glass, sending flecks of light bouncing across the library. My sheer black dress does nothing to minimize the effect.

Lyria shields her eyes and glares at me—as if I have any control over what my body does. Eyes weeping, she reaches into her knitted sweater and exposes a key loop hanging from her neck.

"Which books do you want access to?" she asks, wiping the tears from her face, keeping her eyes trained on the floorboards where the light can't blind her.

"All of them," I say.

Lyria purses her lips, undoubtedly preparing an objection.

"All of them," I repeat, more forcefully this time. It's been a while since I held any semblance of authority, long enough to forget how good it feels. "Malin said I would have full access to this room."

Sighing, she steps in front of me and sets her cane against the glass. "Very well."

Her jaundiced hands shake as she hefts the jingling keys over her head and searches for one that'll open the cases. Doubling over, she inserts a tiny bronze key into the lock then pushes against the panel. It slides sideways on a pair of rollers, giving me access to a small fraction of the collection.

I cough when she starts to put the keys away. "The others too."

Slowly, Lyria hobbles from one corner of the room to the other, doing as she's told, muttering under her breath while she does it. A grimace twists her features as she retrieves her cane and leans on the chalky, crescent handle.

"His Majesty will be quite busy over the next few weeks. If you wish to leave here without him . . ." She lifts her cane just long enough to point it at the entrance. "Guards will be stationed outside who can return you to your chambers. You're not to go anywhere unsupervised."

I grit my teeth.

"Food will be delivered at regular intervals. When you're ready to see more of the palace, you may ask the guards to summon Avum or myself."

"In other words, this library is my dungeon."

Her wrinkled face doesn't waver. Her droopy eyelids don't blink. "Yes. Delegates from Senna and Orinall will arrive tomorrow. Until they leave, your movements will be limited."

Because my father wants to keep my presence here a secret—so much so that he insisted on it as a term of our marriage contract. No parties, no coronations until it's safe—whatever that means. Malin and I married in the dead of night, traveled to Hedra months apart to keep my whereabouts unknown. Currently, less than a dozen people know I'm trapped here in this frozen hellscape.

"Have they told you why I'm being hidden?" I ask.

"I'm not at liberty to discuss affairs of state with you." The corners of her pale lips tilt upward. "You know, it's been a long time since a Varren had the gall to step foot on Carthinian soil. I wonder how our people will respond to having one of *your kind* as their queen."

A shiver rolls through me, but I stand up straighter, unwilling to be intimidated by this decrepit hag. "You can go now, Lyria. I have everything I need."

The receding taps of her cane proceed the swishing of bronze doors.

Hands on my hips, I pivot back to the restricted section, taking in the overwhelming display of books before me. Most of them are written on parchment or silk, some in languages I've never even seen before, despite my extensive training.

My sisters would kill to be granted this level of privacy, this trove of knowledge. Admittedly, it's a greater kindness than I expected, given Malin's reputation and his behavior last night.

Standing on tiptoes, I reach for the prettiest book I can find—a dark blue tome with light silk pages. It reminds me of Kamaran dye, of my *Midnight Sun*. I pull it from the shelf, then another, and another, hefting at least a dozen books to my chosen hiding spot then sprawling them out around a leather recliner and curtainless bay window.

As the sun reaches its apex, I settle into the orgasmically warm chair, crack open the spines, and get to work.

The first title on my agenda: *Body Modification Rituals and Spell Reversals*.

Twenty-seven days, three hours, and forty-seven minutes. That's how long it's been since I stepped foot inside Malin's palace. I've spent twenty-five of them researching spell books, nineteen in orgasm denial.

My clit buzzes, swollen and sensitive around the piercing. Electricity pulses through my veins, setting every nerve ending on fire as I slide a hand past the high slits of my violet dress and cup my throbbing pussy. Skin screaming, I hold my hand there, compressing the overstimulated flesh that's left me raw and wanting. It doesn't help.

Nothing helps.

Rage whirls through me like a hurricane, growing in strength with every minute that ticks by. I want to strangle Malin. I want to ride his face until he's drowning in my come.

Still cupping myself, I glare at the open leather-bound book balancing on my recliner's armrest. It says the same thing all of Malin's spell books do.

Horun dranna vorex—this spell is permanent.

I refuse to accept that.

Moaning, I stroke the metal loop one last time before forcing myself to focus. Wetness clings to my fingers as I slip them free and grab the suede, yellow journal tucked beneath my ass, hidden there so Malin won't be able to find it—not that he ever looks at my stuff when he visits. My husband's too busy bending me over the chair or taking me against the book stacks. He plays with my cunt until I'm in tears then denies me my release even as he takes his own.

It's making me homicidal.

Glittering, golden words fill the white, silk pages of my journal—lists of books to check and notes from the ones worth reading. Thumbing through them, I stop at title number one hundred and ninety-seven, *Sex Magic and Bondage*, then tug the pin free of my balled-up hair. I stab the pointed tip straight into the center of my palm.

Golden locks spill down my back.

Golden blood oozes to the surface of my flesh, pooling there.

The stinging clears my mind, grounds me, as I dip the needle into my wound, gathering my blood at the tip. Frowning, I scratch out the last useful name of the last useful book in my husband's library. Then, I slam the journal shut.

Twenty-seven days wasted. I should have been looking into spell creation, not relying on some ancient magic from some pervy mage three hundred years ago.

Fuck. It's going to take me forever to restart.

Liquid gold drips down my wrist, splatters onto my clothing as I reach for the leather-bound book and set it in my lap. The gold hardens. Layers of transparent tulle grow stiff, and my corseted bodice turns glittery in the afternoon sunlight. It doesn't matter. New dresses come every day—a seemingly endless barrage of provocative, shameful fabrics that no one sees beside myself and Lyria.

I fidget with the dress, peeling gold from it while skimming the book's passages on incantations, ingredients, and tone of voice. Spellcraft doesn't seem as hard as the mages make it out to be. A few herbs here, a few chants there—nothing that warrants the years of study they put into it.

Flipping through the pages, I pluck a strand of hair from my head, then another and another, tabbing the book as I go. Once I'm through with it, I retrieve my yellow journal off the floor and jot bloody notes onto the silk pages. Within an hour, I've repeated the process three times with three different books. Within four, my palm is an inferno of pain, but I have something that resembles a working draft.

Eyes drooping, neck aching, I scroll through the makeshift spell, comparing my most recent edits to the notes that some mage scribbled into the margins of a fiery orange tome. At this point, the words might as well be gibberish. Yawning, I rub the crust from my eyes and stretch my aching back, wincing at the stiffness.

Something dark shifts in my periphery.

I jump, squeaking when I see Malin leaning against a book stack. His arms are crossed, his lips pressed into a hard line.

"How long have you been standing there?" I ask, my voice trembling.

"Long enough to watch you vandalize my ancestors' books."

The stack creaks as he pushes off it and approaches me, hands in his pockets, loafers clicking against the polished wood.

My husband is dressed in full regalia tonight: a topcoat made from black velvet, trimmed in silver, a dark tunic with matching trousers, and an obsidian diadem that blends into his curls. The only sources of color are a purple cravat fluffed around his neck and gaudy, amethyst rings that cling to his fingers.

When he dresses like this, it means he isn't here to stay.

My heart sinks at the realization. The truth is, I'd rather be with Malin than be alone.

"You know, we have ink for that," he says, eyeing my gold-stained hand.

I snap the journal shut then tuck it between myself and the armrest. "I prefer writing in blood."

He snorts. "And people say *I'm* the psychopath."

"Two things can be true."

Malin's black eyes glisten with the need to fight me—a need I feel just as strongly in the rapid pulse of my heart, in the growing heat between my thighs. Over the last few weeks, he and I have become sparring partners—our weapons neither swords nor bows, but tongues that are equally sharp. I'd call it foreplay, but only one of us tends to get off.

As Malin maneuvers around a pile of haphazardly stacked books, I shift my attention to the tome still in my lap and make a show of ignoring him.

Propping my feet onto the ottoman, I thrum my fingers against the armrest and sigh.

"Don't you have somewhere to be?" I ask, flipping the page. My breathing catches when his soft silk pants press against the soles of my feet.

"Didn't you miss me?" he asks. "Just last night, you were begging me to stay."

The very visceral image of Malin massaging oil into my skin and sliding his cock between my thighs has me melting all over again. And then I remember the tingling, yearning sensation that came after, when he left me in the bedroom alone and wanting despite my protests.

I lick my thumb and index finger then flip the page again. "No. Now, go away. I'm busy."

"Busy?" Leaning over the recliner, Malin sets his hand atop the book to prevent me from reading it—as if that had ever been my intention.

I meet his gaze, offering up a sugary sweet smile before waving him off. The gesture isn't at all convincing, but then again, it isn't supposed to be. I want him to touch me almost as much as I want to remove this damned spell. "Shouldn't you be out playing with your nobles or something?"

"I'd rather be playing with you."

I swallow.

Malin kicks the ottoman out from underneath me and my feet slap against the chilly floor.

"Get up," he says.

"Why?" I settle farther into the recliner, wiggling my ass as I cross my legs beneath me. The expression on his face turns absolutely feral.

"What do you mean, why?" Malin snatches the book off my lap and snaps it shut, sending a plume of dust into the air. It stings my eyes, but I don't blink. I stare him down instead.

"That book didn't have any page numbers," I hiss.

"So what?"

"So, it's going to take me forever to find my spot."

"And I care why?"

Malin angles closer, glossy curls falling over his forehead. Right now, there are no black veins on his face, no telltale signs that this is anything more than a game, so I keep pushing. "Were you born this much of an asshole, or have you had to practice at it?"

Starlight flares to life inside my husband's eyes. Throwing his head back, he laughs—a deep, throaty chuckle that sends goosebumps crawling up my spine, down my chest and stomach. Then, he puts his arms on either side of my face, squishing the text between his hand and the cushion, trapping me in the seat.

"Gods, I missed that filthy mouth of yours," he

purrs. "Gagging the other nobles is decidedly less fun."

Blood pounds in my pussy. Moisture pools between my thighs, soaking through a thin layer of black underlace. I force myself to focus on the ancient, wine-stained book, wedging my fingers between it and the recliner.

Malin's grip tightens.

"Give it back!"

The fraying edges spread and rip as he grinds it into my hand, forcing me to let go. Fingers throbbing, I whimper as the tear spreads halfway up the spine.

"Stop! You'll break it."

"Maybe you should have thought about that before you disobeyed me. If you want it back, you'll have to beg me for it."

"You can't be serious." I lick my lips. Heat curls in my gut as I notice just how close our faces are—so close I can smell the burning peppermint on his breath. "Malin—"

"It's Your Majesty. Beg me appropriately or else it doesn't count."

"Your Majesty," I whisper, averting my gaze to my lap. This is Malin's favorite part of our fights—when I give in.

"Look at me when you speak."

Slowly, I raise my chin to his. The stars in Malin's

eyes are so bright, they suck all the light from the room, trapping me in the cosmos. My tongue twists into knots, each word a physical blow to the chest. "Your Majesty, may I please have the book back?"

"Now, that wasn't so hard, was it?" He blinks, and the light returns to normal. A moment later, Malin's fingers slip away, and then the book is sitting open in my lap, the spine fixed, the stains gone.

"There, I even returned it to your spot," Malin says, tucking a strand of hair behind my ear. The gesture is unusually tender and makes my heart flutter in ways it probably shouldn't.

Perhaps the worst thing about being trapped here isn't how much I hate Malin. It's how much I don't hate him—at least not always.

"Thank you," I say, running my fingers over the dark calligraphy, wishing I could run them over his cheek instead. Or maybe under the deep purple circles beneath his eyes. I don't think I've ever seen the man sleep, and in the library's dim lighting, he looks so godsdamned exhausted.

"Malin—"

"Yes, Ezrah?"

Where have you been all day?

Why are you always gone when I wake up?

The stars in his eyes turn amethyst. The rings on his fingers start to glow, a dull pulse emanating from the jewels' centers.

I reach for him, but Tristan's face is there, kissing me, holding me, telling me he loves me. Before I can do something I'll regret, I curl my hand into a tight fist then let it drop.

"It's nothing," I say, because I can't say anything else. Wanting Malin is a betrayal to Tristan. It's letting my father win. And I refuse to give Arrovin another outlet to hurt me from, another person to take away.

"I still need you to get up," he says, all the tenderness draining from his voice. Standing, Malin returns to his post by the book stack and nonchalantly props his foot against a row of priceless, ancient works. "That means now, Ezrah."

My eyebrows knit together. Something feels . . . different. Wrong. But before I can place what it is, Malin clicks his rings against the wooden frame.

I roll my eyes at him. He keeps going until that horrible grating sound is the only thing I can hear. "Oh, for the love of—fine. I'm getting up. Just give me a second."

"You know, I've owned skeletons who move faster than you."

Then why don't you fuck one of them?

Taking a deep breath, I rotate my neck from side to side, popping it. My whole body aches from remaining in the same position for so long, and my eyesight is blurry from reading such small print. In truth, I could use the break, even if it is by force.

"I didn't realize how late it was," I say, yawning as I tab the orange book and place it on the floor.

I've been in the library since sunup, when the outside view was bright and white and filled with snow. Now, dusky grays and deep purples bruise the horizon, and thick storm clouds loom overhead. Even the lantern light has grown dull—its oil all but empty in the glass jar beside me.

If I squint, I can still see the faint outlines of debris cluttering the floor—fluffy blankets sprawled across the walkways, empty fruit bowls stacked beside my chair, bottles of wine on every workstation—but that's it. The other book stacks have faded into shadow, the grandfather clock and expensive rugs disappearing in the gloom.

"Have you found what you're looking for?" Malin asks. "You've been in here all day, every day for weeks. Arrovin must have you searching for something important."

My insides plummet. Frozen in place, I watch him remove my yellow journal from his waistcoat and thumb through its pages.

The purple light.

The glowing rings.

He must've used his magic on me and taken it while I was distracted.

As Malin scans the contents, his playful smirk vanishes. His irises expand into dark voids and the starlight flickers out. "Notes for your father, I presume." His tone is blank. Not cruel. Not bitter. Not anything.

A shiver rolls through me.

I shake my head, but he can't see it. Malin's attention remains on the journal—where the pages are written in blood, not because I couldn't find ink but because the language demands it. Elder tongue is untranslatable, spoken only by monsters and gods, written only in their blood.

"I'm not a spy," I whisper, throat hoarse.

"I don't like liars." Black, thread-like veins weave throughout my husband's body. He marches toward me, grabs a fistful of my hair, and yanks me from the seat. Then, he shoves the journal into my chest.

The golden letters shine in the darkness, the words *"A vassa savna"* twisting and reshaping until they read *"Selmia te amissa."* The sentence has the same meaning as before, or rather the old words mean something new. Elder tongue is constantly changing, which is why reading it is an innate skill that cannot be taught.

"You'll translate this for me," he says.

I know better than to push him when he's angry. "Yes, Your Majesty."

Minus a few omissions.

Malin clenches his jaw and those black veins spread, slithering from his cheeks to his neck, to the space beneath his tunic, covering every inch of exposed flesh.

"I don't have time to punish you right now," he says.

The journal falls open between us.

Malin's fingers dig into my arm as he drags me through the library, into a dark hallway lit by silver sconces and purple flame. His amethyst rings glow steadily now, sending twisted shadows across his face.

"Where are you taking me?" I ask.

Malin stops. "I'm not taking you anywhere. Tonight, I'm meeting with Madam Lyria and Bron to discuss building our road through the Crythian Wilds. You'll be touring the palace with Avum."

I open my mouth to protest, but he cuts me off.

"You've been here for over a month, Ezrah. Now that the delegates are gone, it's time you learned your way around the palace grounds. I'm through letting you sulk around and spy in my library."

"I wasn't spying," I hiss.

"Do you think I'm a fool, Ezrah?"

Malin clenches his hand into a tight fist. Sharp fingernails turn the color of pitch, and inky darkness spreads along his fingertips, then up his wrist and forearm, until it's completely blackened. This is different from the veins I'm used to, which still writhe and slither beneath his flesh. This is as cold as ice.

I slip my arm free, only to have Malin grab my hand and intertwine our fingers. Piercing, burning pain shoots up my forearm straight to my chest, and I let out a pathetic whimper.

"Your father is very particular about the marital arrangements he makes for his daughters," Malin says. He squeezes my palm, and I nearly collapse onto the tile. "I know for a fact Remi asked for your hand months before I did and was denied. Now, his military is twice the size of mine and he controls the Jasmine Strait. I highly doubt my charm is what prompted Arrovin to choose me over him."

"Please, let me go," I say between chattering teeth.

He does, but only to fist his hand through my hair and snap my head back. "If you think you'll get a message out of Hedra without my knowledge and consent, you're grossly mistaken. If you think you'll see your father again—"

"I'm not a spy."

His grip tightens, and pain blooms across my scalp. "I tolerate your duplicitous behavior because I need an heir. But mark my words, Ezrah, if you share any of my secrets with the outside world, I will make you suffer in ways you cannot possibly imagine."

Malin releases me and shoves me to the ground. In the tiles' reflection, my lips are blue with cold, my fingernails the same. They look like aquamarine—sparkly, beautiful, and undeniably Varren.

"You're so pretty like that." Malin smirks, smoothing down my ratted hair. "Knelt at my feet. Your eyes full of tears. I could get used to it."

I flinch but stay put. It'll be worse if I don't.

Malin's cock presses against his trousers, straining through buttons and silk. He reaches for his belt buckle and shoves the leather through its clasp before abruptly stopping. A clock chimes from somewhere deep within the castle, and Malin curses under his breath. "Fucking meetings."

Readjusting himself, he yanks me to my feet and tugs me down the hallway. "We'll play later," Malin says. "In the meantime, mind my general."

Mind my general. As if I'm a child and he's my godsdamned babysitter.

We reach the top of the staircase, and the black lines recede from Malin's body. Avum is already waiting for us at the base of the stairs, his hands clasped behind his back, his posture ramrod straight. He's dressed in a black military uniform with medals and ribbons on full display and a sword sheathed to his hip. I barely notice the glinting weapon or the purple light that shines overhead, turning the hook-shaped scar over his left eye grotesque. No, the only thing I'm paying attention to is the way his serpentine eyes rake over my flesh with unmasked, unbridled hunger.

I scoot closer to Malin. "Please don't leave me alone with him," I whisper.

He snorts. "He's my general, Ezrah. He won't touch you without my consent." Malin grabs my waist and pulls me flush against his chest. Bending, he presses his lips to my ear. "Behave yourself and maybe I won't give it to him."

A chill runs through me. I bite my bottom lip and squeeze my thighs together as I imagine being used by that brute. Bent over a table. Forced to my knees, kicking and screaming as he holds me down.

"You'd probably like that," Malin sneers. "You're probably wet just thinking about it."

"I—"

He slides his hand past the high slit in my gown. I cry out when his fingers slip into my arousal and find exactly what he's looking for.

"That's what I thought."

My shame burns bright hot. I can't look at him, not even when he pulls his hand away and places it firmly on my lower back.

"Behave, Ezrah. Mind him while I'm away."

And then Malin hands me over to the general,

exchanging only a few words with him before vanishing from sight.

"Shall we get going?" Avum asks.

He offers his arm to me then leads me into one of the darkest hallways I've ever seen. My skin crawls . . . with terror or anticipation, I can't tell.

PRINCESS EZRAH VARREN

FORTRESS HEDRA, CENTRAL CARTHINIA

"As you may have noticed," Avum says, "the bottom level of Fortress Hedra is a labyrinth in the truest sense of the word. A single corridor will take you to the grand foyer while all others dead end. Until you familiarize yourself with the layout, the easiest way to locate the correct path is to find the walls with crushed sapphire mixed into the design."

Stepping in front of me, Avum presses his gloved hand to the obsidian wall. A purple-flamed sconce bursts to life, crackling and hissing as it reveals the narrow path ahead. Thousands of gems sparkle in the pale light, each cast in varying shades of purple that makes them indistinguishable from one another.

"If you look closely," Avum says, running his

hand along the wall, "you'll see that these stones are—"

Yawning, I stretch my arms high into the air, fighting to keep my bleary eyes open.

Avum clears his throat. "You'll see that these stones are slightly darker than the others." He pauses over a patch of violet gems then swivels to face me when I yawn a second time. "Are you paying attention?"

No. I'm fucking exhausted.

We've been touring the palace for hours now—winding through nonsensical corridors, peeking into hidden doorways that I'll never find again on my own. What's worse is that General Avum isn't brutish; he's boring. The man could prattle on about ancient kings or master architects for decades without ever growing bored. Me, on the other hand . . . Well, my brain is practically mush at this point.

"Your Highness," Avum says. "I'm not conducting this tour for my own benefit."

"I'm paying attention," I hiss, leaning my head against the bumpy wall. Textureless shadows pool around my feet, climbing up the sides of the barely lit corridor to keep it unnaturally dark. If I stood still long enough—if I closed my eyes long enough—I think I could fall asleep.

Avum crosses his arms and glowers at me like it's my fault we're standing here. "What did I say then?"

"Sapphires. Maze." I gesture to the crushed gemstones and yawn again. "See? I'm listening."

"What I see is that Malin hasn't adjusted you to his schedule yet." Reaching into his breast pocket, Avum withdraws a silver pocket watch attached to a delicate chain. He unclasps the case, reads the time, then sighs. "I'll tell you what, if you can route us back to the grand foyer, we can break for the evening."

I scoff at him. "You want *me* to lead us back?"

Avum nods. The pocket watch snaps shut as he returns it to his breast pocket, patting the fabric to check that it's secure. "As I said, you'll need to find the crushed sapphires and use them as a guide. Malin insisted you be able to navigate these halls before I dismiss you."

Dismiss me. As if I'm not Avum's better. As if he has any standing to control me.

My hackles rise, but I bite my tongue, choosing instead to focus my ire on the stone wall behind me and the gemstones tacked to it. Purple. Slightly darker purple. Almost white. Not quite black. Stones with a darkened middle and others with a lightened edge.

They're all nauseatingly similar.

My body sags with the knowledge of just how long it'll take me to find the grand foyer—*if* I can find it at all. Groaning, I run my finger along a smooth patch of gems and brace for a sleepless night.

"Can you point to the sapphires again?"

"This is asinine," I hiss, glaring at the branching paths ahead. The one to my left cuts at a ninety-degree angle, while the one to my right is so dark, it looks like it could extend straight into the ninth hell. Neither seems particularly promising. "I don't understand how I'm supposed to find anything in this stupid fucking maze."

"It's meant to be difficult," Avum says. "That's why this palace is so defensible." I shoot him a withering look. My eyes burn with exhaustion, and my temples throb in tandem with the flickering flames. I've made no real progress in the last however many hours it's been, and I firmly expect both routes to either dead end or take me back to where I started. Again.

Oscillating between the two, I step left then glance at General Avum and gesture to it. "Well?"

If I'm right, his stony expression gives nothing away.

Shadow and mist swirl up to my knees as I scour

the tunnel-like entrance for scraps of sapphire. Dark purple gems twinkle overhead—several feet above my head—but they could just as easily be rubies, or black diamonds, or amethysts. Without a stepping stool, it's impossible to tell.

"I don't suppose you're going to help?" I ask, folding my arms across my chest.

"I would if I could, Your Highness, but the King insisted—"

"Fuck the King."

He arches an eyebrow and I sigh. Pulling at my hair, I slide down the wall until I'm sitting on the cold, black tiles, surrounded by mist. Maybe I can't escape this hell, but at least I can give my sore feet and burning calves a rest.

"What are you doing?" Avum asks.

"What does it look like?"

Rolling onto my back, I stare at the glittering darkness and imagine I'm at sea. Lapping ocean waves press against my eardrums, and those gemstones become stars.

"When you find my husband," I say, shutting my eyes, "you can tell him I refused to cooperate. I'm sure however he punishes me will still be better than this."

Boots thump beside my head, and meaty hands curl around my waist, lifting me high into the air.

"Put me down!" I scream, flailing in the general's

arms. A second later, I'm fully upright and pinned between him and the wall.

"I don't enjoy this any more than you do, princess." His breath is hot against my skin, his emerald eyes every bit as vicious as the night we met. "Getting trapped down here is the last thing you want. Every year trespassers die trying to solve this maze, and it takes us weeks to find the bodies. This palace is designed to kill. If you were to wander in here and get lost, no one would hear you scream for help."

I swallow.

Jagged rocks dig into my spine as Avum edges closer and drags his thumb along the hollow of my throat. My stomach flutters—a low heat spreading through my middle—but then he steps away and drops to the floor.

"What are you doing?" I ask.

"Demonstrating."

Avum dives into a pushup position, and the black mist consumes him. "When you're down here, no one can see you. You can't imagine how many corpses I've found by tripping over them."

My eyes dart back to the tunnel. A shiver rolls through me as I imagine my lifeless husk rotting away with no one the wiser.

"If Malin and I don't know where you are, there's a good chance we won't be able to find you."

"But the guards . . ." I peer over my shoulders, noticing their absence for the very first time. Since beginning the tour, Malin's hallways have remained empty—so unlike any of the other palaces I've been to.

"The guards won't always be around, nor should you want them to be." Avum's knee cracks as he stands. He doesn't stop to rub it, though his face contorts into a grimace. "The sooner you can navigate these hallways on your own, the better. The servants and staff here cannot lie to Malin; you'll have no privacy under their watch. As queen, your business should be yours and yours alone until you wish to share it."

My eyebrows knit together. In Varren, Kamaran, even Jade, the kings keep their wives on tight leashes. Women have no privacy, no personal desires or power. While Malin might be less tactful than the other rulers, his behavior isn't so far from what I expected.

As if sensing my confusion, Avum clarifies, "When you're coronated—*if* you're coronated—you'll have all the privileges and authority as His Majesty. This is Carthinian law, and one he cannot overturn."

"If I'm coronated?" I ask. "Meaning I might not be?"

"Malin is allowed to marry whoever he wishes,

but to crown you, he needs the council's support as well as your father's. He currently has neither." I open my mouth to speak, but Avum cuts me off.

"No. I'm not one of the council members holding you back. That would be Rayne, Claudia, and . . ." He straightens his shoulders then smooths out the wrinkles in his uniform. "I think this conversation would be more suitable in His Majesty's presence, with His Majesty's blessing. Technically, I'm not permitted to discuss affairs of state with you. For now, let's focus on the maze."

Groaning, I roll my eyes at him.

Avum smirks as he rifles through his breast pocket and withdraws his silver pocket watch, this time passing it to me. "Memorizing the palace's layout will take months," he says for the umpteenth time—all chances of real conversation lost. "Getting a feel for the stones is the simplest solution."

I stare at the watch. The case is a series of intricate metal knots, the backdrop a splattery combination of white opal and something dark. Onyx maybe?

"Why are you giving this to me?" I ask, tracking the silver hands as they tick, inwardly deflating when I see just how late it is.

"It's a cheat. Hold it to the wall and match it to the stones." Avum cocks his head and nudges me toward the right-hand path.

Squinting into the blackness, I do as he says and quickly find the stones that match the sapphire-encrusted dial.

He strolls up to me and places a hand on my shoulder, squeezing it. "You can hold onto the watch until you no longer need it, but let's keep this between us, alright? Malin doesn't want you using cheats."

I nod, and Avum falls back, gesturing for me to lead the way. Smiling, I clutch the pocket watch to my chest and guide us through the labyrinth one corridor at a time.

Left.

Right.

Right.

Left.

The longer Avum and I traverse the labyrinth, the more I lose track of the turns. My blinks get longer, my eyelids grow heavier, and the purple light surrounding us flares so brightly, I have to shield my eyes against it.

"Ezzy!"

Tristan's voice hits me like a fist to the face.

The light clears, revealing a sleek wooden hallway as blue as the morning sky. Tristan's hand grips mine as he drags me past a set of cargo crates brimming with rum, treasure, and confiscated Varronian uniforms. Our surroundings rock back and forth in tandem with the Karmaskus Sea, and the scent of gunpowder burns my nostrils. With my free hand, I balance myself against the wall, bracing as the ship tilts a little too far to the right.

A cannon booms.

Wood snaps and breaks behind us as chunks of metal shrapnel pierce the ship's hull.

"Where are you taking me?!" I hiss, shouting to be heard above the ringing in my ears, the pounding in my skull. In front of us, the hallway splits in two directions—the armory, where guns and swords are bolted to walls, and the captain's quarters.

Tristan turns to face me, his brows pinching together as he says something I can't hear. A dozen scars disfigure his once beautiful face, each of them concealed by thick black ink that takes the shape of a human skull. Each of them caused by me.

Another boom.

Cannon fodder splits the wood in front of us, sending a thousand splinters flying into the air. A burst of golden sunlight streams through a hole in the forecastle, and dust scratches my burning eyes. I cover them with my arm, blinking away fresh tears as I cough up lungfuls of acrid smoke.

"Come on!" Tristan pulls harder, dragging me toward the captain's quarters.

I plant my feet. "Not until you tell me what's happening."

"I don't have time for this," he growls. Letting go of my hand, Tristan reaches for the double barrel flintlock pistol belted to his waist. He withdraws it and points the gun directly at me. "Go!"

I swallow. "What are you—"

He cocks the hammer. "Don't think I won't shoot you, Ezzy. I'll put a bullet in your fucking knee and carry you into that bedroom if I have to."

He angles the barrel lower, his mouth hardened into a flat line.

I swallow. "Please, don't do this."

His expression doesn't waver; neither does the gun. "Now."

I clench my hands into fists but do as he says, slowly stepping around him, the gun, and the cargo crates to reach the sleek black doors that lead to the captain's chambers. The gilded doorknobs never looked so ominous. My gut sinks as Tristan orders me to open them, the gun burning a hole through my back. Slowly, I edge into the dark bedroom and he follows, the floorboards squeaking beneath our heavy boots.

"Don't do anything stupid," he hisses, bringing the gun to my head. The cold metal connects with my temple, sending my heart into overdrive. "I mean it, Ezzy, stay put for once in your godsdamned life."

With his other hand, Tristan grabs my face and

squeezes, pinching my cheeks together. "I'm coming back for you."

He storms out of the room, slamming the door behind him. Keys jingle and the locks click into place. I yank on the knobs. I bang my fists against the wood until pain radiates up my forearms and golden blood seeps from my cracked knuckles.

"Come back, asshole! You can't do this to me!"

But Tristan isn't there to hear my screams.

I sink onto the floor, cursing as a burst of purple light explodes behind me, taking the ship, the door, and everything else with it.

PRINCESS EZRAH VARREN

FORTRESS HEDRA, CENTRAL CARTHINIA

Invisible hands curl beneath my armpits. Something cold and solid presses up against my back. I blink only to find myself in Avum's arms, propped between him and the wall. The hallway in front of us is still blackened by shadows, still filled with an eerie mist that pools around the purple flames.

"Are you alright, princess?" Avum asks, his gaze intense as he assesses me.

The word "asshole" echoes across the stonework like I'm a godsdamned lunatic. Heat floods my cheeks as I squirm free of him. "I'm sorry . . . I . . . I must have drifted off."

Avum's eyebrows knit together. "No apologies necessary. Malin should have let you sleep."

Bending, he retrieves his pocket watch from the

floor and drapes it around my neck. Then, he toes a section of rock. Stone grinds against stone, and a sliver of golden light trickles into the hallway. Reaching into the crack, Avum pulls the rock toward him, revealing a hidden doorway and a secret kitchen behind it.

A plume of white smoke billows into the hallway and I flinch, half-expecting the boom of cannon fire to follow. But it doesn't. The air that hits the back of my tongue doesn't taste like fireworks and metal; it's savory and sweet, like freshly baked tarts.

My stomach rumbles.

"This is normally when Malin takes his breakfast," Avum says. "It's a good time for a break."

Pressing his hand into the small of my back, he guides me inside. The floor is white like snow, the countertops soft shades of pink. In the center of the space is an island filled with cutting boards, mixing bowls, and serving utensils, each of them dripping with goopy yellow batter. Crushed berries stain the stovetop as well as the stack of dishes that overflow the sink, turning the room a kaleidoscope of bright colors so unlike the rest of the fortress.

I squeeze between the island and the counters. It's narrower than it should be—in Varren, I had closets twice as large and half as empty. But my mind isn't on why the palace kitchen is so cramped.

It's on the fruity steam and the woman who's bent in front of the open oven.

Gray robes extend to her ankles, and a tightly bound hood wraps around her face, concealing her features. She removes a pair of tins from the top rack and sets them on the countertops, revealing yellow muffins bursting with red and blue berries. Saliva pools inside my mouth as I watch the juices ooze down the tin, only to mix with an orange stain already marring the marble beneath.

Without thinking, I duck between her and the counter, my sights set on the tray.

The woman turns.

I catch a glimpse of her face and my whole body stiffens.

"Your Highness," Avum says. "It's alright."

"She's . . . She's . . ." I take a step back, then another, not stopping until my ass presses against the island.

"Dead," he finishes for me.

I shove my hands deep inside my pockets to hide their shaking.

The woman's face is nothing but brittle bone and rotted teeth. Her hands—now that I'm paying attention to them—have been picked clean of flesh, allowing her to touch the heated metal without hesitation or concern.

Avum steps between her and me, cutting off my

line of sight. "Under normal circumstances, His Majesty doesn't allow the living to enter the palace," Avum says. "All of the staff here are under his thrall."

He nudges me to the side as the skeleton shimmies past us.

"And you?" I ask. My voice is hoarse as I watch the undead creature dither about the kitchen with morbid fascination. I've never seen one of my husband's creations up close before. For some reason, I expected they would wield knives and swords, not aprons and cookware.

Her—*its*—skeletal hands turn on the faucet and set to work on the dishes, paying us no mind.

"Am I under his thrall?" Avum snorts. "No. Malin only wishes. Lyria, Rayne, and I are all very much alive and in full control of our bodies. But you'll find the rest of the palace is either empty or undead."

I let that settle.

If his words are true, then I'm alone here with no way to make allies and no one to call friends.

My chest tightens. Arrovin bound my magic before sending me to this hellscape. I used to be powerful enough to move oceans, to create hurricanes and cyclones. Since then, I've been reduced to parlor tricks. A spell like the one I researched would've required a powerful caster. I'd hoped to charm one into it, but now . . .

So much for that.

I fight to keep the crippling desperation from reaching my face. It doesn't work.

"Malin is a private person," Avum says, squeezing my shoulder. "And he's been betrayed more times than I think either of us cares to count. When you're the most hated man in Ranada, it's necessary to take these kinds of precautions."

"Of course it is," I say, shrugging out of reach. "You can stop looking at me like that, general. I'm fine. I didn't come here to make friends."

Spinning on my heels, I return to the countertops and use my fingernails to pluck a muffin from a steaming tin.

"This is a Varren recipe," I say, turning it over, blowing on it before popping it into my mouth. The muffin is sour and sweet, lemony and warm. My mother used to make them for me when I was young, but there's no way Malin could know that, is there? I didn't tell him. I would have remembered if I had.

I grab another, moaning as I chew.

"I think our king also prefers your food to Carthinia's," Avum says, withdrawing a pair of mugs from the cabinets. "I hate to see what he's spending on imports. Thankfully, that's not my problem."

In front of him, a pot bubbles with thick, dark liquid—the color of evergreen trees, the texture of mud. Stirring it, Avum pours the contents into both mugs then passes one to me. "Our version of coffee," he says. "It's strong, so it should keep you awake for the remainder of the tour."

I make a face as I swirl it around, watching the liquid form clumps against the sides of the ceramic. "Are you sure it's drinkable?"

Avum laughs. "The texture leaves something to be desired, but the flavor is good."

I bring it to my face and take a sniff. The drink is cold and sharp, like peppermint. Like my husband's breath. The image of Malin's eyes and the deep circles beneath them pop into my head, and I can't help but wonder how long he's been dosing himself with the stuff.

"You said Malin normally sleeps during the day?" I ask, taking a sip. The mushy clumps dissolve on my tongue, and I shudder as the steaming liquid slides down my throat and fills my empty belly.

"Yes. We all do. Our Master of Finance can only meet at night, so we've had to adapt. You remember Bron, right?"

"Vaguely," I say.

"Well, you were a bit distracted at the time." Slowly, Avum's emerald eyes rake over me, lingering on my breasts, my waist, my hips, stripping me bare.

I bury my face into the mug and pretend the steam is what's causing it to heat. "I . . ."

I'm not sure what to say in this situation.

I'm sorry you had to watch me come all over Malin's chair?

I don't normally fuck tentacles in front of strangers?

Instead of speaking, I take a long swig from my cup and breathe in the burning scent of menthol. If only the green liquid could swallow me whole, take me far away from this conversation.

"Malin has always been a bit of a voyeur," Avum says. "But I was shocked you went along with it."

I open my mouth, close it, then take another drink. Part of me wants to deny my willingness that night, but that wouldn't be entirely truthful. After all, I begged Malin to continue even when he offered to stop, and I've replayed the events twice already, touching myself both times to the memory.

With a satisfied hiss, I polish off the rest of my drink and lift my gaze to Avum's. The scars on his face aren't nearly as frightening without the purple light to cast shadows across them. In fact, he's almost handsome: dark-green eyes, hair equal parts black and silver, arms that could rip me in half, but a face that says he'd much rather use his cock to do so.

I bet he'd even let me come.

Do I actually need Malin's permission, or will anyone's suffice?

Pushing past my embarrassment, I jump onto the marble island and cross my legs, all too aware of the metal loop pressing against my panties, of the long stretch of exposed thigh left by my too-high slit. Avum's eyes track the movement, ogling the sparkling flesh.

I shimmy sideways, and the slit rides even higher, exposing the entirety of my leg.

"Malin and I have more in common than you might think," I purr, running my hands up the center of his chest. Avum's corded muscles flex beneath my palm as I trace a line through his military ribbons. "You'd be surprised at the things I like to go along with."

One minute the man is standing right in front of me, and the next, he's gone, refilling our mugs with green sludge.

My smile falters, but only for a moment.

I've taken plenty of lovers who despised being openly seduced, preferring their ladies be proper and their bedmates timid. While Avum doesn't seem the type to care, I don't mind accommodating him either way—not if it means soothing the ache between my thighs.

When I was fifteen, Arrovin taught me how to manipulate men, to become whatever they wanted me to be in order to get my way. For some, that meant shy and sweet. For others, bold and daring. It wasn't until Tristan came along that I learned to be myself, but that luxury is long since gone.

This is what I'm good at. Without my magic, it's

all I'll ever be good at; I might as well take advantage of my assets.

"We should really get going," Avum says, interrupting my thoughts. "We can take our drinks with us."

With his back to me, I get into position, bending in half so I can rub my sore and aching feet. By the time he turns, I've contorted my face into a grimace.

"You're hurt." Avum frowns, his gaze shifting to my feet.

I shake my head and take the cup from him, sniffling as I sip. "I'm fine. My feet are just a little sore from walking so much."

It isn't a lie. Now that I'm sitting, my body screams at the idea of returning to the tour. The last thing I want is to wander the labyrinth shoeless, cold, and aching for the next several hours, forced to exercise more than I have in years.

I bat my long golden eyelashes at him, trying to look as desperate as possible. Men love it when weak girls try to act strong. "You're right, though. We should get going. I've delayed us enough already."

Grunting, Avum takes a drink from his mug then joins me on the island, clambering awkwardly onto the marble counter. The porcelain clicks when he sets the cup down then slides it away. He pats his lap and my eyebrows furrow.

"Your feet, princess."

"Oh."

I hadn't expected that. Cheeks heating, I twist in my seat then wiggle my toes against Avum's thigh. A soft orange glow emanates from his fingertips. Fire-like warmth spreads along my skin as he grabs my ankle and drags me even closer.

I've never met a fire mage before let alone had one touching me.

Avum's thumbs press into my arches and my whole body melts, turning to putty in his hands. Something between a whimper and a mewl crawls its way up my throat as he kneads circles into my tender flesh, hitting all the right pressure points.

"You know, you're really fucking good at that," I say, closing my eyes, throwing my head back in euphoric bliss.

"I should hope so. I've had years of practice."

The heat intensifies like I'm warming myself near a bonfire. It sinks into my bones and spreads until my cheeks are flush with desire and my pleasure-starved center is molten. I shift so that the slit in my dress rides up again, exposing everything.

"I was raised in a brothel," Avum says. Working higher, he massages the sides of my ankle then my calf. "How to pleasure others is one of the first things they teach."

My eyes crack open, wide enough to give Avum a double, then triple take. Something about the facial scars and perpetual scowl stops me from envisioning the man as a prostitute. Yet the way he touches me—only whores have ever touched me like this.

As if sensing my train of thought, he smirks. "I didn't always look like this, princess."

My face grows infinitely hotter. "I didn't mean . . . You're not . . . That's . . ."

"It's alright, Ezrah." Avum chuckles. "I'm well aware of my appearance."

My skin burns so hotly, I doubt I'll ever be able to look him in the eyes again. Biting my bottom lip, I bury my face into my hands and try to will myself out of existence—all the while, his fingers don't stop. He lifts my other foot and massages the space between my toes so adeptly that I almost forget to breathe.

"Tell me something, princess," Avum says. "Why did you come on this tour barefoot when you knew we'd be walking all night?"

I peek out from behind my hands. The coral-painted ceiling stares back at me—yellow stains splattering its bubbly surface. "I didn't have a choice. Malin doesn't let me wear shoes."

There's a long silence.

"Malin doesn't let you wear shoes." He repeats the words slowly, mulling them over. His ministrations stop, fingers resting on the center of my foot. "And the outfit? It's his doing as well."

I offer up a humorless laugh. "It's hard to run away when you're half-naked and barefoot."

He doesn't respond.

The heat of his fingers dissipates, and my foot falls uselessly into the man's lap.

"Avum?" I ask. "Are you alright?" Propping myself up on my elbows, I find his expression pensive, his posture stiff.

"Are you . . . happy?" Avum asks. "Does Malin treat you well?"

"He doesn't beat me if that's what you're asking."

"That's *not* what I'm asking."

I can see what Avum's doing long before he realizes it himself.

It was stupid of me to assume that the general's disinterest in sex had anything to do with my demeanor and not everything to do with his loyalty to my husband. Now, the man is searching for an excuse to touch me, and I'm more than happy to provide it.

"Malin doesn't treat me like anything," I say, running my hands through my hair. "We fight. We fuck. He leaves. I'm basically a living sex doll to him."

I choose not to tell Avum that being used turns me on. It's not relevant that I enjoy having sex with Malin when afterward, I feel more lonely than ever.

"He only speaks to me long enough to strip me down. And he put this horrible spell on me that . . ."

Makes me so fucking horny, I think I might combust.

Makes me want to ride his face all night, suck his cock until I've pleased him enough to earn reciprocation, get down on my knees and beg.

I swallow, trying very hard not to imagine Malin fisting his hands through my hair, shoving those tentacles deep inside me. Now's not the time for that. Maybe later when I'm not trying to seduce his friend.

"I can't come without permission," I finally say. "It's been torture."

"How many days has he . . ."

"Denied me?" I ask. "Three weeks. But *he* still gets off every day."

Avum's eyes darken. His jaw clenches and unclenches as he works through what I've said. And now that I've given him the fuel he needs to justify betraying Malin, I set to work.

"It's not so bad," I say, lifting my leg to his face. I rotate my ankle, not-so-subtly reminding him there's a job that still needs doing. Avum's calloused hands return, hotter than ever, and I relax into them, falling back onto the stone slab. "Honestly, I'm used to it. My father didn't let me have shoes either. And at least Malin doesn't hurt me—not in any way that matters."

I let the implication hang in the air.

Avum's fingers work up the center of my foot and I moan—loudly. He rubs harder, and I swear to the gods I see stars.

"You can't imagine how many times I've touched myself trying to get off," I say, voice breathy. I slip my hand over my pussy to cup it through the black and purple fabrics. "Or how many times I thought about that dinner—the way you stared at me while Malin was finger-fucking my cunt. Do you think I need *his* permission, or will anyone's suffice?"

Avum groans. "Princess, do you want to get us both killed?"

"No," I say, rubbing my hand along my piercing. "I just want to feel you inside me."

He curses under his breath.

Then, his fingers move up my ankle, my calf, my thigh—kneading, squeezing, teasing me in a way that hurts so fucking good. My brain swirls until all there is, is him. His glowing hands. His fiery flesh. Fingers that seem to roam everywhere except the one place I need them.

"You have a scar here," Avum muses, playfully tracing a circle around my ankle. He pulls on my leg and I gasp—my ass practically landing in his lap.

"And here." He brushes a jagged line down my calf then kneels between my legs and moves higher.

"Here." His index finger skims my upper thigh. I

shudder out a breath as he strokes a wide arc from the tip of my knee to the top of my hip, finding an invisible crescent-shaped wound from a lifetime ago. I lift my hips, begging Avum to keep going.

He obliges, slipping his hand beneath my dress.

"I've never seen a princess with so many scars before," Avum says. He traces a triangular indent on my lower stomach, so close to where I want him.

"Technically," I whisper, grabbing his wrist, "you don't *see* me with any, you just feel them. Varren glamor makes them invisible."

Leaning forward, I slide Avum's hand down the front of my black underlace then grab his jacket and tug him to me. There's a protest forming on his lips but I silence it, pressing our mouths together. His fingers find my clit at the same time I find his tongue.

A porcelain mug falls over, sludge pouring into my hair before it tumbles to the floor and shatters. The scent of menthol fills the room, and green clumps spray everywhere. Neither of us cares.

Avum's magic slicks along my piercing, searing my clit. I cry out, but he consumes my scream, kissing deeper, threading his free hand through my hair and pulling.

Gods, I forgot how good kissing feels.

"I shouldn't be doing this," Avum says, but they're just words. He doesn't even bother to remove his hands and instead tilts my head sideways, licking along the column of my throat, taking my earlobe between his teeth. "Malin is like a son to me."

I lick my lips and work my fingers beneath his waistband. "If you want someone to call you Daddy," I purr, "all you have to do is ask."

Avum's cock strains against the front of his pants, the bulge growing impossibly larger. I untuck his shirt then turn my attention to the buttons holding him back.

He puts his hand over mine, stopping me. "You first, princess. You've waited long enough already."

My back arches when his fingers dip lower, teasing my entrance. "I want to feel you burning me from the inside out."

Those fingers plunge deep, curling in a way that makes my whole body quiver. I clench around him. Tears leak past my eyes, and the heat becomes so white hot that black dots blur my vision.

"Oh my gods!" I scream.

"Not quite." Avum buries himself to the third knuckle then adds a third finger and a fourth, stretching me until it feels like I'm going to split in half.

The noise that escapes my throat doesn't sound human.

"Do you think you can take it all?" he asks.

I shake my head. Tears leak past my eyes as he

adds his thumb to the mix, circling my throbbing clit.

"Tell me to stop or this whole hand is going inside you."

My thighs shake so hard, they slap the table. "I can't," I whine.

"You can, princess."

I'm so slick, there's a puddle beneath me. "*Please.*"

"Tell me to stop and I'll stop." He shifts, readjusting his position on the counter. "That's it. Look down. I want you to watch as my hand disappears inside you."

The sight is so fucking profane.

I watch his thumb sink inside my pussy and listen to the squelching noise it makes as he stretches me to my limit, inch by arduous inch. His hand disappears completely, and I sag to the countertop—a useless exhausted heap. Sweat plasters the tulle to my body until I'm suffocating in it.

"I wish you could see how beautiful you look right now."

Panting, I try to speak but can't.

Pain rips through me as soon as he starts to move, pumping in slow, languid motions. I hold my breath and clench my teeth, my vision blurring as the whole world spins.

It's so intense. So unlike anything I've ever felt before.

The pain doesn't fade. Neither does the feeling of being shredded to bits. But pleasure overrides it and soon, I find myself humping his hand, my pussy clenching around it as I near my peak.

"Please, can I come?" I beg.

Avum slips his thumb out and returns it to my clit, arousal glistening on his finger_pad. He rubs circles against my piercing as he pumps me. "Of course, princess."

I throw my head back and wait.

Nothing happens.

Pleasure becomes overstimulation, then agony as I try to tumble over the ledge that Malin's magic keeps me on. And it's in that horrible, awful moment that I realize as long as this spell is on me, I really am nothing more than my husband's living sex doll.

PRINCESS EZRAH VARREN

FORTRESS HEDRA, CENTRAL CARTHINIA

Cold water pelts me from overhead, cooling my fevered flesh. Shivering, I stand on tiptoes and adjust the showerhead so it can rinse the herbal soap from my sudsy hair.

Rosemary.

Sandalwood.

Gunpowder.

Avum's bath products remind me of home. Closing my eyes, I let the scents permeate my nostrils before scrubbing the rest of my body clean. I should be sore and achy but I'm not, courtesy of a very potent painkiller Avum gave me the second we left the kitchen.

The shower in his chambers is small, utilitarian in function, with gray tiles, a hanging basket full of soaps, and a sliding glass door. It reminds me of the showers I'd find back in Laithey, where living in luxury was synonymous with being weak.

Reaching into the basket, I withdraw a round tin and unscrew it. Something brown and grainy spills out the top and I make a face. "What the hell is this?" I ask.

"Smell it." Avum's voice comes from his adjoining room, muffled through the pouring water.

I turn the nozzle, letting the spray reach a toasty lukewarm before sniffing. My eyebrows knit together. "Coffee?"

"And castor oil. It will make your skin soft."

Avum, with his calloused hands and scared flesh, seems like the last person in Ranada who would care about soft skin. Something dark squeezes my chest as I realize the most likely explanation—it belongs to someone else. I shouldn't care. I've only just met him, and I'm Malin's wife. Still, the need to overturn the tin and fling the contents out is almost overwhelming.

I don't.

I slam the lid shut, finish rinsing, then ring my hair out over the metal drain. There's a towel rack hanging outside the shower but I ignore it, letting the cool air and dripping water tighten my nipples into stiff peaks. My skin is the color of rubies, either from Avum's touch or the coldness of the water, I'm not sure. What I am sure of is that regardless of who's been in that shower, I'm the prettiest thing that's ever come back out.

Water puddles beneath my feet as I pad across the bathroom tiles to the open doorway that leads to Avum's living quarters. The other room is sparsely furnished. White animal furs cover the floor in its entirety, and matching leather couches surround a low-lying glass table and crackling hearth. My dress drapes over the table—freshly washed and drying—and Avum sits on the couch in front of it, his bare feet propped against the glass, his jacket gone and shirt untucked. My yellow journal lies open in his hands, and a pair of reading spectacles rest on the cushion beside him.

Avum looks cute this way—all rumpled and messy. It feels strangely intimate to see the man without his uniform, to have him trust me well enough to expose his shoddy eyesight and trick knee.

It's endearingly stupid.

"All finished," I announce, sashaying into the room. Plush carpet tickles my feet, and a roaring fire warms my back as I step into his line of sight.

The book slips from Avum's hands. He whistles low as he drinks me in. "Do you know you're the most beautiful woman in all of Ranada?"

I do.

Smiling at him, I swing my hips as I maneuver

past the glass table. "You got the book for me," I say, scanning the suede cover.

He runs his hands through his hair, gaze shifting between me and it, like he's having second thoughts.

That won't do.

I snatch the book off his lap and set it on the table. Then, I grab his reading spectacles and click them shut before scooting them aside. "I shouldn't have put you in this position, general. I'm sorry," I whisper, making my voice small.

He scowls at me. "You have nothing to apologize for. I put myself in this position. Regardless, I don't approve of Malin playing with you in this way—not if you don't want it."

I blink.

That's not the response I expected.

He ghosts his fingers along my hips and my stomach somersaults. "For someone so obsessed with getting you here, he's certainly made no efforts to keep you happy. Were you my wife, I wouldn't be nearly so foolish."

Biting my bottom lip, I slide my fingers over his and squeeze. "Thank you for helping me."

Avum chuckles. "Don't thank me, princess. It's not at all selfless."

His eyes darken—attention shifting to my taut nipples and slick skin. Though he doesn't touch me,

I can feel the warmth of his magic caress my body. The water dries. My pussy doesn't.

"You know what I *do* want?" I ask.

He shakes his head.

Climbing onto the couch, I loop my arms around his neck and straddle him. The man is already hard, his cock pulsing against me, separated only by a thin layer of fabric and buttons. I lean over him and press my mouth to his ear. "I want to come with you inside me. I want you to finish that spell so I can ride your cock all night."

Avum groans. "Fuck, princess."

He grips my hips then claims my mouth, slipping his tongue between my teeth. Pinpricks burn my lips and they puff up, turning so fucking sensitive, so raw, I can't decide if I should beg him to stop or keep going. He decides for me, devouring my whimpers, pouring more heat inside me.

Each nip, lick, and bite sends a sharp pang of arousal straight to my middle. I cry out, arching my back, grinding my slickness against him. Cupping Avum's jaw, I lose myself to the sensations, letting myself forget for just a moment why I'm doing this in the first place.

It's almost too easy. Manipulating men, turning them against one another, it's what I do best.

Midkiss, I force myself to cry, thinking of the *Midnight Sun* until my vision is blurry and my eyeballs burn. Salt spills down our lips, mingles with our tongues as he sucks my bottom lip into his mouth.

"What's wrong? Are you alright? " Avum pulls away, eyes full of concern.

My heart squeezes. No one's looked at me like that in a long time, and I know if I'm not careful, I'll get attached. Hells, I already am. He's shown more kindness to me tonight than anyone else has in months.

I can barely speak through all my tears, hiccupping as I work myself into a frenzy. "Do you know he's never even kissed me? This is the most I've talked to anyone since Malin's brought me here. I'm so fucking tired of being alone. I had enough of that back in Varren."

Avum wipes my tears away. "Shhhhh, princess. It's alright." Tenderly, he kisses my forehead, then my nose and lips. For a second, I get caught up in the act and part my mouth, letting Avum kiss the pain away. He's so godsdamned tender, so warm in a world of cold and dark.

Avum nibbles on my bottom lip, and I reach for the buttons that separate us, thumbing two of the three free. On the last one, he puts his hand on mine. "No, Ezrah. Not tonight." The words are soft but firm. Resolute.

"Please, let me finish what we started." I sniffle.

"You've been so nice to me. I want to be nice to you too."

His face twists into something pained. "Not until you can come with me. I'll get the ingredients for the spell and then—"

And then I'll run far away. And you'll help me.

I cut him off with another kiss. Minutes later, we break apart panting, and I fumble with the buttons on his tunic, peeling them free one by one to reveal a chest full of jagged battle scars.

"Princess . . ." he protests.

I put my finger over his lips. "I want to see you, general. It's only fair."

With my breasts in his face, it's hard to object. Avum drops his hands to his sides, and I peel the tunic past his shoulders down the back of the couch. The marks on his chest are lumpy and familiar, and I trace each one of them.

"Axe wound," I say, grazing my fingernail down a purple line that runs from clavicle to shoulder.

Avum nods.

"Gunshot wound." I suck on the uneven circle over his left pecs. Goosebumps pebble beneath my tongue and small invisible hairs stand on end. Smiling, I move on to the uneven blobs that pepper the surrounding area, lightly tapping each one of them with an index finger. "Metal shrapnel. It must've been a bitch to pull it all out."

"It was," he says, voice gravelly.

I arch an eyebrow when I see the not-quite-triangle shape on his side. "Scissors? What, did you piss off your tailor?"

The man chuckles, though it comes out shaky. Beneath me, his cock jerks. "I'm afraid I'll be taking that story to my grave."

"Hmmm. We'll see about that." But for now, I let it go. Avum's not mine to keep, and his secrets aren't mine to steal.

"Throwing star."

"Dagger."

"Arrow."

I'm impressed. Most men would be dead by now.

My assessment ends when I reach the hook-shaped scar that splits Avum's left eye. I don't recognize the weapon. It's too messy to be from a precision instrument but too deep to be from most anything else.

Avum pulls my fingers away and threads them with his. "Fingernails, princess. An old lover of mine." He kisses the back of my hand then meets my gaze. "What about the cuff mark on your ankle?"

My spine stiffens.

"I was a prostitute, Ezrah. I know the scars better than anyone."

I shake my head and bite the inside of my cheek, using the pain to ground me. Bile rises up my throat and tears—genuine this time—threaten to spill. "I don't know what you're talking about."

"You have matching ones on your other ankle and your wrists." With his free hand, Avum smooths his thumb along the invisible marks. Then, he brings my wrist to his mouth, eyes boring into mine as he plants a soft kiss at my pulse. "You don't have to tell me about Tristan until you're ready, but I want you to know that I've been through it too, and I'm here for you if you need someone to confide in."

Tristan.

The world seems to collapse around me, everything that I am shattering all at once. I scramble to re-erect my defenses, to redeploy my mask, but I can't. Avum's cracked me wide open, and the splintered bits of me are hemorrhaging onto his lap.

The room grows suffocatingly hot—the fire a million degrees warmer than it was just a moment ago. It feels like I'm drowning in it. "You know about him," I whisper, voice cracking. "They told you."

"Yes," Avum says. "But your brother didn't go into detail."

I swallow the lump in my throat. "What did he say?"

"That your father arrested him for defiling you."

Wetness stings my cheeks as my mind drifts back to that horrible day at the beach. I'd been so stupid, thinking my father would ever allow a man like

Tristan to touch me and get away with it, thinking Tristan would ever agree to leave me. Of course, Arrovin had guards posted on the other side of the rocks, ready to take him away the moment I turned my back.

Everything changed after that. Torture has a way of sucking all the goodness out of a person, twisting them into something wretched and broken. So does heartbreak.

Avum squeezes my hand. "He said Tristan escaped your father's dungeons, kidnapped you, then turned you into his pleasure slave. It took them five years to sink his ship and bring you home."

"Please," I whisper. "I can't talk about this."

"I'm sorry, princess. I know it must be difficult for you, but you know Fontaine's routes better than anyone. Malin and I can't protect you if we can't find him."

Can't find him?

My brows furrow. "The ships . . . The fires . . ."

"Are Fontaine's." He frowns at me. "Didn't Malin tell you?"

No. He didn't.

PORT SERA CAY

PRESENT DAY

(PRINCE) CAPTAIN LOWEN HADE

PORT SERA CAY, INDEPENDENT TERRITORY

Across from me, Tarin's ridiculously oversized tits spill out of a crimson corset, exposing enough skin to make the men at the gambling table granite-hard. Whiskey in one hand, playing cards in the other, she whispers something into my helmsman's ear before readjusting in his lap, parting her legs for easy access. His hand delves beneath the table and disappears down the waistband of her puffy harem pants. Tarin giggles, but all the while, her gaze remains locked on mine.

"I raise," my helmsman says, peeking at the cards in Tarin's hand. A pile of gold coins lay in front of them—a much smaller pile than what he came here with. "Shove the rest in, would you?"

"Sure thing, baby." Tarin knocks the whiskey back then pushes the coins into the center of the table. They clink against an assortment of treasure—gems, gold, drugs, a supposed map to the seventh hell. If I were a bigger dick, I'd point out how paltry his wager is compared to the others, but I'm not. It's bad enough that I'm going to take all his money; I needn't take his pride too.

Squinting through a haze of tobacco smoke and flickering oil lights, I wait for Tarin's signal. As my friend shoves his fingers deep inside her, she bites the bottom right corner of her rubied lips.

A delegation.

Not bad this late in the game. Certainly better than my two-of-a-kind.

Rifling through my trouser pockets, I procure a matchbox, then a cigar case made from crushed seashells and Ezzy's golden blood. I flick it open and select my most expensive cigar.

"You sure about that, Jace?" My tone is measured, arrogant even, as I strike the match against the red ignition strip. A bright flame hisses to life. The harsh taste of spiced wood and burnt leather fills my mouth as I light the foot and roll the smoke across my tongue. "Haven't you lost enough money already?"

He glares at me, and I take another puff, letting the haze out in two distinct blows, relaying my shitty cards back to Tarin.

"Do you fold?" he asks.

Tarin whimpers. The dimly lit, smoke-filled brothel isn't nearly dim or smoky enough to conceal her pinched brows and clenched teeth.

A hellscape.

It's the only hand that can beat him. The only hand that mathematically makes sense, given the discard pile. If Jace is counting cards—and he's always counting cards—then I either play the nine hells or forfeit.

I click my tongue then prop my feet on the table with a heavy thunk. It all comes down to what cards the other players have.

"Aren't we supposed to go in turn order?" I ask.

Muck drips down the soles of my boots onto a filthy green tablecloth. Ignoring it, I take another puff then shift my attention to the man on Jace's left—my quartermaster, Cameron Rost.

A moontouched girl stands behind him, dressed in a wispy silver gown that hangs over her lithe body, the fabric transparent enough that her silver thatch and lavender nipples shine through. Her long silver hair drapes over Cameron's shoulder like a sash, and her skin glows in the near darkness, not so dissimilar to the way a Varren's might.

Normally, a man like Cameron couldn't afford a night with her, but I'm as generous a captain as I am a crook.

As she plants a trail of kisses down his neck, those swirling silver eyes peek at his cards.

Three blinks.

Nothing.

The man's deck is shittier than mine.

"Cameron?" I ask. "You still in?"

He shakes his head and throws his cards onto the table, letting the moontouched girl slide her hands beneath his tunic. As she rubs away the sting of his loss, I puff on my cigar and scan the room for Tarin's sister.

It doesn't take long to spot her.

Pria stands on top of the dingy, cherrywood bar, dancing to the dark rhythm of a damrin drum. As her hips undulate, her scale-mail outfit clinks together, the golden panties and matching bandeau drawing all eyes to her. A crowd of Johns surround the platform. They paw at her curly golden wig, at the *avendessa*—the golden paint—that covers her from head to toe, turning her into an honorary Varren.

She's smudged and messy and beautiful. The prettiest girl here, and her talents the most wasted.

I gesture to her with a series of looping exhales, blowing the smoke high into the air. Then, bending sideways, I retrieve my leather satchel off the floor. Metal rattles inside it as I heft it onto my lap. Crinkly orange fabric pools out the top.

"I raise," I say, knowing damn well there's a fifty-seven-percent chance another player has the cards I need—either Kye or Leston—whether they'd be willing to tattle on me is an altogether different story.

Reaching inside the bag, I withdraw a pair of metal shackles. *"Amaron,"* I say, tossing them onto the treasure heap. Jace's golden coins slide down the pile, tinkling against each other as they hit the ground and roll. "My father's creation. Imbued with his magic to stop others from casting spells. Works on innate power too."

Greed flickers in my helmsman's eyes as he no doubt calculates all the damage an anti-magic weapon could do. "How does it work?"

In my periphery, Pria hops down from the bar, a bottle of whiskey in hand. Another minute of distractions and she'll be ready to go.

"It electrocutes people," I say, taking a final puff from my cigar. I jab the smoky, ashy tip into the tablecloth and wait for the flame to sizzle out. "When someone tries to use their magic, the amaron activates. It starts as a dull pinprick—nothing more than a vibration—but if they don't stop, the pain increases until the shocks are so strong, it'll kill."

"Gruesome," Cameron says.

Jace withdraws his fingers from Tarin. "Has Arrovin ever used it on you?" Leaning forward, he examines the pale metal as if waiting for the magic to reveal itself. It won't—not until something magical comes into contact with it.

I shake my head then fling the remnants of my cigar across the room. It hits the back wall and explodes into a plume of brown powder. "No, but I've seen it used on our prisoners. It's nasty but effective."

To my left, Pria snaps into focus, sashaying her hips as she walks, dancing to the ever-present drumbeat. She sets the whiskey bottle on the discard pile then grabs me by the ankles, scrunching that dainty little nose of hers when the dirt rubs off my boots onto her painted flesh.

"You owe me a bottle of avendessa, Captain Hade." Pria forcefully pries my boots off the table, and I rock forward, the front two legs of my chair slamming into the hardwood floor. My satchel tumbles from my lap, disappearing beneath the tablecloth.

"Can't you see I'm a little busy right now?" I growl.

"Can't you see, I don't care?"

She shimmies onto the table and sets her gilded ass in the mud puddle. Parting her legs, Pria slides her feet up my knees then leans forward and grabs me by the shirt collar, tugging me so close, I can smell her chalky paint. Avendessa stains my shirt, permanently imprinting her finger pads into the fabric.

Damn. I really hate it when she ruins my things.

"You promised me avendessa, then left port without paying," Pria hisses.

I snort. "It's not my fault you spread your legs without taking payment first. Besides," I say, rubbing her shoulder, streaking the paint. "I prefer you when you don't look like my sisters."

Smack!

Fire burns my cheek, radiates down my jaw. Acting on impulse, I clench her hand in mine and—

"Lowen, don't!" Tarin's frantic voice cuts through the music, stopping me just before I squeeze down— something that would have shattered every bone in Pria's pretty hand thanks to my magical strength.

This is why we rehearse things.

This is why we don't go off script.

Clenching my teeth, I force a smile to my lips then kiss each of Pria's gilded knuckles, no doubt getting the avendessa on my lips. "There's no need for violence, sweetheart. Your payment is in the bag."

I lift the tablecloth and point to the satchel. Its contents are half-sprawled on the floor, the orange shawl covered in bar grime. A corked bottle of avendessa lies on its side and a crystalline jar of crushed seashells sets beside it—a new shard added for every port I've traveled to.

Pria crawls beneath the table, and I slap her ass, wincing when the scaley panties dig into my palm. She sticks her tongue out before disappearing beneath the green fabric.

"Now that I've paid you," I say, plucking the whiskey off the discard pile. "Can you be on your way?"

The table rattles, coins and jewels spilling over the edge as Pria thumps her head against it. All eyes shift to her, to the spilling treasure, except for mine. As she maintains the diversion—making hasty apologies, bumping her head a second time—I reach beneath the whiskey bottle and grab the hand of cards stuck to it. Then, I replace them with my own, pushing them into a clear tack that coats the glass bottom.

By the time Pria crawls back to the surface and returns the fallen goods, I've already finished and am leaning back in the chair—no one the wiser. I return my muddy feet to the table then forcefully pass the bottle to her, shoving it into her jeweled navel while she smooths out her hair.

Pria glares. "I can't believe I ever let you touch me."

"Baby, we both know I can touch you whenever I please. After all, I'm the only one in Ranada who can get avendessa to you. Now, take that shit off your face and meet me in my room. I'll be up in an hour."

Her cheeks flush bright pink, the color seeping through gilded smudges. "You're an ass, Hade."

"And you're a whore. Now that we've stated the obvious, get going. You're ruining our game."

With a huff, she yanks the bottle from me, her spine straightening like I've shoved a lightning rod through it. Every man at the table watches her walk away—not to the bar where the Johns still wait for her, but upstairs to the rooms I keep.

Good girl.

A smile creases the edges of my lips as I glance back to Tarin, who's now running her fingers through Jace's hair, messing up the carefully and meticulously applied gel. "Now that that's over with, let's get back to the game."

HUNDREDS OF GOLD coins spill from my satchel, clinking together as they hit the low-lying glass table. Buried beneath them are Cameron's map, a dozen leather pouches filled with *tannix*, and more sapphires and tourmaline than my father wears in his pompous crown.

I overturn the bag and give it a handful of shakes, ensuring every last piece of treasure has been thoroughly discarded. Beside me, Pria kneels on a fur rug and eyes the winnings, a smile plastered to her pale, freckled face. Wet brown hair clings to her cheeks. A plush bathrobe covers her freshly washed body.

The air around us is thick with incense, masking the stench of mildew that clings to the walls. Pria's bedroom is a strange combination of decrepit opulence. Dozens of animal furs hide the rotten floorboards, jeweled and glossy furniture presses up against the peeling, green-painted walls, and vibrant silk canopies hang from a leaky ceiling, separating the room into quadrants. All of Pria's luxuries were provided by me, and while they're nowhere near good enough for her, it's the best I can manage until I'm king.

"We did good," Pria says, pilfering one of the coins, rolling it between her fingers.

Water droplets patter to the floor, landing in one of my discarded boots. I kick them away and frown. "*I* did good. *You* went off script. I could have broken your hand back there."

"Oh, please. I'm not afraid of you, *Prince* Lowen Hade." She rolls her eyes at me then gives a mocking bow.

"I wish you would take this more seriously."

Pria flicks her coin back into the pile then runs her hand along the glittering trove, ignoring me like she always does. "Why do you steal all this shit anyway? It's not like you need the money."

I shrug. "Because it's fun . . . I dunno. Ezzy and I used to run cons all the time when we were young. I guess I never really grew out of it."

"She's the only sister you talk about."

"She's the only sister *worth* talking about. The other ones are conniving bitches."

Metal scratches against glass as I dig through the coin pile and withdraw the pilfered map. The paper is chalky and thin—transparent like the skin on a leaf and worn along its folded edges. Gingerly, I open it, smoothing out the creases on the hardwood floor. The paper pulses beneath my palms, but the sheet itself is blank.

I refold it then tuck it into the waistband of my white breeches. "You lot can have the rest. Like you said, I don't need it."

"Is it real?" she asks, gesturing to the map.

I grunt. "Hard to tell. There's an enchantment on it that'll need a mage to break. Supposedly, Ezzy's new husband—"

I realize the mistake a second too late. For months, our kingdom has kept their marriage a secret, which in turn has kept Ezzy hidden. Safe. And while I might trust Pria with my life, I certainly don't trust her with my twin's.

My tongue knots, but the bedroom door swings open before I'm forced to elaborate.

Golden light pours from the hallway. Raucous music carries up the stairs—fiddles, tambourines, a bloody shawm, all clashing together as my drunken soldiers break out into a vulgar folk song.

My eyes smart against the sudden brightness, adjusting in time to see Tarin appear arm in arm with the moontouched girl.

"I hope you two are getting along," she says, shutting the door behind her.

The music stops the second the latch clicks into place. Pria's magic—the reason why a night with her sells for so much—allows her to control the sound in a room. The words spoken inside it are private, the words outside, as noiseless as a fallen feather. A great trick when someone needs to have clandestine meetings or when their sexual proclivities are too deviant to risk being overheard.

"We always get along," I say, rising from my spot on the floor. "Especially when she sticks to the script."

I can feel Pria flash me a vulgar gesture even though I can't see it. I offer one back, waving my pointer and middle finger high into the air.

Fuck yourself.

Ignoring us, Tarin unhooks her sandals and fumbles with the laces on her too-tight corset.

Meanwhile, the moontouched girl shuffles awkwardly into a corner, her glowing arms folded over her glowing tits.

"I keep men's clothing in the closet," I tell the new girl. "Nothing fancy, but it'll be more comfortable than that."

She bites her bottom lip and squeezes herself even tighter.

Ducking behind Tarin, I bat her hand away and take over the lacework, my fingers much more nimble than hers. "You think you'd be better at this, given what you do."

"People enjoy undressing me," Tarin says. "Something you probably can't relate to."

Pria snorts.

I narrow my eyes at them, fighting back a smile that would only encourage their bad behavior. Gods, I missed them.

"You know I'm still a prince, right? I could have your tongue for that."

"But my tongue is what makes you all that money," Tarin purrs, inclining her head to the treasure heap. Goosebumps spread along her back, pebbling beneath my fingertips as I unknot the final bow and peel the corset free of her sweaty skin.

It tumbles to the floor between us.

"Your tongue is more trouble than it's worth," I say, stepping around her. "Honestly, you're no better than Pria. You shouldn't have called me Lowen in front of the others; it's too familiar."

"*Pfft*. You would have broken her hand if I hadn't, and then I would have listened to her whine about it for the next month."

Pria glares at us. "Gods, the two of you are so uptight. Lowen wouldn't have hurt me."

The faith she has in my self-control is grossly misplaced. Tarin says as much, and then they're off to a bickering match I want no part of.

Sighing, I shrug the white justaucorps from my shoulders and toss it to the couch. Next, the matching tricorn. Then, my white and gold tunic. By the time I've stripped down to just my pants, their little tiff is over, and Tarin is fully naked, her thighs spread wide on the seat across from me. Yawning, she undoes the pins from her hair and a tangled mess of red curls spills onto the cushions as she throws her head back and closes her eyes for what must be the first time all night.

"Can we divvy up the winnings in the morning?" Tarin asks. "I'm exhausted."

"There's no need," Pria says, lifting a sapphire to the candlelight. "Lowen says we can have it all."

Tarin opens one of her eyes and sets it on me. "Why? I want a real answer, Lowen. Don't pretend you're being nice."

I push the shaggy brown hair from my face and

glance at the leaky ceiling, considering my words. I loathe goodbyes almost as much as I loathe being stuck at sea; I'd hoped to sneak out in the morning and leave a note.

"Arrovin ordered me back to the palace, and I don't know when I'll make port again," I finally say. "I want to make sure you're taken care of while I'm gone."

"Knew it," Tarin snaps.

Pria drops her sapphire, and her smile falls with it. "You're leaving? But you only just got here."

"I know." Normally, I'd be relieved to have my military tour shortened, but not when it means abandoning my hunt for Fontaine or leaving my two dearest friends behind. "I wasn't supposed to stop at all, but I needed to check on you."

"I don't want you to check on me," Pria hisses. Sniffling, she balls her hands into fists and rubs her rapidly reddening eyes. "I want you to take me with you."

"No." My tone is harsher than I meant it. I take a deep breath and restart. "When you and Tarin come to the palace, it'll be as my advisors, not as my whores, and it'll be after the crown passes to me."

She shoves the treasure heap to the floor and the coins go rolling, clinking together as they vanish under tables and chairs. "That could take years! I don't want to be stuck here anymore."

And this is why I prefer the notes.

Groaning, I run my hands over my face; it's always a fight with her. "My father would never accept you or Tarin in a position of authority," I remind her. "If he allowed you to stay, it would be as our slaves, and my father is not particularly kind to the women he keeps. I refuse to see you broken by him."

"He's right, Pria," Tarin soothes. "We're safe here. Lowen takes good care of us."

Pria crosses her arms. "Do you know how much money I could make selling my services elsewhere?"

"None," I growl. "Because the kings would find out about it, snatch you up, then use you for breeding. At least here, you can choose who you fuck. King Saril, Remi, Therin—they wouldn't give you that option."

It's naive of her to think any differently.

"I don't keep you here because I enjoy it," I say. Crouching beside her, I begin picking up the spilled coins, returning them to the table one clink at a time. Soon, she joins in, refusing to meet my gaze as she dives beneath the couch.

I let her mope.

In another world, things would be different, but in this one, magic is in short supply and the kings are ruthless. Usually, it takes two mages to produce magical offspring, which makes Pria invaluable to any king looking to expand their empire. Arrovin has several illegitimate children with women just like her, and he's assigned all of their offspring—my half brothers and half sisters—to fight in his never-ending wars on permanent deployment. What he does to the mothers is even worse.

Images of Pria covered in avendessa, collared and chained at his throne come unbidden. I shove them aside, swallowing the bile that churns my gut.

I won't let that happen.

The floorboards squeak, and I snap my head toward the sound, remembering for the first time that we've got company. "What are you staring at?" I ask. The moontouched girl hasn't taken her silver eyes off me since entering the room; she hasn't moved either. "I know I'm good-looking, but hells, woman."

She wrings her hands over her stomach, shuffling her feet against the sagging floorboards. "You're . . . I thought you'd be more . . . glittery."

I snicker, imagining myself as a walking, talking geode like my sisters—thank the gods, I was born normal. "Sweetheart," I say, plucking a ruby from the white seal-fur rug, "that's not how Varrens work. The bloodline is only passed to the women in my family."

She bites her bottom lip, brows drawing down into a frown.

Tossing the ruby onto the heap, I clarify, "I'm from Varren, but I'm not *a* Varren. That's why my father and I have different last names. The country and the title are separate."

"Oh." She drops her arms.

"You're from Carthinia, right?" I ask, already knowing the answer. I've never met a moontouched girl who wasn't from the hinterlands of Malin's kingdom, deep within the Crynthian Wilds, where the Varren are so detested and feared that to speak their name is to bring a curse upon one's family. Malin's father used to claim the Varren made her what she is—moontouched, cursed to never see the sunlight again. According to their legends, one touch from a Varren is all it takes to ruin a bloodline forever, although from experience, I can all but attest that isn't true.

The girl nods. "I'm from a small village near Rannith."

Small towns make for small minds.

A decade ago, I might've tried convincing her that my family isn't what they seem, but after a dozen arguments with religious zealots, I no longer have the patience for it. That's Ezzy's job now.

"You can relax," I say, staring at her glowing, pale skin. "Even if I shared my sisters' powers, which I don't, I can't curse you any more than you already are."

Pria smacks me in the shin. "Be nice to her, prick. Livi is the reason we won tonight." She smiles at the girl. "He's harmless, really."

It's not true, but I decide now isn't the time to point that out.

The new girl—*Livi*—slowly scans the three of us, her cheeks flushing light purple. "Are you guys . . ."

The noise Pria makes—somewhere between a cough, a gag, and a laugh—is almost enough to wound my ego. "Fucking? Gods no."

"I prefer blonds," I say.

"And cock," Tarin mumbles, half asleep on the couch.

I flash her a vulgar gesture and rise from my seat. "And with that, I'm taking the bed tonight. I'll wake you both before I leave."

Pushing the curtain aside, I step into the bedroom. It's as beautiful and disgusting as the rest of the space, with a bright golden rug, a plush golden bed, and golden curtains that frame a small window overlooking the city streets. The side of the mattress lies flush against the wooden wall, pushed into a corner just beneath the window. I elect to leave my pants on as I crawl into bed and settle into the downy pillows, tucking myself beneath the sheets.

Half-asleep, I stare outside the window where oil lanterns hang along the deserted cobblestone, omitting an eerie glow across Sera Cay. A single carriage clicks along the path, kicking up dust as it passes by, likely venturing to a more reputable part of the city. The docks are close enough that I can see the outline of my prized frigate from down the hill but far enough away that I don't have to interact with most of my crew.

For nine years I've been on conscription, stopping by this dingy room every three months like clockwork. The girls are my confidantes, this brothel my home, more so than the palaces have ever been. The stench of liquor, sex, and tobacco smoke are so familiar to me now that I crave them when I'm at sea, not the luxuries of Varren or the prestige of being my father's only legitimate heir.

Losing the brothel and my girls is worse than if Arrovin had shot me.

The bed squeaks and dips. Soft fingers curl around my stomach as Pria crawls into the empty space beside me. "I'm going to miss you, you big dummy."

"It's not forever," I say, throat tight.

It very well could be forever. I'm as subject to my father's will as anyone.

"Promise?" she asks.

"Promise."

And for a moment, I let myself believe the lie.

ORANGE LIGHT FLICKERS outside the bedroom window, shining brightly in my eyes. Blanketless and shivering, I roll onto my side and come face-to-face with Pria. She's overtaken the bed, spreading herself like a starfish, tangling the gilded sheets around her legs. When I try to peel them free, Pria grunts, flips me her pointer and middle finger, then rolls far away.

Snores come shortly after.

Groaning, I wipe the crust from my eyes and reach for the window. I'm about to pull the curtains shut when I see it.

A plume of midnight blue smoke billows from the docks, pouring over the city streets like fog. Fire licks across the sea as every ship along the harbor burns, including mine.

Shit.

Shit. Shit. Shit. Shit. Shit.

Fire blazes across the street from us, running up the sides of buildings, crumpling and crumbling them into a smoldering heap. Torches bob along the cobblestone streets, held by pirates dressed in dark uniforms and skull paint. Their guns and blades glint in the firelight as they gather below the brothel and charge the entryway.

Fontaine's crew. I'd recognize the getup anywhere.

My military training has me conjuring up a dozen plans of defense—none of them viable.

I rush to Pria instead, shaking her arm. "Get up!" I hiss.

Her brown eyes snap open, and I cover her mouth with my hand before she has time to argue or scream.

"Get up. Get to the closet. Keep your mouth shut. Do you understand?"

Pria nods, her body shaking as she scrambles out of bed. The room is unnervingly quiet. I should be able to hear something—the mob outside, my men downstairs—there's no way Fontaine could coordinate something as stealthy as this.

And then I remember.

"Pria, your magic. Shit. Turn it off."

She blinks, and a thousand noises slam against my ears. Shouting from downstairs. Gurgling. Hissing and snapping flames. The blast of cannon fire and the bang of guns.

A deep, male voice comes from the other side of the bedroom curtain. "Come out, Hade! Stop hiding behind your whores."

"Lowen," Pria whispers. "Please, don't go."

I put a finger over my lips and gesture to the closet. "Hide. Now."

As soon as she's out of sight, I sweep the curtain aside, duck into the living room, and freeze.

The door to the staircase is open, and golden light filters into the room, illuminating the white couch where Tarin sits. She's not alone. Two pirates flank the couch, while another has forced her into his lap. A flintlock pistol presses against her temple.

"I'm sorry, Lowen. I didn't—"

The pirate slams the butt of his pistol against Tarin's forehead and red blood gushes, pouring into her eyes. Tarin's head lolls. Her skin turns unnervingly pale.

I clench my teeth. "Let her go."

"On your knees, Hade," hisses the pirate with the gun. It's impossible to recognize him with the paint on, but I do what I can to commit his face to memory. Crooked nose. Dimpled chin. Hair the color of ravens.

He'll die first.

Slowly, I lower myself to the floorboards and scan the carpets for something to hurl. The one good thing about my strength is that it can turn anything into a weapon, especially shiny metal coins. One good toss would put a crater through his skull, and once he's down and the gun is no longer a threat, I can handle his shitty friends.

I don't see any coins, though.

The one time Pria finishes picking up her mess . . .

"Hands in the air," the gunman says.

I hesitate.

"Hands in the fucking air." He slams the butt of the gun into Tarin a second time, and a resounding crack splits the air.

Tarin moans, body slumping, eyelids fluttering as she drifts in and out of consciousness.

"Try anything clever and I'll put a bullet through her head."

"Lowen," Tarin whispers. "Run. Please."

We both know I'm not going to do that. I'd never leave her; I'd never leave either of them.

I do as the gunman says, my lip curling in disgust. "How exactly do you plan on keeping me," I growl. "I can bend any bars, put holes in any ship. I can break your bones as easy as I draw breath."

The pirate grins, flashing me a mouthful of gilded teeth—gold likely bled from my sister at Fontaine's command. "Livi here is going to cuff you and you're going to let her."

My gaze swivels to the moontouched girl hidden in the recesses of the walls. Her wispy silver gown is gone now, replaced by a midnight blue uniform and matching head wrap. Amaron shackles gleam in her palms—*my* shackles—and blue electricity sizzles across the metal. No longer nervous or shy, she approaches me with a smooth gait, her posture tall and haughty.

"You fucking bitch!" The need to lunge at her tugs deep within my bones, but I hold my ground for Tarin's sake.

Stepping behind me, she clicks the metal cuff around my wrist. A low vibration travels up my arm, across my shoulder blades, and down the length of my spine. I hiss when she wrenches the other arm back and secures the second cuff. Electricity crackles in my ears, the vibration turning sharper, hotter, until I bite my tongue.

Copper floods my mouth.

Livi grabs my hair and yanks, dragging my gaze to the ceiling. Voice low, she whispers, "Try to stay alive, *prince*. Malin will be furious if I get you killed."

The gun goes off.

A plume of thick smoke fills the air, and something heavy thumps to the floor. When the gunpowder clears, Tarin's glassy, empty eyes stare up at me, her red curls spilling over a bloody face. I throw myself at her, screaming till my lungs burn.

Her olive irises are the last thing I see before the pirates toss a bag over my head and the world goes dark.

CARTHINIA

PRESENT DAY

PRINCESS EZRAH VARREN

FORTRESS HEDRA, CENTRAL CARTHINIA

My fingers glide along the smooth curve of Avum's pocket watch, playing with the tiny, hook-shaped clasp that keeps it shut. My other hand is tangled up in Avum's, his fiery warmth pouring into me as he guides us into the grand foyer. I expect purple-flamed sconces to burst to life as soon as we emerge from the cramped corridor, but they don't. Aside from a few candles atop the black chandelier, everything around us is dark and quiet—strangely so.

Squeezing Avum's hand, I glance between him and the large obsidian staircase that will take me to my rooms. At the foot of the steps is a striped, purple rug made from sleek animal fur. At the top is a hanging clock twice as tall as I am that displays the hours in phases of the moon. There are no windows on the lower floors of the palace—likely meant to disorient people the same as the pooling mist and nonsensical pathways—but here the clock confirms what Avum's pocket watch showed just moments ago. It's almost sunup.

Tick.

Tick.

Tick.

The minute hand inches ever closer to the top of the hour, its echoing movement the only sound besides our shuffling footsteps. Scooting closer to Avum, I worry my bottom lip between my teeth, wondering if Malin will be upstairs waiting for me, if he'll notice the missing journal or the fact that I smell like Avum's soaps.

"If you keep working the clasp like that, you'll break it," Avum warns.

I stop my nervous fidgeting, wishing I had pockets to store the watch inside. "I'm sorry. It's just . . ."

"You're safe, Ezrah."

Avum pulls me tightly to his chest. I wrap my arms around him and inhale the scent of charcoal and woodsmoke, knowing the falseness of his words but wanting more than anything for them to be true. I've never been safe a day in my life—not with Tristan, or my father, or any of the lovers I've been forced to take. Varrens don't have the luxury of safety.

Neither do pleasure slaves.

Tenderly, Avum strokes my hair and I sniffle, trying very hard to forget about all the people who have failed me. Avum isn't the first man I've seduced, thinking he'd be the key to my salvation. In the end, they all end up leaving. Or else they end up dead.

Pulling away from him, I peer at the obsidian staircase. *What will Malin do if he catches us?*

Avum cups my cheek and forces me to meet his emerald eyes. "His meetings don't end until this afternoon. His Majesty doesn't sleep in the same rooms as you, correct?"

I nod, though I have no idea how he knows that.

"Then you'll be safe until sundown. I'll get the ingredients and we'll cast the spell before he wakes. I have connections in Laithey who will know how to hide you. If you don't want to be here, then you don't have to be."

"What about you?"

"Don't worry about me, princess." He kisses my forehead and lowers his voice. "Go to your rooms and wait for me there. I won't be long."

I latch onto his puffy white tunic when he tries to pull away. The military uniform is gone now, replaced with disheveled nightclothing and bare feet. Avum said he didn't want to wear shoes when I couldn't, which I think fundamentally broke something inside my brain. Perhaps the last sane part of me that knows it's impossible to keep him.

The gesture was so simple, yet nobody has ever made it before—not my lovers back in Varren, or the privateers at sea, not even the guards who escorted me to Carthinia through barren tundra and pelting ice. While my feet blistered in the sand or froze in hip deep snow, they wore soft furs and hiking boots, figuring it would be easier to carry me through the elements than risk incurring my owners' wrath.

In three years, nobody has ever pitied me enough to shoe me, let alone to share my fate.

The longer I stare at Avum's naked toes, the more my throat tightens. Already, the thought of losing him makes me feel things I definitely shouldn't.

"Please let me come with you," I whisper. "I don't . . . I don't want to be alone." The admission tastes like acid on my tongue. It makes me sound as weak as I feel.

Sighing, Avum tucks a strand of hair behind my ear then smooths his thumb along my cheekbone, the warmth of his skin turning my bones liquid. "Alright, princess, you can come, but if we run into anyone, it's important you let me do the talking."

I quirk an eyebrow but before I can speak, Avum grabs my biceps and scoots me off the purple rug.

His knee cracks as he bends, rolling the fur into a bundle to reveal the smooth stonework beneath.

"Only six of us live in the palace," he reminds me, lowering himself to the stony floor. "Rayne in the east wing, Lyria in the west. Bron in the crypts. You, Malin, and I are the only ones allowed inside the central keep. When we leave, we're supposed to bring His Majesty or his guards with us, so we'll need to be quiet, and we'll need to be fast."

"He keeps you prisoner too?"

Avum shakes his head. "The guards are for our protection, princess. Most of us can't stand one another. Years of history and betrayal make for awkward company."

Digging through his pockets, Avum procures a pale silver key attached to a worn leather strap. Its bow is shaped like a crescent moon and glows as if it's made of starlight. I'm not sure where, and I'm not sure how, but I think I've seen it before, or at least something like it.

Avum runs his hands along the glossy obsidian, pausing over a small divot. He inserts the key and twists. A mechanical whirring fills the chamber, followed by a *click-click* as part of the stone slab rises from the ground, shifting to reveal a black wrought-iron staircase that extends far beneath the castle. There are no lights leading down it. No railings either.

Sweat pricks at the base of my skull, and I take a nervous step back. Then another.

Avum blessedly stands, blocking my view of the hole in the ground. "Our arrangement works well until we're trapped in the same room for too long. You've seen Malin and Rayne when they get together; it's worse in the winter when their sister isn't around to serve as a buffer."

Malin has a sister?

"I'm not trying to make excuses for him," he says. "And I would never expect you to stay given everything that's happened, but you should know Malin would do anything to protect you from Fontaine. He's been enthralled with you ever since the Oksas Ball."

My eyebrows furrow. "The one six years ago?"

It's the only one I've been to, yet my memories of that event are dominated by the fight I had with my father—the fallout of it. It was the day Tristan left me, and the day my whole life changed for the worse. "Malin never mentioned—" Footsteps shuffle behind me, and I cut the sentence off, a chill seeping into my bones as Malin emerges from one of the many winding corridors, arm and arm with Madam Lyria.

Avum's eyes dart to the pocket watch I'm not supposed to have which Malin will certainly confiscate if he sees. With no pockets to store it in, I do the only thing I can. I hide behind Avum, shove it past the slit in my dress and down my panties, cringing when the cold metal bites into my skin. He arches an eyebrow, trying very hard not to snicker. I elbow him.

"I see you two are getting along," Malin says. His expression is unreadable as he unlinks himself with Lyria and approaches us. "It's not polite to gossip about me when I'm not around."

"If you were around, it wouldn't be gossip," I snap. Apparently, a month of constant bickering has made it impossible for me to play nice.

Malin narrows his eyes, but there are no black veins on his skin, and Lyria's liver-spotted face is smiling, so he must be in a halfway decent mood. "How's the tour?" he asks, directing the question at Avum rather than at me.

"Fine." If Avum is nervous, he gives no indication —no sweating, or fidgeting, or glancing around the room. The man's poker face is impressive.

An unspoken conversation passes between them as my husband hooks his arm around my waist and pulls me close. The touch is possessive and, despite everything, sends heat pooling at my middle. I can't help but envision those hands snaking lower, bringing me to the precipice of release again and again as they punish me for what happened in the kitchen and tease me for the hundredth time.

Once the spell is gone, I'll be back to normal. I'll stop melting at his touch or daydreaming about the way his cock feels inside me—at least that's what I keep telling myself because anything else would be unacceptable.

"We just finished the first floor," Avum says.

"And the crypts were what?" Malin asks. "A quick detour?"

"I was planning on—"

"What in the nine hells are you wearing?" Malin's eyes trail over Avum's nightclothing and bare feet. The tension between them becomes so palpable, I can practically taste it.

In need of a distraction, I suddenly remember that our "gossip" got derailed. Not to be deterred, I pick up where Avum and I left off. "We met at the Oksas Ball?" I ask, turning to Malin.

Those black irises flare to life, silver starlight swirling inside them.

"We did," Malin says, words clipped. It takes a second, but his gaze shifts back to me. "But like all Varren, you were too good to speak to me." He releases my waist then runs his hand down the curve of my ass, squeezing hard. "But you're not too good anymore. Are you, Ezrah?"

I bite my lip to keep from crying out.

"Are you?" He squeezes harder, and this time a small whimper eeks past.

"No, Your Majesty." I clamp my thighs together, shuddering when the pocket watch shifts against my piercing.

"Good girl." Malin smacks my ass, then returns his attention to Avum. "Does Bron know you're coming?"

Avum shakes his head. "No, but we're on speaking terms again so our company should be well received."

A smirk appears on my husband's pale face and again, I wonder how I could have forgotten those curls, those eyes, those spiderweb veins that send shivers running through me. Had I truly been so distracted at the Oksas to have missed him?

"I'll go with you, just in case. Lyria can handle Rayne without me." Malin rakes a hand through his messy locks, tugging the diadem free as he glances at the hole in the floor. Then, he unknots his cravat and slips the waistcoat from his shoulders, letting it all tumble to the ground.

"Is it wise to ignore him, Your Majesty?" Lyria asks. She hobbles between him and Avum with her shoulders raised and her back ramrod straight. The woman's skin is pulled so tight, I can see every bone in her brittle body, and her long-sleeved dress is practically slipping off her. It's strange to witness someone so small hold their own against my husband, and I can't help but wonder what kind of magic she must possess.

"I'm not worried about Rayne," Malin says. "His claim to the throne is tepid at best, and the second Ezrah is swollen with my child, there's not a noble in this kingdom who would support him. Slut or not, the Varren are considered rulers by divine right. My days are much better spent buried in her cunt than engaging my brother in conversation."

My mouth falls open, but words don't come out.

"Let's go." Clicking his tongue, Malin places a hand on the small of my back and guides me to the staircase.

My knees buckle when I peer into the hole. Sweat clings to my palms, my back. The last time I got trapped inside a dark room, I didn't come out for months. Where my father couldn't break me, his jail cell did.

"After you," Malin says.

He pushes me onto the platform and the darkness consumes me.

PRINCESS EZRAH VARREN

FORTRESS HEDRA, CENTRAL CARTHINIA

The wrought-iron staircase creaks beneath my feet. Cold metal bites into my blistered soles as I descend past the hole in the ground and into foggy blackness. The platform shudders and sways when Malin joins me on it. Suspended chains, support beams, and a cobweb-covered pulley system are the only things standing between us and a floor that I can't see.

I release a shaky breath. Each step is torture, made all the worse by the shrieking, groaning sounds coming from the twisting metal.

"Malin, I . . ." The words lodge inside my throat. Even on the precipice of reliving my worst nightmares, I can't tell him the truth about my past.

Stars flare along the edges of my vision just as

Malin puts a soothing hand on my shoulder and squeezes. "I won't let you fall," he says.

But it's not the falling I'm afraid of.

I can handle a broken bone or missing limb. I can even handle bleeding to death at the bottom of a darkened stairwell. It's the claustrophobia that's eating at my bones. Malin has no idea what it's like to live in silence, deprived of sunlight and touch for so long, he'd be willing to do anything—*sacrifice anything*—for the slightest bit of human connection. While I don't know what kind of relationship he had with his parents, I do know he couldn't even begin to fathom what it's like to be Arrovin's daughter.

My husband is a monster, but my father makes him look like a stuffie bear.

The staircase rumbles when Avum enters behind us. There's a *click-click* followed by a resounding boom as the trap door snaps shut, taking the rest of the light with it. I swallow hard and force myself to take another step forward.

You can do this, Ezrah. It's just a little dark. Stop being a baby.

"What has your father told you about our marriage contract?" Malin asks.

I blink. "What?"

"Our marriage contract. What do you know about it?" Malin keeps his hand on my shoulder, holding onto me as we descend. "Have you forgotten how to speak?"

I shake my head, though I'm certain he can't see it. "No, I just . . ." *I don't understand why we're talking about this right now.*

"Would you rather we walk in silence?"

"No." Intentional or not, this conversation is a welcome distraction from our surroundings. I'd do anything to keep my mind off where we're going, even if that means discussing our sham of a marriage.

Malin groans. "Then speak, Ezrah. For the love of Daliah, answer my question. You have a special gift for trying my patience."

I bite my bottom lip. "My father didn't tell me anything," I whisper. "Just that he expected me to obey you and to keep hidden until he said otherwise."

"Hidden from Fontaine," Malin corrects, as if that should have been obvious, as if he and Avum have already discussed our conversation from earlier.

Fear manifests itself as sweat against my palms. I wipe them on my tulle skirts, ignoring the shifting pocket watch in my panties. Malin doesn't know what happened in Avum's bedchambers or in the kitchen—he *can't* know. The man isn't psychic, and outside of Avum's quick trip to the library, the two of us have been inseparable. Still, my stomach knots.

Why would he wait until now to bring Tristan up? What's changed?

"Your father insisted that we keep the marriage a secret so Fontaine wouldn't know where to find you," Malin says. "According to Arrovin, he accepted my proposal because Carthinia is the farthest kingdom from the coasts and the hardest to invade."

I can tell by his tone that Malin doesn't believe my father's reasoning, yet the logic makes total sense to me. The icy wasteland isn't exactly a pirate sanctuary, and although Malin suspects me a spy, I'd rather jump off the balcony than serve Arrovin. I could say as much, but I don't. We don't know each other, or trust each other, or even like each other outside of sex, so the words would be wasted breath. Instead, I take the opportunity to pry.

"What were the other terms? How much did you pay to bring me here?"

"Ten-thousand skeletons to the Varren coasts, ten thousand living to their eastern border, and enough wood to rebuild the Varren fleets ten times over."

Behind us, Avum's baritone voice cuts through the darkness. "Then there's the matter of the road, which will open up trade between our kingdoms for the first time since their inceptions."

Twenty-thousand men and a couple of trees. That's exactly how much I'm worth to Arrovin.

Perhaps I should feel honored—my older and much more pious sisters went for half that amount—yet my freedom means so much more to me. I try to numb myself to the information, but all I can do is think about Malin's words in the library, his doubts now.

Twenty-thousand men and a couple of trees? Is that all?

Remi would have offered more ... much, much more. Sure, his coastal palaces would've been too dangerous for me, but the man's empire stretches half as wide as my father's. He could have hidden me in a jungle or desert and I'd be equally safe, equally unreachable. Not to mention, the man was half in love with me when I left. I have no doubt he would have given Arrovin control of the Jasmine Straight, access to the Bronze Road, and a hundred-thousand soldiers to fight the Kamaran Fleets. Yet I'm here...

Why?

The staircase spirals, winding lower and lower beneath the floor, bringing with it the burning stench of ammonia and decay. We must be nearly a mile beneath the ground, beneath anything living. Scratching at my arms, I glance up at a ceiling I can't see and take big gulps, trying not to panic or claw the skin clean off my bones.

Malin grips the back of my neck and forces my

head to the path in front of us. "Eyes ahead," he growls. "Mind on me."

I don't have time to interpret his words before Malin is speaking again. "Avum, why don't you fill her in on the war? Since we're publicly discussing Fontaine now, I see no reason to spare her any details."

"Yes, my king." The stairwell warms beneath my feet as if Avum is reaching out to comfort me. And it does. I don't feel quite so alone with him by my side. "Fontaine's men have destroyed seventy-five percent of the Varren fleets, but nobody knows how he's outgunning and outmaneuvering Ranada's fastest ships. Tristan doesn't take prisoners or leave survivors."

"That's not entirely true," Malin interjects. "He leaves one survivor from every attack. Cuts their tongues out so they can't speak and breaks their fingers so they can't write. Each of them carries a letter bearing the same message. *Bring her back.*"

I feel sick, trapped, boxed in from all sides, both on this stairwell and in Ranada. Between Malin, my father, and the Kamaran fleets, I truly have nowhere to run.

Avum and I made a mistake.

I made a mistake.

If we can't break the spell and he can't spirit me away, then all I've succeeded at doing is worsening the situation . . . and perhaps condemning an innocent man to die.

"Their most recent attack was on Port Sera Cay," Malin adds. "But we managed to get a spy on the inside who can learn Fontaine's strategies or assassinate him should the opportunity present itself."

Assassinate?

I dig my nails into my palms and use the pain to ground me even as my whole body sways. Sticky warmth drips down my fingertips, gold glistening at my feet as sounds drift in and out of focus. Avum says something, but I can't hear it over the ringing in my ears.

Assassinate.

It feels surreal.

"You can't kill him," I whisper.

"Why the fuck not?"

"He . . ." My tongue feels heavy. My heart feels heavier. "He's . . ."

Malin's fingers turn icy. "The man forced you to service half of Ranada. Do you really hold that much compassion for him?"

"Malin," Avum growls.

"What? It's a perfectly valid question."

The room is so quiet, I can hear water trickle through the walls. I clear my throat and force the words past. "You can't kill him because Fontaine is as much an idea as he is a person. Every captain in the

Kamaran fleet takes on the title, but most of them don't have a clue where the real Fontaine is or if he's there at all. You can kill every captain in their fleet, but they'll keep coming."

"Do you know which ship Tristan sails?" Avum asks, voice gentle.

I shake my head. "The flagship was destroyed when Arrovin brought me back."

"Well, this has been enlightening." Malin snorts. "Seems your father left out some key details. Ultimately, it makes no difference, though. We'll find the bastard and kill him, and if his crew doesn't let up, we'll kill them too."

He makes it sound so easy—it won't be.

I lived with those pirates for years, and I know them better than I know myself. They won't forget about me. They won't abandon me. I'm far too valuable.

My toes connect with sleek, cold stone as the staircase comes to an end. The tension in my body lessens ever so slightly as I step off the ancient metal deathtrap and shuffle deeper into the crypts, waiting for someone else to take the lead or at least light the path ahead.

Avum obliges. With a snap of his fingers, a dozen torches ignite into bright orange flame. The floor warms beneath my feet—not stone, I realize, but gems. Ruby tiles polished to perfection make up the entirety of the floor, while obsidian walls glisten in the firelight.

I rub my eyes, adjusting to the brightness. When the searing in my corneas dulls into a low simmer, I give the room another scan.

It's a large, elliptical space with recessed loculi built into the walls and dark tunnels between them. The shelves of bone are organized by type rather than person—a row of only hands, another of only feet, then ribs, then ones I'm not quite sure of—all of them stacked so tightly, it's difficult to tell where one bone starts and the other stops.

I stare at the skeletal remains, then at Malin, who appears to be gauging my reaction. Shrugging, I approach one of the many loculi and run my hand over a section of bleached white skulls. Then, I pick one up. His brows pinch together, a deep crease forming between them as he joins me near the shelf.

Pursing my lips, I toss the skull into the air and catch it over and over again. "How much magic does it take to keep ten-thousand skeletons animated?"

Malin swipes the skull midair. "Trying to usurp me already?"

There's a playful edge to his tone, and he offers me a sly half-smirk before returning the bone to its proper shelf. If we were on better terms, I'd make some sarcastic retort like, "I'm only interested in stealing things of worth," but I manage to bite my tongue at the last second.

"Don't worry, Ezrah," Malin says. "I have more than enough power to keep our kingdom protected and you in line. Come along now. It'll take a while to show you everything before sunset."

"What happens at sunset?"

Ignoring me, Malin and Avum start down one of the tunnels with me at their heels, scurrying to keep up. Their legs are so much longer than mine, their strides double the length, and soon I find myself sweating. The heat of the corridors doesn't help. Avum's flames span as far as I can see, framing the narrow walls and the doorways within them.

"What happens at sunset?" I repeat, peeking into chambers as we go. More loculi fill the spaces, tombs as well. We stop in front of a thick metal door.

"This is where we keep prisoners for long-term storage," Avum says. His expression is blank, his emerald eyes worlds away. The pocket watch in my panties suddenly feels like a powder keg and all I want to do is fish it out. Any time I've been led to a dungeon, it hasn't ended well for me.

Malin doesn't know.

He doesn't know.

He doesn't . . .

"It's alright," Avum whispers. As Malin unbolts the door, his fingers find mine, just long enough to graze the inside of my palm. And then they're gone like they'd never been there at all.

It helps more than I care to admit, and I can't help but smile at him.

Wiping the sweat from my brow, I brace myself for prisons like the ones in Varren—iron cells made from crisscrossed bars, floors soaked with pus and piss and gods know what else, rusty manacles mounted to the walls and ceilings. Then, I follow them through.

All the air whooshes from my lungs when I see what's inside and I stumble backward. It's nothing like the prisons back home. It's nothing like anything I've ever seen before.

PRINCESS EZRAH VARREN

FORTRESS HEDRA, CENTRAL CARTHINIA

"Can they talk?" I ask, staring at the severed heads in front of me. The room is covered floor-to-floor in white, cube-shaped pedestals, each containing its own head—not a skull, but a head, complete with eyes, noses, ears, mouths, and scalps full of hair.

"When I want them to," Malin says, slinking an arm around my waist. "They can hear and see just fine though."

Nasty scars split some of their faces, while others are perfectly preserved save for their ashy skin. Beside me, a pretty brunette blinks her glassy blue eyes at us and her red lips part, mouthing the words, *"Help me,"* over and over again.

I can't stop the shiver that rolls across my spine.

A day ago, I considered Malin's sunny library a

cage, but apparently, my husband's idea of trapping someone is infinitely more creative than I gave him credit for. To be unable to move, unable to speak or eat, stuck in a permanent state of undead—it's unthinkable. I'd do almost anything to avoid it. Then again, Malin probably knows that. Why else bring me here if not to threaten me with a similar fate?

Trying to hide the horror from my face, I avert my gaze to the woman's pin-straight locks. They flow past her jagged neck, down the limestone she's mounted to, before brushing against the ruby floor.

"What did they do to end up here?" I ask.

"Treason." Avum clasps his hands behind his back then moves to stand in front of the now-closed doorway. "When Malin took the throne, there was a schism in our kingdom."

Malin chuckles, sending ice through my veins. "That's one way of putting it."

"A civil war then," Avum corrects. "His Majesty is the youngest of his siblings, so by tradition, the throne would normally default to Rayne first, Claudia second, and Malin last. But Rayne wasn't born with magic, and their sister never wanted the throne."

"You're giving her the diplomatic version. If she's to be my queen, then she needs to learn the truth. Rayne is her enemy as much as Tristan is mine," Malin says.

Avum bows his head. "Yes, Your Majesty. Would you like me to explain, or do you wa—"

"It's good to see you again, Kyree," Malin coos. Releasing his hold on me, he turns to the brunette and strokes her cheek the way a lover might. Her murky eyes widen, and her mouth curls into a soundless scream. "I'd visit more often, but I've been busy entertaining my new bride. Her Varren cunt requires so much more attention than yours ever did."

My cheeks burn.

The woman's gaze shifts from Malin to me, a sympathetic look crossing her features. I work to keep my own expression neutral. Humiliation. Pain. Fear. I've been trained to enjoy all those things—forced to enjoy them. The moisture pooling between my thighs isn't my fault, but it certainly feels like it is.

Avum's jaw clenches. A vein pulses in his forehead. "Must you speak about Ezrah in that manner?"

"It's Ezrah now, is it? I didn't realize the two of you were on such familiar terms. Remember your place, Avum, or I'll be forced to remind you." The starlight in my husband's irises swirl so brightly, they almost look silver. His attention settles on me, so intense I can't stop myself from squirming. "You're mine, Ezrah Varren. Do you understand that?"

My tongue sticks to the roof of my too-dry mouth. "Yes, Your Majesty."

"Good. Now, I believe we were discussing treason." He flashes both of us a pointed look, and I wait for him to mention the kitchen, the spell book, or the pocket watch that keeps grinding against my pussy. My eyes wander to the other severed heads—to the sheets of skin hanging off their gray musculature and to their missing eyelids and pustuled lips.

Kyree is one of the few undead who's still intact. Would I look more like her or like them?

Stroking Kyree's hair, Malin leans toward me and lowers his voice. "Don't worry, Ezrah, you're far too valuable to end up in a place like this. I can't exactly skull-fuck a child into you."

My spine straightens. Adrenaline pours into my veins, but before I can react, Malin winks at me then resumes his story where Avum left off.

"My mother was King Ranin's concubine, not his wife," Malin says. "By Carthinain law, I shouldn't be allowed to rule. But the law also states only a powerful caster can ascend, which excludes Rayne as well. Succession was always going to be contentious. Rayne's mother was beloved by our people. Mine was some random whore my father found at a brothel in Tarinth—the same brothel Avum grew up in, actually. My father saved both of them from that shithole."

When I peek at Avum, his gaze is trained on the floor, head hung low as Malin does just what he threatened to do—*reminds him of his place.* Everything Avum has, everything he is, can be taken away with a snap of my husband's fingers. With no nobles to fight for him and no lands to call his own, Avum's fate is at my husband's whimsy.

I'm a horrible person.

I'm every bad name I've ever been called and then worse.

My title protects me. My body ensures I'm worth more to others alive than dead, but him . . .

Malin snaps me from my thoughts. "Our people rioted when my father declared me his legitimate heir, then rioted again when my powers manifested as *this*." He gestures to himself. "It turns out, the only thing my people hate more than you is a king who aligns himself with the dark god."

The dark god? Surely, he doesn't mean that. He *can't* mean that. To align himself with Enen would be to forfeit his immortal soul, his chance at an afterlife.

I wait for an explanation that doesn't come. Behind Malin's cruelty and bravado, I see the pain lurking, cracking him in two. So does Avum.

"It wasn't your fault," he says.

"Don't patronize me," Malin snaps. "I did what I had to do."

They exchange looks and suddenly, I'm all too

aware that I'm missing something crucial to this conversation. I want to ask about it but manage to keep my mouth shut. This kingdom isn't my problem, and neither is its king.

Malin grabs his shirt cuff and begins rolling up the sleeve. "I didn't want to rule. I even tried forcing Claudia to ascend, but you can't make that woman do a damn thing. When I seized power, the fallout was exactly what you'd expect."

"A coup," Avum says.

"Led by Rayne. Backed by half the country." Malin shifts his attention to the other sleeve, folding it to expose a muscular forearm. "When it failed, I sentenced him to death, but that triggered a three-year civil war. Rather than see the sentence through, I negotiated peace with the insurrection, formed the council, then put him on it. I don't have the absolute authority my father did, but giving up some power was better than seeing my people die. Despite whatever rumors you might hear about me, I have no interest in ruling over a kingdom of bones."

"Each of us gets to vote on a law before it's passed," Avum says. "Malin gets two votes, as will you upon your coronation. Queens break ties. As you can imagine, no one thought His Majesty would wed a Varren, so tensions are . . . more heightened than usual."

Malin snorts. "I rather enjoyed breaking Rayne's nose against the table. He's lucky that's all I broke."

My gaze shifts to Kyree as Malin resumes stroking her head. "And where does she come in? Was she involved in the coup or the war following it?"

"Neither. She was the bitch I fell in love with who tried to kill me in my sleep."

I can't help but envision the scars on Malin's chest—a half dozen stab wounds, any of which could have been fatal. Without thinking, I reach for him, touching a spot on his tunic where I know one of the scars is hiding. "She's the reason you don't sleep in our bed," I whisper.

He places his hand over mine. "She's the reason I'll *never* sleep in your bed. I trusted her with my life. I trust you even less than I trust your father." His heart thunders against my palm. Without breaking eye contact, he addresses Avum. "You're dismissed. Wait for us in the hallway."

The doorway creaks open then shut. In Avum's absence, an icy coldness settles over the room, and an uneasy feeling forms a pit in my stomach.

"Do you want to talk about her?" I ask, not sure why. I shouldn't care about Malin's pain, let alone want to soothe him. But I do.

He grips my hand and pins it to his chest. "There's nothing to talk about. I loved Kyree, and she used that love to get close to me. The details don't matter." Malin pulls me with him as he leans against Kyree's pedestal, his ass nearly touching the woman's face. "I suppose I should thank her, though. If she hadn't betrayed me, I would have never bought you, and it's nice having your Varren cunt all to myself—or mostly to myself, as the case might be. Tell me, Ezrah, do you think Avum would still find you charming if he knew Tristan used you as an assassin as well as a whore?"

The cold air catches in my lungs.

I try to pull away, but Malin's grip tightens. "You like pretending to be a damsel in distress, but we both know your body count is higher than mine. And I'm not talking about in bed."

"I..."

...didn't want to?

...didn't mean to?

I most certainly did. I've done horrible things for both Tristan and my father, either out of obligation, love, or fear. I'd do it all again, too, because I'm not strong enough, or brave enough, or *nice* enough to act otherwise.

"Deny it. Tell me I'm wrong." Malin slides our hands down the hard planes of his chest, those dark eyes igniting with mischief. Black veins seep down his face, and desire pools low in my belly—the fear of what he'll do to me enough to make me weak-kneed. "I can't hear you, Ezrah. Tell me how sweet and naïve you are."

Our palms sink lower.

"You're just a weak little girl trapped in a big scary castle, aren't you?" His cock jumps into my hand, straining against the two silver buttons holding it back. Groaning, Malin forces me to stroke him through the fabric. "Your husband is so cruel to you. Fulfilling all your fantasies. Playing with your pretty little pussy for hours on end. You must really hate having to touch him."

Gods, he's a dick.

Squeezing my thighs together, I nod emphatically, doing my best to ignore the ache between them.

It's not my fault I like dicks.

"Show me how much you hate it," he says. "Shove your finger up your pussy and prove it to me."

I glare at him.

"Would you rather *I* do it?'

Maybe.

"No." I flash him a vulgar gesture before shoving my hand past the slit in my dress, over the front of my soaked panties. Malin smirks knowingly, and I just barely resist the urge to flash him another cruder gesture as I sink that finger deep inside me, avoiding the pocket watch as best I can.

Moaning, I pump myself a few times, putting on

a show for him before pulling out entirely. Arousal glistens on my fingertip as I flash it in front of his face.

Malin catches me by the wrist and bends, slowly sucking my finger into his warm mouth. He groans like I'm the best damn thing he's ever tasted, stroking me with his tongue so adeptly, I can't help but imagine it elsewhere. *Everywhere.*

Cheeks burning, I stare at his chest, watching black, spiderweb veins writhe beneath the skin's surface like parasitic worms. When Malin's finished, he pulls my finger free with a pop.

That's what I thought," he says. "You say you hate my games, but you're always *so fucking wet for me.*" He emphasizes the last words, drawing them out as he squeezes my ass and grinds me against his cock.

The pedestal rocks beneath us.

With a sickening smack, Kyree's head tumbles to the floor, hitting the ground face-first. Stringy tendrils of her hair fan across my feet before Malin toes her aside and spins me around, lifting me to the pedestal in her place.

My stomach clenches.

This is so fucking wrong—so disgusting. I shouldn't let him touch me like this, not in here, not in front of these . . . *things.*

My attention flickers to the other prisoners, whose milky eyes rest on us. Yellowed teeth form a dozen too-wide smiles like this is the most entertaining thing they've seen in years.

I think I'm going to be sick. I am sick—as sick as my husband, maybe worse.

"Eyes on me," Malin says. Cupping my cheek, he drags my face away from the severed heads and threads his fingers through my hair. "Good girl."

My body melts as his hand slips beneath my dress and rubs a path up my thigh. I lean in closer, ignoring the fact that somewhere behind us, Kyree's hate-filled eyes are probably glaring up at me, judging me for the slut that I am. At this moment, all I want is to taste him.

"Kiss me," I whisper.

Malin's lips part.

Cool, pepperminty breath tingles my cheeks, his mouth finding my ear at the same time his fingers find my dark underlace. "I'm not like Avum," he says, teeth grazing my earlobe. "I don't kiss sluts, Ezrah. I fuck them."

In one swift motion, he yanks the panties down my thighs and cups the pocket watch to my pussy—not the least bit surprised to find it there. Metal scrapes against metal as Malin strokes the watch over my piercing, sending shockwaves through my body, across my clit. Eyes watering, I throw my head back and rake my nails across his scalp.

Gods, it hurts.

"Do you want me to stop?" he asks.

I shake my head as the metal case pushes against my entrance, stretching me wide. There's little resistance. I'm so fucking wet—so stretched from Avum's fist—that it slips in as easily as a finger, filling me so fucking good. My eyes roll to the back of my skull as Malin grabs the chain and yanks, pulling it out before shoving it back in.

Thighs quivering, I moan as he fucks me with it, bucking my hips in tandem with his hand.

"Louder, Ezrah. I'm not sure Avum can hear you yet."

I shriek when the pocket watch turns icy. Goosebumps spread across my skin and I squirm, trying to push it out of me. Malin holds it firmly in place. "That's it, baby. Scream for me. I want to lick the tears from your face."

It's so fucking cold. My nipples tighten into painful points as I shudder around him.

"T-t-take it out," I beg, teeth chattering.

Malin runs his tongue along my cheek, licking up a stray tear. His chuckles fill the room. "But we're having so much fun."

His fingers find my clit, and I grip the edges of the pedestal so hard, my knuckles turn white. Stone bites into my fingernails, splintering them as he moves the watch inside me. My muscles tighten, pleasure climbing higher and higher until I can barely breathe. "P-p-please let me come."

"Baby, this is a punishment, not a reward."

I buck against his hand as he pulls the watch loose, my slickness dripping off it onto the ruby floor. Slowly, the warmth returns to my body as he edges his other hand free, giving my pussy a final pat before smoothing the dress over my thighs.

"Malin, please."

"Look at the mess you made." He dangles the watch in front of me. "Now lick it clean."

I glare at him, scrunching my nose in revulsion. *Absolutely not.*

"I said, lick it clean." Malin thrusts the watch into my hand and holds it there. "I may not be able to put you in here, but Avum is expendable."

The threat looms heavy between us, realization creeping in. Malin wasn't threatening me when he brought us here; he was threatening Avum. Swallowing, I clasp my fingers around the slippery metal and, with begrudging slowness, glide my tongue along the case.

He grabs my chin and lifts, forcing me to look at him as I clean it.

"Such a pathetic slut," he muses, gripping my jaw until it hurts. "That's it. Clean the chain next. I love watching your tongue work."

When I'm finished, he snatches the watch from me and examines it. "Good girl. Now you can come."

"What?" My brows pinch together.

"Come for me."

Malin smirks. Before I can figure out why, a mind-shattering orgasm crashes over me. Moaning, I arch my back, spiraling into what can only be described as paradise. Starbursts cloud my vision. Sounds become cotton in my ears.

It lasts a lifetime—or at least it feels like that.

As the tremors in my body slow, I wrap my arms around Malin and sob into his chest, thanking him, promising him I'll be good. I'd say anything at this point if it meant not having to be denied again.

All I want to do is pass out on the floor and rest for a thousand years.

"Again," Malin says.

My muscles convulse as another orgasm ravages me from the inside out. Tears run down my cheeks and my bones turn to gelatin.

I didn't know he could do that.

"Again."

The pleasure becomes white-hot fire. My shrieks echo off the walls as Malin pries me from his arms, and I go sprawling to the floor. I need air. I need—

Chest heaving, I wrap my arms around his legs and beg for it to stop. It doesn't.

Malin shakes me loose, chuckling as he

commands me to come until my voice is too hoarse to object. Then, he pulls me from the floor and tosses me over his shoulder like I'm nothing.

"We're not finished," he says, "but I'll need Avum for the next part. Behave yourself and maybe I'll spare your gullible fucktoy. Don't and you'll see firsthand how I make my monsters."

The door slams shut—the severed heads behind it forever imprinted into my memory.

PRINCESS EZRAH VARREN

FORTRESS HEDRA, CENTRAL CARTHINIA

Ranin's milky eyes stare up at me, unblinking, unmoving, from behind a glass coffin. Brittle fingers clutch a silver crown to his chest and tufts of wispy silver hair frame his gaunt face, fanning across a dark pillow down a military uniform made of black leather. The man's skin is yellow—cracked in some places, missing in others—rendering him entirely unrecognizable were it not for the plaque outside his box.

I touch my palm to the glass then jerk back, shuddering at how cold the panels are. It's like they were carved from ice.

"This is the Room of Kings," Avum says. Coming up behind me, he places a hand on my shoulder and the coldness disappears. "It's where we lay our rulers to rest, including our queens. The name is a holdout from generations ago."

A line of coffins spans the length of the room, each corpse dressed in the same attire as King Ranin, posed in the same position behind a glass barrier. A thick, black mist pools around them, obscuring the coffins until they vanish into nothingness. The air around us is cool and humid and so dark, we might as well be trapped inside the ninth hell.

Enen's hell.

Malin grunts from somewhere in the distance and Avum withdraws his hand from my shoulder, but not before giving me a reassuring squeeze. It's anything but.

This has arguably been the most stress-inducing tour of my life. Despite our confrontation in long-term storage, Malin hasn't spoken a word to us since—not beyond insisting Avum finish the tour. For almost an hour, we've walked in near silence, the tension so thick, it feels like a living, breathing thing.

I'm not stupid enough to think Malin has decided to let this infraction go. Rather, he's drawing out our torture, fucking with our sleep-addled brains by keeping us on high alert. But two questions remain: how much does Malin know, and *how* does he know it?

"To the left, you'll see a silver door with guards

stationed outside it," Avum says. "That's Bron's bedroom."

He points past a pair of thick obsidian columns into the foggy gloom. Squinting, I can make out the faint golden glow of firelight but nothing else.

"To the right is Malin's."

I squint harder. A hint of silver glints through the blackness, and I spin on my heels in search of my husband. When I can't find him, I address the coffins instead. "*This* is where you sleep?"

"And work, among other things." Malin materializes in front of us, his feet as silent and as predatory as a cat's. Eyes on Avum, he hooks an arm around my waist. "Is something wrong?"

You would rather sleep in a room of rotting corpses than share a bed with me? Is my company truly that awful?

I wipe my face on the back of my hand, hating myself for how fucking emotional I get around this man. I shouldn't care where he sleeps. I *don't* care. After Avum and I complete the damn spell, I'll be a thousand miles away from him, drinking rum on a beach, surrounded by men who can actually stand the sight of me.

"It's nothing. I'm fine." Smoothing out the front of my dress, I clear my throat then do what I do best —deflect. "What's next on the tour?"

"This is the final room," Avum says.

Malin smirks, and a lead ball settles low in my stomach. "You and I both know that isn't true. There's one room left."

Threading our fingers together, Malin drags me past a pair of coffins to a thick metal door at the back of the chamber. Chunky iron chains loop through its twin handles, and a padlock the size of my face keeps it shut. On either side of the doorway, two skeletons stand at the ready. Musty, moth-eaten fabrics hang off their bloodstained bones, and they hold in their hands a set of twin daggers made from carved bone and amethyst. Flames the color of pitch burn inside their chest cavities, suspended in midair where their hearts should be.

Malin releases my hand and I step closer. The skeletons track the movement, following me with their unseeing eyeholes.

"They won't hurt you," Malin says. "That ring protects you."

I stare at the wedding band, twisting it in circles as I close the distance between myself and the guards. A painful coldness leeches into my skin, the flames in their chests emitting ice rather than heat. Cocking my head, I study the flame for a moment before sliding my fingers through one of their ribcages and—

Malin pulls me back. "Don't. Not unless you want to be like them."

Goosebumps pebble along every inch of my skin. Shivering, I wrap my arms around myself and vigorously rub my arms. "What is this place?" I ask.

The room behind us reeks of chemicals—disinfectant, maybe?—and emits an indescribable aura of dread that sucks the light from my body, dulling its glittering sheen. I can't bring myself to look away, even as footsteps shuffle behind me.

Avum's footsteps.

He doesn't touch me, but I can feel the fire radiating off his body in waves.

"Avum," Malin says, "since you're the one leading this tour, would you care to tell my wife where we are?"

Arms crossed, Malin moves in front of the doorway and leans against it. Shadows curl around him, slithering over his arms and legs until they blend almost seamlessly into the dark walls. Spiderweb veins spread down his face, turning what little skin I can still see the color of volcanic ash. All the while, Avum keeps silent behind me.

I turn away from the now-hidden door to find Avum's jaw clenched and his hands balled into fists. Refusing to meet my gaze, he glares at Malin before spitting the words out. "He calls it his playroom. It's where he ... It's where ..."

"It's where I torture prisoners. And where I punish the women in my life who misbehave."

The ground ripples. Shadows snake around my ankles—sleek and cold like metal—pinning me in place. "It's also the part of the tour where General Avum leaves us."

"Your Majesty," Avum says. "I implore you, don't do this. She's not—"

"Ezrah, before Avum leaves, why don't you thank him for showing you around all day? It must have been incredibly inconvenient for him to clear his schedule like that."

My eyebrows knit together. *Where the fuck is he going with this?*

"Go on," Malin says, a smile twisting his features.

The shadows pull me forward until I stumble into Avum's chest. His arms are fast to catch me, righting me until I'm standing up straight. Staring into his emerald eyes, I swallow, hands shaking, whether from cold or nervousness, I'm not sure.

"Thank you, general," I say. "I really appreciate everything you've done"—*and tried to do*—"for me. I'm sorry I wasted so much of your time."

My lips quiver as he takes my hands in his. His touch is soft and gentle, despite the fact that Malin might be seconds away from sending him to long-term storage.

I'm so godsdamned unworthy of Avum's kindness.

"It wasn't a waste, princess," he says. "Don't ever think—"

Malin grunts. "Not like that, Ezrah. On your knees."

Avum sucks in a breath, his eyes darting between Malin and me. "Your Majesty, that really isn't necessary."

"Ezrah, on your knees. Now."

This is bullshit.

My cheeks flame as I lower myself to the icy floor. The shadows surrounding my feet climb higher, winding 'round and 'round my thighs like a constrictor, tightening until it burns.

"Thank him, Ezrah," Malin hisses.

The shame is white hot as I meet Avum's gaze—this time from the floor like I'm some kind of . . . of . . .

Pleasure slave.

My stomach flips, but I force the words out. "Thank you, Avum."

"Now, Ezrah," Malin drawls, "when a woman is on her knees, she should already know what's expected of her."

My teeth clench. So does my swollen pussy. "You *can't* be serious."

"You're the one who wants him. If you're going to have him, it'll be on my terms for *my* amusement. Now be a good girl and thank him properly."

One of the shadows grazes my clit, slipping through the metal loop just long enough to have my thighs quivering, my pussy aching. And then it's gone, inching around my waist, growing bigger and wider until—

My dress rips.

Tiny scraps of tulle puddle around my knees, leaving me entirely exposed. As the air hits me, my nipples tighten into points. I'm so embarrassed, I can't breathe. It doesn't matter that Avum has seen me naked before. That was on my terms, and this . . .

I don't want this, right? I mean, I *can't* want this. Servicing him in front of Malin is demeaning and cruel—made all the crueler by the fact that Avum is my lesser. Yet, if there's anything I've learned to enjoy, it's cruelty.

The ache between my thighs is unbearable, *undeniable*, as I take Avum in. A simple pair of drawstrings are the only things standing between me and the erection already tenting his silky, green pajamas. An erection so big and so close, it nearly brushes my face. Avum's body is as stiff as a board, his face a mixture of guilt and desire as he watches me shudder and squirm around Malin's snake-like shadows.

"Your Majesty?" I ask. Peeking over my shoulder, I wait for him to stop me, to tell me that he's changed his mind or that this is all a joke.

Malin reaches into his trouser pocket instead. Something silver shines through the darkness.

The pocket watch.

He snaps it open and pretends to read it. "Tick-tock, Ezrah. General Avum is a busy man. He doesn't have all day."

Avum's throat bobs. He puts his hand over mine and shakes his head, his salt-and-pepper hair ruffled from where he's raked his fingers through it. "You don't have to do this."

"It's okay," I whisper. "I want to."

And I do. I wanted to touch him an hour ago, and I want to touch him now, even if it is at my husband's command—maybe because it is.

I like it when Malin uses me, even when I hate it.

Biting my bottom lip, I unknot Avum's drawstrings then work my fingers past his waistband. He's so fucking thick. And smooth. I peel the fabric down his muscular thighs and his cock springs free, leaking precum from the tip. The fabric floats to the floor where my own gown lies in shambles.

Slowly, I open my mouth and slide my tongue along the underside of his shaft, moaning as I lick higher and higher, flicking my tongue across the salty tip. Avum groans. His hands fist in my golden locks, eyes snapping shut as I part my lips and slide him into my mouth.

Fuck he's thick. *Too* thick. My jaw screams at how wide I have to open for him, the corners of my lips nearly splitting. There's no fucking way I can take it all, and I'm not going to try. Gripping Avum by the base, I hollow out my cheeks as best I can and stroke him while I bob on his cock, watching his face as I learn exactly how he likes to be pleasured.

Avum's fingers tighten in my hair. "Fuck, princess. You're so good at that."

"I know." Malin appears behind me, his fingers joining Avum's on the back of my scalp. "Doesn't her mouth feel amazing? Almost makes buying her worth it." He pushes down on my head until Avum's cock hits the back of my throat and I gag on it. Drool oozes from my mouth. My eyes water as I cough and gasp around it.

"I fucking love the sounds she makes." Malin holds me there, grinding my nose into Avum's pelvis.

I slap at Avum's thighs. I thrash my head from side to side, my chest on fire, my thighs slick with need. My fucking jaw feels like it's going to crack open.

"I know you can take it, baby. Look at how good you're doing." Malin pulls me back just enough to let me suck in air, then he shoves me down. "Don't be gentle with her. Ezrah likes it rough."

My garbled cries fill the air, throat constricting around Avum as he takes control of my head, sliding me down his cock until it's brushing my throat with every stroke. The pace is unforgiving—cruel even—and my whole body tingles the longer I choke on him.

"That's it," Malin says. "Show him what a good little slut you can be."

Shadows wriggle around my torso. Between my legs. I'm so focused on breathing through my nose that I barely notice one of them pushing against my cunt until it's sheathed inside me.

Moans slip past my lips. Tears blur my vision as the need to draw breath reaches a fever pitch. "Please," I beg, the words gibberish around Avum's cock.

His movements get sloppier, his thrusts deeper. The tentacle spreads me so wide, I shriek.

Avum slams my nose into his pelvis, thighs tensing as he spurts wave after wave of salt down my burning throat. I swallow all of him, panting as I collapse onto the ground, sucking in ragged gulps of air. The tentacle continues slipping in and out of me, moving slower, deeper, but I don't have the energy to fight it. My legs are heavier than lead, my brain a messy jumble as I watch the shadow fuck me.

Malin kneels over me and rolls my nipple between his thumb and forefinger. "She's my favorite toy," he says, the words cutting deep. "Next time you want to play with her, all you have to do is ask. You know I don't mind sharing. I just hate to be excluded."

The shadow curls inside me and my whole body jerks.

"Allow me to let you in on a little secret though." Malin pinches my nipple until I scream. "Ezrah Varren is the most arrogant, manipulative creature in all of Ranada. She'll let anyone between her legs if it means getting her way."

He pinches me again, but the second I open my mouth, a shadow fills it, wrapping around my head as it gags me.

"Your point?" Avum asks.

"The journal. I expect you'll hand it over."

They glare at one another as the tentacle in my pussy slips loose.

"It's in my chambers," Avum snarls.

"And the translation?" Malin holds out his hand expectantly.

The tension festers between them, neither moving or speaking for what feels like an impossibly long time. Finally, Avum reaches into his trouser pocket and slaps a folded sheet of paper into Malin's palm. "What you're doing to her is unacceptable."

Malin snorts. "Try telling that to her dripping cunt."

"She's not a prisoner here," Avum says.

"But she is," Malin spits. "You're delusional if you

think Ezrah could survive out there on her own. It takes an army to protect a Varren. The moon-touched would kill her on site. The peasants would flay the skin from her bones and sell her body in parts. Tristan would turn her back into a pleasure slave, and the other kings ... Fuck, you know as well as I do what they're capable of. For Daliah's sake, Avum, think with your brain, not your cock."

Avum's throat bobs.

I wriggle on the ground, trying to sit up, but the tile turns sticky. Glue-like.

"Did it have to be that spell?" Avum asks.

Malin grins. "Of course not. But it keeps her nice and wet for me."

"Gods, you're an asshole."

"And you're dismissed." Malin snaps his fingers, and the gag vanishes from my mouth. "Ezrah, thank Avum for allowing you to pleasure him."

This can't be happening.

I lie there, frozen, waiting for Avum's softness, his warmth, but whatever sway I had over him seems gone now, my efforts wasted. A thick desperation washes over me as I realize I truly am nothing more than Malin's living sex doll and no one is going to help me change that. I'm alone here. I'm alone always.

"Thank you, Avum." I bite the inside of my cheek to keep from crying. Somewhere far away, the sun is on my face, the sand squishing between my toes. Tristan is there too—not Captain Fontaine, but the lieutenant I fell in love with. The lieutenant I still love even after everything he's put me through.

"Thank you for what, Ezrah." Malin snaps his fingers in front of my nose, and the illusion blinks out of existence. "Use your words."

"Thank you for letting me suck your cock," I mumble, the words mechanical, far away.

"Look at Avum when you speak," Malin says.

This time, when I pull myself to my knees, the shadows let go, turning as textureless as they were when the tour first began. My golden eyes meet Avum's dark green ones. There's this stony, blank look on his face that wasn't there before. Sniffling, I force the words out. "Thank you for allowing me to suck your cock."

Malin nods, happy with my obedience.

Avum says nothing.

"I'll see you at sunset." Malin pets my head like I'm a dog but keeps his gaze on Avum. "She and I are going to play for a little while longer."

If I had any lingering thoughts that Malin's general might save me, they die the moment he spins on his heels and leaves. He doesn't even give me a second glance.

PRINCESS EZRAH VARREN

FORTRESS HEDRA, CENTRAL CARTHINIA

"... Jemmin root, crushed akadian petals, the blood of a caster, the bone of a king, ash from a reaching tree . . ." Malin crumples the sheet of paper in his palm then hurls it across the room. It disappears into nothingness. "Were you planning on ingesting that?"

I don't answer him, opting instead to keep silent from my spot on the floor.

"Akadian petals are toxic when you boil them," he says, looking at me like I'm an idiot. Maybe I am.

"I didn't know that," I whisper.

"Of course, you didn't. Mages spend years learning their craft. It's not something you can wake up one day and just do." Malin leans against the shadow-filled wall and sucks his teeth. "This spell would have gotten you and Avum killed. I assume you didn't tell him you weren't trained to do this."

I shake my head. "I didn't think he'd help me if he knew. I didn't want to hurt him. I just . . ." *Wanted to be free.*

When I glance back up, Malin is scowling at me. "Gods, you even got the basics wrong. I didn't cast a blood spell, and if I did, it wouldn't be the blood from *a* caster, it would be blood from *the* caster. As in my blood."

"Oh."

The words are a physical blow to my plans, to my ego, to any hope I had of escaping this wretched life. I'm not used to being bad at something.

I hug my knees to my chest and bury my face in them.

"For future reference, the root of my magic comes from Enen, so unless you choose to become a necromancer, any spell you cast is moot. I plan on informing Avum of that as well, although I doubt he'll be helping you anymore." Malin sighs. He paces the room, raking his fingers across his scalp. "You know, I didn't want this. When you arrived, I had every intention of doing things the right way between us."

My throat is so dry, it feels like swallowing nails. "What changed?"

"I found you on that balcony. You were ready to

jump before I'd ever spoken a word to you." Malin clenches his fists. His throat bobs. "I suppose this is fine too. Being a villain is much easier than being your husband. Crawl to the coffin and wait for me."

"Malin—" My voice trembles.

"The coffin, Ezrah." His belt clicks as he unfastens it, freeing it from his trousers.

Head hung low, I crawl through the dark mist to the glass box he's pointing at. His father's emaciated, rotten face stares back at me as I lean over the icy panels.

Malin joins me a moment later. Belt in hand, he sits on the coffin and pats his lap expectantly. "Bend over my knee."

My body shakes with nervousness.

I've been beaten so many times before that I already know what to expect—stinging welts and deep bruises, sore skin that aches for days, maybe even weeks, if he uses the right technique. It's my least favorite kind of punishment, and the only type that doesn't get me wet. Still, I know better than to think I can say anything to change Malin's mind.

Heart thumping, I crawl onto his lap, smushing my breasts against his thighs, readjusting until my ass is fully in the air. I clamp my eyes tightly shut as he lays his arm across my back and pins me in place.

Malin raises his hand and my breathing stops. I flinch as his palm finds my ass, but there's no sting, just the smooth stroke of skin against skin. "Relax, Ezrah. When have I ever done anything to you that you didn't like?"

Never.

Every cruel and wicked thing he's done, my body's begged for—even the damned spell. Malin pushes my boundaries; he doesn't break them. And when we're done playing, I'm not plagued by the memories of it. I'm aroused by them, even though I shouldn't be.

"I'm going to punish you, Ezrah. But I'm also going to make you feel so fucking good in the process." Malin rubs my cheek again, and I wait with bated breath to see if he'll notice the invisible scars there, just as Avum had. But he doesn't. People rarely do.

"When you've had enough, say mercy and I *will* stop." Malin raises his hand, and all the muscles in my body clench.

Smack.

He strikes me across the left cheek. I jerk forward, whimpering at the sting. It doesn't burn nearly as bad as what I'm used to, but it still fucking hurts.

Another slap sends fire coursing through my skin. I grapple for something—anything—to latch onto, and my fingernails scrape across the icy glass.

Malin groans, his cock hardening beneath me. "You're so fucking cute when you struggle."

Face heating, I moan the next time he strikes me, squirming to escape the sting even as I arch my ass to meet it.

"See? I told you you'd enjoy this." Malin spanks me again and again, massaging my ass between each stroke—his fingers so fucking close to where I want them. "Are you going to behave from now on?"

"Yes," I whisper, tongue sticking to the roof of my mouth. "I'll be good."

Another slap.

Another massage close to my slick center.

"No more seducing my friends?" he asks.

"No." I shake my head.

He keeps spanking me, and I thrust forward, my clit pounding, my pussy aching. I'm so fucking wet I can't stand it, but when I try to spread my legs apart, Malin shakes his head. "Not yet, baby. I don't believe you yet."

He takes the folded belt from the hand that's pinning me, and I wriggle against him. "Malin, please."

"Say mercy and I stop. I'll send you upstairs, and you can go straight to bed. You must be so exhausted."

I know he's baiting me. And like an idiot, I take it, too stubborn to let him win.

The leather slides across my skin, between my legs, and I shiver—terrified and exhausted and hot. So fucking hot. Sweat beads across my forehead as I grind my pussy against his thighs.

Snap!

The leather cracks against me and I cry out.

Snap! Snap!

Two more sharp flicks of the wrist, and I'm even needier than before. Tears drip down my cheeks, disappearing into shadow.

"You did so good, baby," Malin says, rubbing away the burn. "So fucking good."

Carefully, he slides me off his lap, stroking my hair as he repositions my body over the coffin, my ass in the air. The cold glass soothes my sweltering skin even as King Ranin stares up at me with those milky, haunted eyes.

The leather wraps around my neck, tightening into a makeshift leash before I have time to realize what's going on. Rolling the slack around his palm, Malin yanks, forcing my head back.

"You know I have worse spells," he whispers. "I could make every place on your body as sensitive as this." His free hand delves between my thighs and pinches my clit.

Tugging against the leash, I yip, begging him to let go. He strokes me instead, tracing circles against my piercing.

"I could make it so the only way you come is if I fuck that tight little ass of yours." He spreads my cheeks and spits, the saliva dribbling over my asshole before dripping to the floor. I buck against the leash and his fist tightens, the tension choking me.

"There are so many fun ways I could play with you, and someday, I'll try them all out." His finger pushes against my tight hole and my entire body freezes, my pulse pounding so hard, it's the only thing I can hear. Malin's never touched me there before—only one person ever has.

"Next time," he says. "For now, let's try something more basic." Malin chants something beneath his breath and amethyst light floods the room, blindingly bright and everywhere. For a second, the shadows recede just long enough to see the ruby floors and high archways. Flecks of color blind me as I readjust to the darkness.

"What did you do?" I ask.

"You'll see."

One hand on the leash, Malin unbuttons his pants and knocks my legs apart, seating himself between my thighs. Slowly, he rubs his cockhead along my slit, getting it all slippery—getting me all slippery. I moan, wanting him deeper, needing it. Shifting my hips, I work him lower until the tip of him sinks inside me.

Malin hisses out a breath and yanks on the leash. "Behave yourself, Ezrah, or I'll bend you over my knee again."

My pussy clenches at the thought, but I keep painfully still as Malin fills me, his cock sliding so fucking deep that his balls hit my piercing. Back arching, body aching, I moan when Malin tugs on the leash, yanking my head back. The belt tightens around my windpipe. My vision tunnels until I'm sputtering for breath—choking on it—so focused on air, I barely notice the way my breasts grind against the glass panels or how the casket groans beneath us.

I want him harder. Deeper. I don't give a fuck what *or who* is underneath us.

As if reading my thoughts, Malin pulls out then grabs me by the back of the knee. Maneuvering my leg onto the coffin, he spreads me infinitely wider—fills me infinitely deeper—sinking into my pussy in a single thrust. Gods, I feel so fucking full. So alive and tingly all over.

Gripping my hips, Malin sets a brutal pace, each thrust sending me a little closer to the gods. Pleasure builds fast, fire coursing up my center as he spits again and presses his thumb against my narrow opening.

No.

Nuh-uh.

I shake my head and squirm to get away. The leash holds me there.

"Don't think about it, Ezrah," Malin growls. "Just take it like a good little slut."

It burns as he fills me.

My body shudders around him, the pain of his thumb and the fullness of his cock too fucking much. I scream out my orgasm—choked off by the belt around my neck. Malin doesn't stop. He rides me hard and fast, slamming my hips against the glass casket over and over again. And then he's pouring into me, grunting as his own control snaps.

The leash goes lax.

My vision clears, breaths coming easier as my head falls forward. "That was . . . intense." I pant.

"I wanted to put on a good show for him."

I look down.

Behind the glass panels, King Ranin's white eyes blink.

Fuck.

Shit.

I scramble off the coffin and wrap my arms around myself, trying to ignore the cum leaking down my thigh. "You . . . You . . ." I have no words. I am completely and utterly speechless. What kind of person reanimates their father and fucks a girl on top of them?

My insides sour as I take a step back, then another, nearly tripping over my own feet. "Why?"

Malin rolls his eyes. "Because my father said the only way he would allow me to marry you was over his dead body. This seemed fitting."

"You killed him?" My voice quivers.

Malin's responding silence is an answer in and of itself.

I shake my head in disbelief, my brows pinching together. "You killed him to marry me? Why?"

VARREN

SIX YEARS AGO...

MALIN THE TITLELESS

THE KARMASKUS SEA, VARRONIAN WATERS

This bucket isn't big enough.

The ship thrashes and my stomach thrashes with it, spewing mushy biscuits and sour wine into the metal tin. Cold sweat plasters the tunic to my shaking body. Between retches, I peel it free, shucking it off the bed where it hits the wooden floor with a splat. Beside me, Kyree stirs. A woolen blanket slips down her nightgown as she leans forward and gathers my wet hair into her palm, holding it as I vomit yellow bile into the bucket until there's nothing left.

I want to insist that she not baby me, but it's hard to insist on anything when I haven't had the strength to leave the cabin for three whole days.

"You should see the doctor," she says after the vomiting subsides.

Panting, I set the bucket on the floor and roll onto my back, staring at the artwork above our mattress. Unlike the beds at home, this one is built into a wooden box, attached to the wall so that it can't shift or rock. The frame is insufferably claustrophobic and the artwork is grim. Carved sea monsters attack ships. Brave sailors fight valiantly only to be swept up by hurricanes and riptides. Looking at it, however, is still an improvement to looking at the putrid bile in that bucket.

The entire room reeks of my sickness, yet I know if I venture to the galley to toss the bucket's contents overboard, I'll be sick in the hallways. The last thing I need is Ranin hearing that I can't hold my stomach.

"No doctors, Kyree. I'm fine," I say.

She strokes the silver curls from my sticky face. "You're being stubborn."

I catch her wrist. "No, I'm being pragmatic. Ranin would rather see me die than be attended to by a Varronian physician. I'm merely avoiding the confrontation."

Sighing, she pries my fingers away and crawls over me, slinking off the bed.

"What are you doing?" I ask.

"Emptying this." She retrieves the bucket and my stomach tightens. Bile sloshes way too close to the top to allow anyone besides myself to handle it.

"Please don't—"

"It reeks in here, and I'm not going to have you living like this. Rayne would never be subjected to it. He would have servants caring for him—he *does* have servants caring for him."

Ignoring me, she pads to the door and opens it. It screeches on its hinges. Rain pounds against the sides of the ship, and thunder booms in the distance. I'm not sure my stomach will last the time it takes her to leave and come back, but before I can voice that concern aloud, Kyree slips into the dark hallway dressed in a silky blue gown that barely reaches her knees.

A gentleman would call her back and insist she don a robe, but Kyree enjoys being ogled, and despite the ship being owned by Varren ingrates, its sailors aren't foolish enough to be forward with my fiancée. Bastard or not, sick or not, I have more power in my left foot than they have in their bloodlines.

When Kyree returns, she isn't alone. A yellow lantern swings in Avum's fist, illuminating four windowless walls, a wardrobe, and a writing desk. He hangs it by a hook above the desk and approaches me, the floorboards squeaking underneath his military boots.

"You look awful," Avum says.

I glare at Kyree, who sets my now empty bucket on the floor. "Why the fuck did you bring him?"

"You're his charge," she says. "It's his responsibility to look after you."

Kyree jumps on top of the writing desk, folding her arms as she observes us. Avum is fully dressed—because of course he is—and not the least bit affected by these godsforsaken waves. I loathe him seeing me like this, and I loathe Kyree for allowing it.

"He's my mentor, not my nursemaid," I snap.

Avum orders me to sit and I'm too fucking nauseous to object. Groaning, I readjust against the back of the wooden headboard and fight the turning in my stomach. He presses his unbearably hot palm to my forehead and tsks.

"When's the last time you drank any water?" he asks.

"When's the last time you minded your own business? I'm fine, Avum."

He rolls the blankets off me and wads them into a pile at the bottom of the bed. "There are hammocks in the forecastle with the rest of Fontaine's crew. We should move you there; it'll help with the nausea."

I snort. "And let word reach my father that I'm living with Varronian peasants? I'd rather not." Shivering, I reach for the blankets, pulling them up my goose prickled legs. They're not halfway to my thighs when Avum rips them away and tosses them to the rocking floor.

"The captain's quarters then. I've been inside

them. The accommodations would be much more suitable and discreet." Avum offers me his hand, to which I respond by inching closer to the wall. "It's not good for you to fester in a room like this, Mal. The small space and poor ventilation are only making things worse."

Kyree sticks her tongue out at me and mouths the words, *"I told you so."*

I love her, but gods help me the woman can be completely and utterly insufferable.

I can tell I'm not going to get anywhere with these two so, knocking Avum's hand aside, I crawl from the boxed-in mattress and brace myself against the cabin's narrow wall. My legs wobble beneath me, knees buckling from how rarely I've used them in the last few days. I fucking hate the ocean. And Ranin for insisting I come on this wretched journey.

"Are you certain Fontaine will have me?" I ask. The ship veers left and I swallow back a mouthful of sour saliva. "I have no interest in trapezing across the deck in the middle of a storm only to return here."

Avum retrieves his lantern and orders me to dress. "I'll speak with him. If he refuses, I'll switch accommodations with you. My room isn't much larger than this, but there's a porthole in it that allows for fresh air. Meet me at the stern once you've finished packing. In the meantime . . ." He reaches into his breast pocket and withdraws a red, spider-shaped ball of . . . something. "Open your mouth."

"No thank you."

"It'll help with the nausea."

Fuzzy tufts of hair protrude from the squishy substance. It oozes something sticky and yellow as Avum smashes it against my lips, forcing it past my closed teeth. Bitterness seeps into my sinuses, down my throat, and behind my bloodshot eyes. Coughing, I swallow the hairy substance and scramble toward the desk, frantically throwing open drawers in search of a canteen.

Kyree places a metal cylinder in my hand, saying nothing as I unscrew the lid and guzzle an entire container's worth of warm water. The unease settles in my gut, though the flavor of whatever the fuck that thing was lingers. Gasping for breath, I sling a dozen curses in Avum's direction, but he's already gone.

Kyree hops off the desk and rubs soothing circles into my back as I fall into bed.

"You shouldn't have brought him," I hiss.

"You're sick, Mal. For once, let us help you." She pulls the clothing from my wardrobe and tosses it beside me.

I packed lightly for this voyage: two outfits for combat training, another two for sleep, and a fifth formal suit for the last night of the Oksas—the only night someone of my station is allowed to attend.

It takes her no time to have it all laid out. Then, she reaches for the leather duffle slung over the bedframe and stuffs it while I finish dressing.

A fresh tunic, a pair of silk nightpants, and a comb through my damp hair is all it takes before I'm ready to go. Holding the bucket to my face, I glance at my reflection for a third and final time, coming face-to-face with a person no amount of grooming can fix—sunken silver eyes, gray lips, and unnaturally pale, luminous skin that always looks sickly even without the motion sickness to contend with.

"Ready?" Kyree asks.

She hefts the duffle over her shoulder and urges me out of the bedroom for the first time all week. The ocean roars in my ears and I no longer see the hallway, but the hand-carved artwork above our bed—great monsters of legend bashing their scaly bodies against the ship's hull, dragging us down into that graveyard of salty blue. Any number of things could be lurking below us, waiting for a strong enough wave to make their move.

The ship lurches sideways and I slam my shoulder into the hallway's wooden wall, bucket swinging.

"Are you alright?" Kyree asks, helping to right me as I rub my aching shoulder.

"How are you so good at this?" I ask. "You've never sailed before."

She kisses my clammy forehead. "Neither has Rayne or Bron. I think you're uniquely terrible at sailing, sweetheart. I love you, but maybe don't buy a ship anytime soon."

I flash her my middle and index finger, but Kyree only laughs, leading me down the hallway and through the galley like it isn't tipping from side to side every several seconds. Outstretching my arms, I mimic her movements, leaning into the rocking in a way that doesn't feel intuitive at all. I much prefer the snow, where I'm more likely to get stuck in hip-deep ice than flung about.

Water drips from the leaky roof and cool wind whistles down the open stairwells that lead to the upper deck. The faint screams of Fontaine's crew and the stomping of feet have me clenching my jaw, wondering how close this vessel is to fucking sinking. My insides feel like they're being squeezed, and my glowing skin is so translucent, veins poke through. It's nothing short of a miracle that I make it to the stern without dry heaving in the hallway.

True to his word, Avum meets us in front of Fontaine's closed cabin door with his arms clasped behind his back and his gaze straight ahead. He nods when he sees us—not smiles. Avum never smiles—and takes the duffle from Kyree. "It took some bribing," Avum says. "But he'll keep you until the end of the voyage. It turns out Fontaine's girl has a taste for expensive rum. I expect it to be replaced on our return home."

Noted.

I wipe the sweat from my brow and grab the gilded doorknob. "Thank you, Avum."

"You're my ward," he says. "Your father might not care what happens to you, but I do. Who will lead my ninth division if you die?"

The edge of his lip twists up.

"Are you . . . making a joke?" Kyree asks.

"No," Avum deadpans before gesturing at me to get my ass inside.

I squeeze Kyree's hand one last time then bid her goodnight, pushing on the black double doors that will take me to my new home for the next week. At least it can't be any worse than the broom closet Ranin was storing me in.

Right?

Fontaine's quarters are . . . empty. I expect to find opulence—expensive furniture, exotic rugs and artwork, formal dining spaces, and smokey parlor rooms. I find nothing. It's like he doesn't live here. Two hammocks hang from wooden posts in the cabin's epicenter. Behind them, the storm rages against an enclosed balcony, waves crashing against the sides of the ship and surf spraying over glass panels. A single writing desk, Avum's crystalline decanter of expensive rum, and a ship schematic on the wall titled *"Midnight Sun"* are the only things I see in the entire, massive space.

"This isn't normal, right?" I ask.

Avum discards my duffle underneath the desk where it won't get knocked around or slide across the floor. I set my bucket beside it.

"No," he says. "It is unusual. Best not mention it to the crew though; it'll spook them."

I arch a brow, stumbling my way toward one of the hammocks. "Spook them how?"

"If I had to guess, he's abandoning ship," Avum says. "Rumor has it, they seized the *Dorina St. Clara* before we boarded, but the frigate isn't following us, which means he's ordered it somewhere else against Arrovin's orders."

Interesting.

Pushing down on the hammock, I crawl onto its stretchy mass. Knotted, white cords tighten beneath me and the sides fold in, smothering me until it feels like I'm being swaddled. The rocking stops—or rather, my body adjusts to it, the rolls smoothing into something almost bearable. I close my eyes and breathe.

Just...

B r e a t h e.

It feels so fucking amazing to not touch the gods-damned floor.

"Do you require anything else?" Avum asks.

"You aren't my servant," I remind him, cracking open an eye. "And you've done more than enough. Go back to sleep. I'm certain Bron misses his bed warmer."

His cheeks turn apple red. The expression looks entirely ridiculous on him; the man is a decorated soldier, old enough to be my father and well versed in bedplay.

"You know about us?" he asks.

I wave him off dismissively. "I know and I don't care."

"But he's . . ."

"Too young for you?" I suggest. "Easily bored? Terrible at fighting?"

We both know what Avum is concerned about. Bron comes from a noble family. He's an only child, expected to marry and carry on his family's bloodline—and Avum is lacking some very specific organs needed to see that job through. It can't end well for them; it never does for any noble seeking the company of the same sex, but that doesn't mean it isn't worth the effort.

"I'm happy for you, Avum. I'm glad you've found someone who can tolerate your incessant mothering."

His lips form a thin line. "Next time, I'll leave you to your vomiting. Goodnight, Malin."

"Goodnight, Mom."

The door clicks shut.

I settle into the hammock and close my eyes, not sleeping but not awake either. The rain slows to a drizzle. The ship steadies, bobbing up and down rather than lilting from side to side. An image flits past my closed eyelids as my mind and magic wander, reading the thoughts and dreams of anyone within reach. Surface-level prying comes to me as easily as blinking. It's memories that are difficult to access and impossible to navigate.

Golden hair.

A melodic voice that sounds like the heavens bursting.

> "I know a lass,
> A maiden fair,
> Who took my dreams
> When I left her there
> Along the coast."

The tune lulls me.
Beautiful.
Perfect.
Mine.
The door bursts open and a rage unlike anything

I've ever felt before tears at my chest. How fucking dare he break my concentration? Eyes open, body alert, I whip my head around, glaring through the corded hammock.

A man no older than me trudges through the room. Barefoot. His white and gold uniform is soaked all the way through, leaving a trail of water in his wake.

Sighing, the man—Captain Fontaine, I presume—yanks the bandana from his scalp then discards his clothing into wet clumps on the floor. I blink a few times, certain he'll maintain enough fabric to stay modest, but he doesn't. Within seconds, the man is ass naked aside from a belt around his waist, a dagger made of seashells fastened to it.

Bastard or not, I'm still a dignitary. Still Ranin's son. His behavior has rendered me completely speechless.

Without saying a word, he rakes his fingers through his dripping hair and climbs into the hammock, the cords squeaking beneath him. The urge to throw a blanket on him gnaws at the back of my skull.

Even soft, the man is hung like a horse, with metal barbells down the length of his cock. They glint in the moonlight as do the gilded tattoos on his thigh.

Blood Empress

Kamaran's Ghost
Black Bonnet
Golden Hand
Sythe
Silverbells
Dorina St. Cl—

"Should I commission a portrait?" Fontaine asks, staring up at the ceiling, his arms behind his head.

My brows furrow. "What?"

"Should I commission a portrait so you can stare at me longer? I know a man in Kamaran..."

I turn away, my temper smoldering. He can't speak to me like that. He's a Varronian. A nobody. But before I have time to dress Fontaine down or snipe something back, the man turns onto his side and his grating snores overtake the room.

This is going to be a long nine days.

MALIN THE TITLELESS

THE KARMASKUS SEA, VARRONIAN WATERS

"Get up."

Fontaine looms over me, his cock unnervingly close to my face. The man sleeps nude every night. If there's an unexpected visitor, he answers the door nude. If something goes wrong with the ship, he repairs it nude. If I didn't see him with pants on during the day, I'd suspect he didn't own any.

Groaning, I roll onto my side, putting as much distance between myself and that *thing* as humanly possible. The hammock stretches, enveloping me like the cocoon of a luneri moth.

"You're not sick, you're not busy, and you've slept *all fucking day*," Fontaine says. "Now get your ass out of bed and come to the crews' quarters with me."

"Why?"

"Because I'm the captain of this ship and you're sleeping in my bed." In my periphery, Fontaine messes with the post, loosening the eye of the hammock. "Wait . . . that didn't come out right."

The cords give and I go flailing. My back hits the ground with a distinctive smack, and the hammock falls on top of me, getting salty strings in my mouth. Spitting them out, I rip myself free then scramble to my feet, narrowing my gaze as I readjust my clothing. "You are the most inappropriate soldier I've ever met."

"Thank you." Fontaine climbs into a pair of white breeches, and I arch an eyebrow.

"Have you finally learned to dress yourself?"

He grins. "My girl wouldn't like it if another girl saw my dick." Rifling through his desk drawers, Fontaine procures a dark, billowing shirt and pulls it over his head. "Kyree's coming tonight. My first mate invited her. You better watch out or he'll snatch her away; girls love sailors."

I snort. "Yes, bad manners, a poor bathing schedule, and lack of reading comprehension are the quickest ways to a woman's heart."

"Are you always so uptight?" Fontaine grabs my wrist and pulls, dragging me barefoot from the room. His grip tightens as I attempt to pull away. At this rate, he's going to leave a bruise.

"Are you always so insistent?" I snap.

"Always."

He leads me to the central staircase, where a thin fishing net droops from the ceiling. Clear stones hang inside the net, filled with bright golden liquid that illuminates the steps. At the bottom of the stairs, human shadows crawl up the wall, their spindly limbs hanging from swinging hammocks. Laughter buzzes through the air. Idle chatter carries into the hallway—too many conversations to keep track of and useless ones at that.

Nearly a week of prodding and I'm no closer to learning the depth, *or cause* of Fontaine's treachery. If the crew realizes he's stolen Arrovin's ship, they've given no indication. Heavy labor leaves little room for complex thoughts, and their memories are too disturbing to sift through. Wanting to procure a turncoat for my father's militia isn't worth watching sailors piss on their roommates' clothes or pretend the tail end of a mop is a woman.

"After you," Fontaine says, gesturing me forward.

Staring at my shoeless feet, I mutter a curse under my breath. The man runs a tight ship. His crew is constantly sweeping and scrubbing, bolting down furniture, and clearing walkways. Most of Fontaine's sailors traverse the decks shoeless, finding it easier to grip the wet ropes that way. Still, I prefer my leather loafers.

Once you've had a nail through the foot, you never forget the feeling.

I keep my eyes on the ground as I descend, checking for debris, barely registering how hot the stones are above my head—like molten metal or a blacksmith's forge. More netting and more stones illuminate the crews' quarters below, converting it into a muggy sauna. Fog mixes with yellow light, partially concealing the throngs of people who've piled onto wooden crates or corded hammocks.

I shouldn't be here. My father would have my head if he caught me below deck with the peasants and shiphands. Still, if Kyree's down here, then I don't see much choice in the matter.

"Hey, you made it!" Bron appears through the haze, damp red hair clinging to his ruddy cheeks. He's naked except for sleep shorts that adhere to his body like a second skin. Apparently, Fontaine's disposition toward clothing—or lack of it—has spread like an infectious disease, which could be amusing were it not for the fact that Kyree is the only woman aboard.

"Avum and ReeRee are in the back," Bron says, wiping the hair from his face. "We saved you a spot."

"For what?"

I make no effort to hide my lack of amusement. Bron knows that I don't enjoy surprises, nor being carted around like a dog.

"Relax, Mal." Bron rolls his eyes and my blood boils. "We made port an hour ago and the crew wants to celebrate."

Made port?

Now that I'm paying attention, it's clear the ship's rocking has leveled into gentle bobs. My stomach is calm for the first time in weeks and I no longer feel the need to latch onto support beams every several seconds. It's late enough that the docks will be closed, the Varrens asleep in their gilded beds and safe from us until sunrise.

My skin itches in anticipation. Soon, I'll have to meet those monsters. And then I'll have to break them.

"Douse the stones!" Fontaine shouts.

I'm imagining how good it'll feel to snap their gilded bones beneath my fist when the crew scrambles to their feet. Unfurling the netting above our heads, they shake golden rocks into water buckets on the floor. Steam hisses. Fog spurts into the air as the water's reflection turns golden, the stones' bright light dimming into almost nothing.

"Come on," Bron hisses. He weaves past a group of shirtless men and waves at me to follow.

Sighing, I pinch the bridge of my nose and attempt not to inhale as I traverse the unwashed masses. Rum. Sweat. Oranges. Salt. Tobacco. With the close proximity, this place is a breeding ground for disease.

Somewhere near the back of the space, Kyree and Avum lie belly up on a single hammock, his arms around her stomach in a way that's entirely too familiar. I bite back a grin. We've discussed it—inviting Avum into our bedroom. Bron has played with us for years now, since the three of us were teens still learning what sex was. Avum's never been open to it, but he's never been in a relationship with Bron before either.

Nodding at her, I claim a hammock close behind them, and Bron joins me, both of us sitting crisscross on the cords.

The room's walls form a half-circle around a stack of wooden crates in the center—a make-shift stage? Tristan approaches it, crowbar in hand, shoving it into the crack. The wood splits open, and he withdraws several dark bottles full of amber liquid, passing them around to the crew. A bottle finds its way between Bron and me, another between Avum and Kyree.

Tristan empties three crates. He stacks them one on top of the other then sits on them, legs spread wide, a rum bottle in hand. Jamming the cork between his teeth, he wiggles it from side to side until it pops then spits it out. The cork shoots across the room, rolling beneath a hammock.

"I've never gotten seasick," Tristan declares, raising his bottle and waving it in my direction. "That one's for you, Malin."

I arch an eyebrow.

Beneath his breath, Bron whispers, "You're supposed to drink if you've done it." He hands me our uncorked bottle, and I glare at Fontaine.

The rum burns on its way down. I'm not the only one who drinks though. Several other crewmates take a long swig before passing the bottle to their companions. Tristan cocks his head and the guy closest to him clears his throat.

"I've never shit in someone's hat."

I squint through the darkness and fog. No one's drinking except Tristan. He tips the bottle back, greasy hair shining in the light of the water barrels. The crowd snickers. The next crewmate speaks. Then the next and the next.

"I've never killed a man who's pissing."

"I've never killed a man *while* pissing."

"I've never drank so much korrack juice my piss turned blue."

Tristan's mouth never leaves the bottle. Over the hooting and hollering crowd, I can almost hear the liquid glugging. Chest heaving, he gasps in air, a broad grin revealing every pearly white tooth in his mouth.

"Why is everyone so obsessed with my piss?" He

chuckles. "Surely you lot can come up with something better."

To my right, a hammock squeaks. A man half my age—a boy really—probably too young to drink, let alone throw his lot in with glorified pirates, raises a bottle. Gilded tattoo ink forms a sick tapestry over his dark-brown skin. When he smiles, a golden tooth gleams.

"I've never gotten my cock stuck in the bilge pump." He snorts.

The crew snickers. Tristan flips the boy off but raises the bottle, still smiling.

"I've never licked One-Eyed Nick's good eye either. Or snuck a girl into the navigation room. Or let Samin pierce my dick. Ten times."

Tristan's face turns scarlet. "Alright, alright, you've proven your point, Jordie." He brings the bottle to his mouth and chugs, finishing off the whole damn thing like it won't fucking wreck him.

Kyree turns back to me and arches an eyebrow. "Would you let me pierce your dick?"

Absolutely fucking not.

Something whooshes through the air, past Jordie's head. Glass shatters against the polished blackwood. It takes a second to register that Tristan threw it.

"Target someone else," he says, sweat beading on

his forehead. "I'm meeting my girl in the morning and I need to be coherent."

Coherent my asscheeks. The man will be lucky to be alive. Fucking lunatic.

On heavy feet, Tristan rises. Reaching for the crowbar, he inserts it into another wooden crate and jerks, splintering the box. Swathes of bright fabric spill out: tulip pants, mesh netting, bandeaus with jingling bells attached. I might be sheltered, but I know a pleasure slave's outfit when I see one.

I swallow the nails in my throat, wondering if Fontaine is involved in the slave trade. If there are girls aboard this ship. If he put them there or if Arrovin commanded it.

A stolen ship filled with magical women could buy him anything he wanted. Enough to actualize those blueprints in his office. The *Midnight Sun* feels sinister now and my mind is reeling. Assessing. Recalibrating.

The game continues.

Tristan hastily throws the lid onto the fabric box before opening up another—the one he'd clearly intended to crack open in the first place—and reaches for a fresh bottle. Slowly, he clambers toward us, plopping into Jordie's hammock.

Opening my mind, I hear dozens of thoughts, see dozens of images. Parsing through them would take time, and my head already throbs with the effort.

"Mal?" Bron nudges me. I start to yell at him when I notice all eyes on me. Before I can ask what they said, Bron whispers it. "I've never been moontouched."

How original.

I bring the bottle to my lips.

"What's it like?" one of the crewmates ask.

It takes an incredible amount of effort not to flash him a crude gesture. "What do you think it's like?" I spit. "Not fucking great."

"How'd it happen?" Jordie this time.

"Sorry." Tristan clasps him on the shoulder. "There aren't any moontouched in Varren. A lot of what we know about your people is hearsay. Don't feel obligated to answer."

"My people are born with it. It's a curse the Varren put on our bloodlines centuries ago." I take another swig, gripping the bottle until my knuckles ache. The burn of the alcohol is nothing compared to the inferno raging in my chest. The gold on this ship, the wealth, it's all a reminder of where I am and where I'm headed.

The boy peers at me with wide, curious eyes and the tension tightens in my chest. He honestly doesn't know. Perhaps no one here does. It doesn't surprise me that their wretched family has rewritten history, pretending they didn't make us into the monstrous creatures that we are.

Time to set the record straight.

I clear my throat. "Four hundred years ago, the Varren made it illegal to worship any god but Eliah. Whoever was caught breaking the ordinance was punished. Worshipers of Adrian were drowned. Worshipers of Kathen were burned. Worshipers of Daliah were moontouched." I stare at my pallid, glowing skin and clarify. "Cursed to never see sunlight again. Later, banished to the farthest reaches of Ranada to die alone, cold, and in the dark. But we didn't die, and the curse persisted through our bloodlines."

"Could they cure you?" Jordie asks. "The Varren, I mean."

"That's what I'm here to deduce."

Avum shoots me a look against giving away the parameters of our mission. I swallow down another gulp of rum then turn the bottle in my hands. When I look up, I've forced a smile to my face.

"I've never slept naked."

Everyone in the room drinks.

MALIN THE TITLELESS

THE GOLDEN COAST, CAPITAL OF VARREN

My skull is throbbing.

Begrudgingly, I open my eyes, vision blurring as I lean forward, attempting to sit up. Slender arms wrap around my chest, tugging me back into bed—not bed, I realize. The surface is too hard. The texture is too slick and hot and . . . *wet?*

Something nudges my shoulder.

I groan, turning into the soft skin and silky hair beside me. I'm in no mood for combat training—no shape for it either. "Avum, for the love of Daliah, I'm trying to sleep."

"Wake up." King Ranin's voice cuts through my foggy brain. In the span of a single breath, I'm on my feet, disentangling myself from a pile of sweaty limbs and sticky skin.

"Your Majesty." My throat is so fucking dry, I might as well be swallowing sandpaper.

Ranin's nose scrunches in disgust as his silver eyes scan over my nude body, then Kyree's, Bron's, and Avum's. I can't remember a damn thing from last night, least of all how the four of us ended up naked on the quarterdeck.

"Get downstairs, get dressed and don't embarrass me anymore than you already have," Ranin hisses.

Avum is next to rise, combing fingers through his black hair.

My father spins on him, adjusting his silver crown. "I expect this behavior from the boys, but you?" His lips curl. "Perhaps I should have left you in the whorehouse."

Avum lowers his head. I've never seen him cowed before. "I'm sorry, Your Majesty. It won't happen again."

Ranin's jaw clenches. The two of us look nearly identical with our long silver hair and moontouched skin. When my father is angry, though, I don't see myself. I see an unmovable force. A demon behind a mask of formality, good breeding, and cordiality.

"Malin's sex toy stays on the ship," he says coolly.

My spine straightens. "She's my fiancée."

"Call her what you like. She stays on the *Black Death* so long as we're in Varren."

"Like hells she does."

"Malin." Avum grabs my fist before I can fully process that it's clenched and ready to swing. "I will prepare him, sire. We'll be ready to depart in time for the greeting ceremony. You have my word."

"Good," he says, straightening the edges of his tunic.

Ranin usually dresses in animal furs and thick leather, but today he's the mirror image of any other king: a black, long-tailed coat with a high-necked collar, matching knee length breeches, silk stockings, and buckled shoes. Everything is embroidered in silver, except for the purple sash across his chest.

"I want Malin in his formal attire today. He will be included in the procession with Rayne," my father adds.

I'm never in the procession. I'm a bastard, a son made for fighting not breeding.

"Yes, my king." Avum bows low.

My father's expression remains indignant. Sighing, he spins on his heels and marches toward the forecastle, disappearing behind raised sails and a dozen fully dressed, fully uniformed crew members.

I glance down at my nude body, then at Kyree's and Bron's.

Shit. Of all the places to fall asleep like this.

Our clothing lies in a sopping heap, either from rain or mop water, it's impossible to tell. Using only my fingertips, I pluck a shirt from the pile and make a face. This is revolting. The thought of putting it on makes me want to puke. Gently, I nudge Kyree awake and pass her the shirt. Rubbing at her eyes, she stares up at me with a hazy, confused expression.

"We passed out on the upper decks. You're naked, sweetheart." Her cheeks flush and she snatches the shirt from me, hugging it to her chest. The dirty water seeps down her skin onto Bron's sunburnt cheek.

As they rouse themselves to consciousness, I turn to Avum. "I can dress myself. Can you help Kyree get cleaned and settled? I don't want her returning to her chambers like that without an escort."

I might love it when men ogle Kyree, perhaps even more than she does. I might love it when they play with her too—so long as I can watch and participate—but the idea of her being alone on this ship for the next nine days has my hackles rising. Sailors are pigs. Filth. They're lonely too. Some of them haven't seen another woman in months.

I rub my throbbing temples.

This was not the arrangement Ranin and I agreed to.

"I'll put soldiers outside her cabin," Avum says, already sensing my thoughts. "No one will touch her, Mal. You have my word." He cocks his head and gestures for me to leave. "Get dressed. I'll handle these two."

I nod, though the last thing I want is to leave her to these vultures.

Keeping my head low, I ignore the sharp whistles and catcalls the sailors lob at me. I haven't had time to see how close our ship is to the harbor. Certainly, it's close enough that a person with a spyglass could see me like this, but I refuse to be embarrassed. A Carthinian officer doesn't get embarrassed by Varronian peasants or unwashed sailors scrubbing vomit off the upper decks. Still, it's a huge fucking relief when I arrive at the stairwell.

At least, I thought it would be.

Loud, cheerful humming comes from the other side of Fontaine's cabin. It's too early for this nonsense. Groaning, I throw open the doors and find him sitting at his desk, looking at himself in a foldable mirror.

My brows furrow. Fontaine looks nothing like the greasy, unkempt soldier I've come to know. Dressed in a white and gold uniform, the metal gleams. His hair is brushed, hidden beneath an officer's tricorn, and he smells like spicy, expensive cologne. The kind my brother uses.

In the mirror, Fontaine dips a round shaving brush into a metal tin, lathering white soap and spreading it across his stubbled chin. He grabs a straight-edged razor off the desk and slides it across his skin, still humming.

"You've got to stop staring at me like that," he says, wiping the blade on a hand towel. "You're making me blush."

I shake my head and pray to Daliah for patience. "How are you not hungover?"

"Practice." He *shinks* the blade across his chin, wipes, then *shinks* again. "I heard you and your friends had a little too much fun upstairs last night. I suppose next time you drink with us, you'll have to come up with a new *I've never*."

Shink.

Ignoring him, I snatch my duffle off the floor and unpack my formal military uniform. It's nearly identical to Fontaine's—straight pants, a stiff, long-sleeved jacket with a braided front, and knee-high boots. But where his is white and gold, mine is black and silver. The braiding is more ornate as well, and thick ropes dangle over my left shoulder.

"I've got a washing basin in the other room," Fontaine says, staring at himself in the mirror, playing with his hair like he's a gentleman. The only thing gentle about this man is the way he prowls about the ship.

"There's a fresh water pitcher beside the basin," he adds. "Soap. Oils. Whatever you want, feel free."

"Since when do you care about looking and smelling like a respectable human being?" I ask.

"Since I haven't seen my girl in three months." He

takes the tricorn off. Puts it back on. Takes it off again. "My hair is getting too long, I think."

I roll my eyes.

While Fontaine preens himself, I do the same, stepping into the adjacent room where a claw tub overlooks the balcony. True to his word, an assortment of crystalline bottles form a line outside the tub. Prisms of light shoot off them, casting rainbows across the polished floorboards.

One by one, I pick them up, unstoppering the bottles. Sniffing, I scrunch my nose at the potency. They're more feminine than I'd imagined. Floral. Sweet. The oil is so thick, it could almost be honey.

I put them down.

The nagging voice in my head—the same one from last night—grows louder, warning me something is off with him. Feminine oils. Those harem outfits. Peering into the adjacent doorway, I watch Fontaine wipe the lather from his smooth face.

If there were slaves on this ship, where would he keep them? Would he carry them out for the king's enjoyment or his own?

If Ranin were here, he would tell me to mind my business. He would say Fontaine isn't my problem, that we came here to destroy the Varren, not play hero to a handful of desperate girls. But the thought has rooted in my brain and I can't get it out.

For all my father's faults, and there are many, he's

never kept slaves. He pays our servants nicely, and the only women he's ever kept were my mother and Rayne's—Rayne's out of obligation, mine out of love. The moontouched aren't monsters like the Varren or brutes like their king.

With concerted effort, I force myself to ignore Fontaine, grabbing a lumpy bar of soap off the tub's edge. This isn't my problem. This isn't my responsibility. More than that, I'm in no position to stop it.

Stepping into the empty, bronze tub, I stare out into the harbor. Black sky stretches over sandy beaches, dense tropical rainforests, and a sprawling city that's stained by wealth. It's so green and vibrant and ... *alive*. The complete opposite of Carthinia.

White tenement buildings tower over walkways made from crushed seashells and gold. Potted plants hang from gilded balconies, so full of ivy and jasmine that they drip down the sides of the railing onto alleyways and sidewalks. The people here dress in vibrant colors, their clothing tight enough and short enough to display eyefuls of dark, sun rich skin. Even though I can't see it, the light is so bright, its reflection makes my eyes burn.

Squinting, I avert my gaze to the castle, which is every bit as gaudy as I imagined it would be—two ramparts twice the height of our ship, a white and gold spired keep, and blooming gardens between them. Soldiers clad in gold plating pace the fortifications, armed with guns? No, arrows. No, guns, I think. From this vantage point, it's difficult to tell. At least nine emplacements face the harbor, but there could be more.

"Sizing up Arrovin's defenses?" Fontaine asks.

I jump when he appears behind me, snatching an oil bottle off the floor and pocketing it. Before I have time to answer, he adds, "Varren is impossible to invade, you know. The barrier reefs protect its eastern borders and the Pearl Islands protect the rest. You could maybe slip a frigate through the reefs, but only if you'd mapped it out in advance. You certainly can't get a navy through."

I stare at him blankly and keep my tone neutral. "Carthinia is surrounded by snow. We have neither the means nor desire to invade Varren."

We simply wish to burn it to the ground.

I scrub my body quickly and efficiently, drinking from the pitcher of water before I pour it over my sudsy skin. Once I'm finished, I step from the tub, drying my face on a towel that Fontaine offers me. "I didn't realize Arrovin's palace was so close to the city," I say. "Carthinia's nearest village is several miles away."

"It's pretty convenient."

"Convenient for what?"

He slaps me on the back and drags me to the main cabin. "Hurry up. The greeting ceremony starts in . . ." Fontaine withdraws his pocket watch. "Fifteen minutes."

As I dress, I focus my mind on his. Most people think loudly, but not Fontaine. His mind is so quiet, it's like he doesn't think at all. I push my magic deeper, angling for the barriers to his subconscious. Normally, they appear in my mind's eye as a physical barrier—a towering wall, an endless sky, a depthless sea—each a reflection of the person's soul. With Fontaine, there's nothing there but a black, gaping hole.

Buttoning my pants, I try again. Same result.

Strange.

It wouldn't be boastful to say I'm the best psion in Ranada, and this has never happened to me before. Frowning, I don the rest of my uniform and comb through my mop of curly, silver hair, still seeking out Fontaine's subconscious. Still failing.

"You look like you're trying to take a shit," he says.

"Fuck off." I rub the crease lines from my forehead and let it go. Another time. Another place. Knowing what Fontaine thinks is not within our mission parameters, even if the man is more suspicious than white rocks in a snowstorm.

Together, we approach the mezzanine deck. Both Carthinian and Varronian soldiers part for us, giving low bows as we pass. It makes my skin crawl. I'd rather be invisible. A wraith in the shadows. Fontaine, on the other hand, seems to live for this shit. He's all broad smiles and perfect posture when we reach the pre-appointed meeting spot.

My father, Avum, Rayne, and Bron are already waiting for us—Avum in an outfit that mirrors my own, the others in fine jewelry and silks. My brother's obsidian crown and purple sash is surprisingly absent from his ensemble, but in my father's arms is a folded purple cape so dark, it could almost be black. An intimidating jacket is hardly enough to make up for Rayne's lack of power. I'm about to say as much when Avum points.

"There they are."

I follow his finger.

Across the harbor, golden-caped figures glide along the docks, forming a single-file line as they descend into a crystalline rowboat. Their movements are graceful, almost like a dance. Behind them, a man in a white suit—with no cape or ornamentation—climbs in last. It's difficult to see him against the glare of the boat. His skin is the same sandy brown as the shoreline, white hair combed into a fishtail braid.

I don't need to be told who he is. Only one man could look so haughty and unassuming at the same time. Only one man would be allowed to accompany the Varren without guards at his heels.

King Arrovin Hade.

My jaw clenches. He may not be one of those gilded, glittering beasts, but he's still my enemy. They all are. Every person who's helped perpetuate the Varren's reign will fall. Slowly. Brutally. Someday, I'll flay the skin from Arrovin's bones and stain that white suit red. I'm imagining the squishy sound his flesh will make beneath my blade when Ranin grasps my shoulder.

"You will be expected to give a demonstration of your power," he says. "Do not reveal your psionics."

I snort. *Does he think I'm an idiot?*

Ranin unfurls the cape, blowing humid, hot air against my face.

I quirk an eyebrow. "What are you doing?"

"Preparing you." He fastens the cape to my left shoulder, hooking clasps together, straightening the velvet until it's flat against my uniform. "In Varren, it's customary for royal families to meet in neutral territory as a sign of peace." He lowers his voice. "Make no mistake though, Fontaine's crew are more than capable of shooting us down. Behave yourself."

"Why bring me at all? I'm not royal."

He doesn't answer. Instead, Ranin procures a diadem from his coat pocket and places it atop my head, squishing down my messy curls. It takes a minute to process that it's Rayne's crown I'm wearing. "What—"

I'm cut off by Fontaine. "Time to go, Your Majesty." His eyebrows go all the way to his hairline when he looks at me, dipping into a low bow. "Your Highness."

My stomach sours at the honorific. For the first time in my life, Ranin doesn't correct him, keeping silent beside me.

Hanging from the ship's hull is a rowboat large enough to haul twenty men. At Fontaine's command, sailors raise it on a pulley system until it's flush with the railing, metal chains clinking against darkwood. Fontaine places a stepping stool in front of the railing and gestures us forward.

Confused, hungover, and exhausted, my insides clench when I see the drop, the dark-blue ocean waiting to devour me. I shouldn't have read all those books on sea creatures and sailing before we left.

Ranin thrusts me forward, hissing impatiently. If he knows I'm afraid, I'll never hear the end of it, but that doesn't stop me from grimacing when the wood groans and wobbles beneath my weight. Half scrunched over, I fumble toward the back of the boat until Ranin redirects me to sit beside him at the center. Rayne tumbles in next on my father's right. My brother's expression is as perplexed as mine, eyebrows furrowed as he takes in my accessories—the ones he should be wearing.

We both know I shouldn't be here—that I hate

being here. I belong with Kyree below deck, unseen and ignored.

Fontaine leaps into the boat and it rocks, slamming against the side of the hull so hard, my legs vibrate. Sour saliva pools in the back of my throat but I swallow it down.

Don't show weakness. It's only a thirty-foot drop to certain doom.

Four sailors join us, picking up oars as Fontaine takes position at the front. Avum and Bron remain at the railing, waving us goodbye.

"Lower the boat!" Fontaine says.

The scraping chains and heaving grunts are all I hear for the next several seconds. I close my eyes until the boat hits water, my breaths coming in uneven gulps. If I never see the ocean again, it'll be too soon. Beside me, Ranin squeezes my shoulder—tight.

"Keep it together. Do not embarrass me."

My skin itches. The sleeves on my uniform are too hot, too restrictive. The sun burns into my upper back and stinging sweat streaks my forehead, though the sky is dark around me. I put my head between my legs and count backwards from one-hundred, ignoring the scowls everyone casts my way.

Ranin's fingernails dig in. "Look up. Now."

I force myself to listen, willing my shaking, useless body to cooperate. Closing in on us is the

Varrens' boat, sparkling in the afternoon light. Their gilded cloaks burn my eyes, though I see nothing of their infamous golden skin. Arrovin Hade doesn't paddle the ship, he commands the waves beneath it, propelling it forward with nothing but magic. The closer we get to him, the more of his face I see. Storm clouds churn in his foggy, gray eyes. Though his hair is white, there's not a wrinkle on him.

Our boats line up beside one another.

Fontaine speaks first. "Your Majesty." He nods to Arrovin, then to the hooded figure directly behind him. "Your Grace. I present you with—"

My father raises his hand, cutting him off. "King Ranin Varuz. This is my son Rayne." He gestures to my brother who inclines his head. "And my other son Prince Malin, Commander of the Grays and my heir apparent."

What?

Ranin refuses to meet my gaze, and Rayne's gone pale, his shoulders stiffening, hands tightening into fists. The kings shake hands while the two of us stare at one another, my dread mixing with his anger.

I close my eyes and reach for his consciousness. *"I didn't know. I didn't want this. I swear."*

If Rayne can hear me, his face gives no indication.

"This is High Priestess Lyenna Varren," Arrovin says. The figure behind him lowers her hood, revealing swirling golden eyes, golden hair, and gold-painted skin. Her body glows so bright, it could be the sun for all I know.

My mouth drops. My blood sings. Every part of me wants to touch her, to bleed for her, to—

"Malin. A demonstration," my father growls.

The woman—the creature—smiles at me knowingly, her pearly white teeth transforming into razors. When I blink, they're smooth again. Her expression is serene.

Knee bouncing, I reach for the blade at my hip. It's a dull ceremonial thing, just functional enough to work for my purposes. Opening my palm, I carve a stinging line through my pale flesh and watch blood bubble to the top. I show it to them then close my eyes and imagine the flesh cinching back together. It starts as a tug on my skin, like stitches or tape. As the new skin forms, I hear spectators clap.

"Healing magic, very impressive," Arrovin says.

"Rare too." Lyena's tongue darts out to lick her lips. A patch of glittering skin reveals itself beneath the golden paint. *Avendessa*, they call it. "You would be a nice addition to our court," she adds.

A shiver rolls through my spine. *What the fuck has my father done?*

PRINCE MALIN VARUZ

LYENNA VARREN'S MIND, THE GOLDEN TEMPLE

A gold wall blocks my path to Lyenna Varren's mind. It reaches into endless darkness, stretching to my left and right for infinity. I press my astrally projected hand to the wall and it ripples, the shockwaves spreading higher and higher until they smooth out into a flat sheet.

I shouldn't be wending minds right now, but boredom does strange things to a person.

"Let me in," I whisper, spearing my false fingers through the sleek, liquid metal. It doesn't burn. If anything, it feels cool to the touch.

My hand disappears first, then my arm. I step closer, holding my breath as the gold encapsulates me, seeping into my nostrils, ears, and mouth. It's tasteless. Soundless. Suffocating. When I emerge, I'm standing in the center of a golden temple before an altar in the shape of an open hand. Arrovin Hade towers above me, tucking a strand of hair behind my ear—not my ear, I remember, *Lyenna Varren's*—I'm in her memory, her body, experiencing this moment exactly as she had.

"Don't touch me like that," we snap, raising our chin to meet his smug stare. Arrovin Hade is twice our weight in muscle, but his hair is white and crows' feet age his eyes. He might be strong, but he isn't immortal like us, and he can't boss us around. "I want the Jasmine Strait and I need Ezrah married to Remi to secure it."

"She isn't ready to be placed at court," Arrovin says. He touches us again, placating us, and it makes our skin crawl with spiders. The man is revolting but he's powerful. He's a means to an end.

We slap his hand away and pivot, moving toward a long line of golden pews. "You're too attached to her, Arri, and it's clouding your judgment. Ezrah was ready last year and the year before. People will talk if she isn't at the presentation ceremony."

People are talking now.

"What's wrong with her?"

"What's wrong with him?"

"Twenty-one is too old to be unmarried."

Arrovin crosses his arms. "Let them talk then. She's my daughter. I'll present her when I'm ready."

Lightning flashes in his eyes. The scent of rainwater washes over the room, thunder crackling in the distance. We're under-impressed. We've seen his tantrums before, watched him level buildings and flood entire islands. His worst isn't scarier than ours.

Ducking between the pews, we find a man tied, gagged, and unconscious lying on the bench. His clothing is dirty—probably some pissant from the gambling dens or whorehouses. He moans when we climb on top of him but doesn't open his eyes. Not yet.

"We want her placed in Kamaran or Jade by the end of this year. Marry her to Remi or Corvin—we don't care which." Our words are meant for Arrovin, but our eyes are on the man whose dirty cheek we stroke. He reeks of booze and tobacco; they're better clean and fresh, but it'll do. "She's useless to us here. I—we have a visitor."

The memory turns grainy, like looking through dirty glass.

Our head snaps forward so the sharp angles of our face are reflected in the polished golden walls. Our irises flash silver, then gold, then silver again. A masculine nose appears behind ours like a mirage or a ghost . . . or a spy.

"Get out," she hisses, gripping onto the sides of her head. "Get the fuck out of my head, you disgusting worm!"

The temple shakes. The metal walls groan,

collapsing inward. Like elastic, my consciousness snaps back into my body, my chest heaving, sweat drenching my military uniform.

When I blink, I'm in Arrovin's parlor room surrounded by royals.

What the fuck?

Flashing blue and silver light disorients me as lightning zaps from one wall to the other, arcing over a high-rise ceiling through hundreds of thin glass tubes. Obnoxious chattering muffles the low buzz of electricity and my father throws his arm around me like we're the best of pals.

"Malin commands our ninth division," he says. "My son is the best tracker in Ranada."

"The ninth division?" Emperor Remi Scalen leans forward in his lounge chair, brown eyes gleaming in the pulsing light. Arrovin's parlor room is dark and unnerving—a symbol of power more than a comfortable meeting ground.

I take slow, rehearsed breaths and attempt to remember where our conversation left off before I got bored of it and fucked off to places unknown. To anyone at the table, I would have been absent for a small stretch of time, short enough to feign daydreaming.

"You might be more familiar with the term Grays," my father says.

"You mean the monster hunters?" Remi's face

perks up. He's younger and more feminine than the other rulers, with ornate silk robes that cinch at the waist and eyes outlined with kohl. His long brown hair is tied into a simple bun, and oil greases his light-brown skin. The man strikes me as the type to spectate fights rather than partake in them. I wonder if he's ever hunted a damn thing in his life.

Remi's eyes scan me slowly, like he's stripping me nude. "You lead them?" he asks.

"Someone has to."

Slipping from my father's grasp, I reach for the wine glass between us, my eyes landing on a portrait of the Varren family. My hands shake as I sip from my drink, but I smile like I'm supposed to and sprawl out on the couch, sinking into the cushions with a confidence I don't feel.

Lyenna Varren saw me.

No one's ever seen me before.

Memories are supposed to be stagnant. Set in stone. Lyenna Varren should not have been able to interact with me, let alone kick me out.

My father's forehead creases, the question, "What's wrong with you?" hanging on his tongue. If I tell him I was using my gifts on a Varren, he'll rip me a new asshole. If I keep it to myself . . . I swallow, swirling the wine like I haven't a care in the world.

Perhaps she didn't recognize me. Perhaps I wasn't in her mind long enough to be identified.

"This is your first Oksas?" Remi asks. Like everyone here, he already knows the answer. Carthinia has never been invited to Varren for any reason; we've been at war with them since our kingdom's inception.

"Yes," I answer plainly. "I'm not searching for a wife though—"

"Like hells you aren't," my father says. "Malin's got it in his head he's going to marry his mistress."

Remi smiles. "Marry her then. I've taken three wives and I'm looking for a fourth. The fathers don't care if you offer a high enough price."

The gods care.

I keep my mouth shut. Remi has been uncharacteristically kind to us and it wouldn't serve to make him an enemy. He rules over Jade, the second-largest land mass in Ranada. If we were to attack Varren, we would need his support and access to his waterways.

"I've been courting Aliyah Varren since last year," says the man beside Remi. He's my age with white hair and light-blue eyes. "But the real prize is Ezrah."

Other men grunt in agreement.

Over two-dozen royals gather at our table—not an ordinary table, but a glass box of iridescent sand and saltwater. Tiny fishes dart through porous coral reefs, and crustaceans crawl along the bottom, their shells translucent enough to watch their hearts beat.

I imagine that's what the women at the Oksas feel like, creatures to be gawked at.

At least with the Varren, that's not far from the truth.

"I've placed a bid on her," Remi says. "Her father didn't seem inclined to take it."

But Lyenna Varren did.

"That's because Ezrah is Arrovin's favorite daughter," says the white-haired man. "If he had it his way, she'd join the Maidenhood. I doubt she'll be in attendance this year."

I can't stop the words from rolling out. "What makes her so special?"

Remi snorts.

The other men look at me like I've asked, "What makes water wet?"

Before anyone can answer me, three loud bangs vibrate the marble floors.

The collective room turns, our conversation fizzling out as a gold-plated guard opens the gilded entryway. "My lords, I present to you High Priestess Lyenna Varren and His Royal Majesty, King Arrovin Hade."

Everyone stands.

I force myself to do the same, not breathing as they enter the room one after the other. Lyenna doesn't walk; she glides. Dressed in a puffy, long-sleeved gown, her golden eyes latch onto mine, lips upturning into the faintest of smiles. I imagine razors behind them, ripping out my esophagus and eating my heart.

"You would taste so good," she whispers.

All the blood drains from my face as I realize I'm still linked to her. Those images weren't *my* fears; they were *her* desires.

Lyenna's smile widens. Her thoughts twist until I'm lying flat on my back inside the temple, my arms and legs tied as she crawls on top of me. Her sharp fingernails rip through my jacket like it's made of gossamer. *"Be careful whose mind you enter, little prince. You may not like what you see."*

"Malin, are you alright?" my father asks, voice low in my ear. "You don't look well."

In my mind's eye, she leans over my chest. Her hands cover my nose and mouth, pinching off my airways.

"I can't . . ." I glance at my father, each word, each breath a desperate struggle. "I need air."

I stumble from the room, not caring that I'm making a scene. Lyenna practically beams as I brush past her and Arrovin, exiting into the outer courtyard.

The images grow darker.

My blood drips from her teeth. My cock fills her fist, the pain needling as she squeezes me through layers of thick cotton.

Calves burning, I sprint from the palace and keep sprinting, swatting at ferns, ducking under branches until the grass beneath my feet turns to mushy sand. Her cackling laughter follows—merciless and unyielding. It penetrates deep inside my skull.

"I could break you, little prince. It would be so easy."

An invisible knife slices at the backs of my knees and I collapse into the foamy surf. My head hits the wet sand, bitter saltwater spraying into my open mouth. I can't close it. I can't do anything. My limbs refuse to cooperate no matter how hard I struggle.

Groaning, I swallow back a mouthful of sea spray, then another, choking as the tide moves higher.

"That's right, love. I could drown you and nobody would ever know. The tides would wash you away and turn you into fish food."

I close my eyes and reach for the invisible strings that connect my consciousness to hers. If I can sever them, I can—

"I love it when they fight back," she purrs, her breath searing into my throat. *"You're strong too. So much stronger than your oaf of a father. Remi and the Jasmine Strait seem like a consolation prize when I could have you. I hear Carthinia is beautiful."*

A thin silver thread appears behind my eyelids. I reach for it and pull, snapping the cord in half.

Lyenna Varren vanishes.

A weight lifts from my body and I scramble to my feet, coughing as I claw my way through the slurry sand. Tiny sand granules burrow beneath my fingernails. My vision swirls as I brush myself off and peer into the harbor, legs shaking as I seek out the *Black Death*—specifically the forecastle where Kyree remains confined. Dozens of ships swarm the port, hoisting royal banner flags in every color. For the first time in Carthinian history, our flags fly amongst them—purple and black with a crescent moon in the center. Sighing, I rub my eyes, embedding scratchy sand into the corneas.

It wasn't supposed to be like this.

My mission was simple—learn Arrovin's defenses and assess his weaknesses while his guard is down. My father never said anything about mingling with nobles, least of all interacting with Arrovin and Lyenna. Now there's a target on my back and Kyree isn't here.

She isn't here.

I fist my hands in my hair. I kick the sand, slipping in it and falling on my ass. Water splashes onto my sticky, wet uniform, and I curse whatever god had the audacity to fill the gaps in the world with disgusting fish water.

"This whole situation is fucked," I say. Running my fingers through the clumpy sand, I stare at the captain's quarters on the *Black Death*, where a golden light brightens the balcony. I imagine Kyree there, painting the skyline on her weather-worn easel.

Gods, I fucking miss her.

"How am I supposed to find a wife who isn't you?" I ask. "How am I supposed to steal a nation my brother spent his whole life preparing to lead?"

If she were here, she would know what to say to soothe my troubled mind, but instead, I'm left with nothing but lapping ocean waves, whistling wind, and Lyenna Varren's threat to take my kingdom from me.

I PACE THE GOLDEN COAST, shivering, shoeless, and sopping, with no destination in mind. My arms sink with the weight of my swollen leather boots—still dripping after all this time. They drag through the sand, tracing a path from Arrovin's palace to the rocky outcropping at the edge of the estate.

Sighing, I stop in front of the outcropping and hang my boots to dry. Unhooking the buttons on my military jacket, I toss it to the rocks as well. It makes a soggy slapping sound when it hits, darkening the limestone with dripping water. Shirt next. I leave my sand-covered pants on if only to spare Ranin the humiliation of having an indecent son—who knows who could be watching me from those ships.

Hopefully, no one.

The port is silent, the docks are closed for the night, and silver starlight is the only light for miles. This place is as good a place as any to fall asleep, collect my thoughts, and avoid that bitch Lyenna Varren.

I sink into the sand. Groaning, I lean my head against the rock wall and close my burning, bloodshot eyes. It's been a long fucking day.

"That's it, baby. You're doing such a good job."

My eyes snap open.

I'd recognize that annoying voice anywhere. *Tristan-fucking-Fontaine*. What in Daliah's name is he doing on Arrovin's property? More aptly, *who* is he doing?

"Relax your throat, princess. Just like that. I'm so fucking proud of you."

A woman's sloppy, throaty gags fill the space between us, and fuck if it doesn't get me hard. I bet Kyree would look so fucking sexy taking Tristan's giant dick. All swollen and red-lipped. Kohl running down her cheeks. The tightness in my pants is too fucking much. I stroke myself through the wet, salty fabric and stand, seeking a better visual that'll hide me from them as well as the ships at sea.

Maneuvering past the waves and up the jagged

rocks, I'm met with a burst of gold, glimmering light. I duck into a recess and blink a handful of times, waiting for the starbursts to subside before peeking out again.

That's when I see her—a creature so beautiful, she could make the gods weep.

Kneeling in front of Tristan is this golden, glowing beacon dressed in a midnight-blue pleasure slave's outfit. Her glittering bronze skin is more akin to gemstones than flesh . . . and there's so much flesh on display. Her toned stomach. Her perfect fucking breasts. She lures me in like a moth to a flame, and I'm certain she could destroy me just as easily.

I stroke myself again.

"Mind your teeth," Tristan says. "Open wider."

He fists the back of her long golden hair and pushes down, forcing her to take the entire length of his dick. Tears streak the sides of her pretty face, and drool drips past her ruby lips.

Fucking hells.

Seeing a Varren without their avendessa feels almost surreal. Watching one supplicate themselves to an asshole like Fontaine . . . damn. I bet people would pay good money for that. As she bobs on his dick, it finally clicks. The stolen ship. The pleasure slave outfits. The oils. Tristan Fontaine isn't capturing girls for Arrovin; he's preparing to kidnap one.

This one.

"Too much?" he asks, pulling her back. She comes off panting, a thick string of saliva connecting her lips to his swollen tip.

The Varren shakes her head, humming as she licks a path up the ladder of metal barbells from base to tip. Fontaine groans in pleasure. His muscles tense when she sucks him back down, hips thrusting into the back of her throat.

"That's my girl," he says.

No, she isn't.

Fontaine's head jerks up and his eyes meet mine. He doesn't stop, doesn't slow. Instead, he fucks her face harder, winking at me when he comes in a mess of shuddering, disgusting moans. From my hiding place, I watch Fontaine pull out of her and coat her glowing, sparkling face in his release like a fucking animal.

My jaw clenches.

A fiery possessiveness burns through my chest, unbidden and unwelcome.

She isn't his. She's mine.

Fuck anyone who tries to get in my way.

CARTHINIA

PRESENT DAY

KING MALIN VARUZ

FORTRESS HEDRA, CENTRAL CARTHINIA

Mine.

The word forms a mantra in my head as I stare at Ezrah's naked, glowing body, pale now from her time in Carthinia.

Mine to punish.
Mine to fuck.
Mine until I say otherwise.

I killed my father to marry her. I'd kill Avum too, and Remi, and Fontaine, and any other man who tries to tell me what I can and can't have. I'd kill my entire kingdom—every moontouched in Ranada—if they threatened my claim on her.

What Ezrah Varren doesn't know is that she was mine the moment I saw her on her knees. Except now, I'm the only one who'll put her there.

"Bedtime," I say. "Now."

Buttoning my pants, I lean over Ranin's glass coffin and flip him off. His milky silver eyes glare back at me, eyebrows narrowing with an intelligence he should not possess. Ranin was my first resurrection. I waited too long to bring him back, leaving holes in his memory, but he's present enough to remember who I am and what I've done. He's also present enough to watch me fuck the glitter out of my wife's shiny Varren cunt.

I hope he enjoyed the show.

With a simple thought, I force Ranin's eyes closed. A serene smile curls his mouth, and his worry lines disappear. He looks at rest, but I leave him conscious so he can feel the rot desiccating his bones, the stiffness of his unmoving limbs. Somewhere in the back of my mind, I hear Ranin's whimpering protests and rejoice in them. The asshole brought this on himself, denying me what's rightfully mine.

I never wanted this fucking kingdom. I only wanted her.

"You didn't answer my question," Ezrah says. She makes this cute little huffing sound that has my cock at half-mast again, pushing uncomfortably against the front of my trousers.

I could fuck her all night if I wanted. I could drag

her to the playroom, lock her in a cage, and pull her out whenever the mood strikes. She would love every godsdamned second of it—caged and leashed like a dog, like my bitch.

"I wasn't aware I took orders from you," I say instead, readjusting myself. I've punished her enough for one night. Between Avum's fist and my cock, her cunt must be a sloppy mess by now. Playtime will have to come later.

Threading our fingers together, I drag Ezrah past the Room of Kings, down a hallway that leads to the foot of the stairs. Enen's darkness hides the steps from view, turning this part of the crypts into a void-like, hell-like space.

I breathe in, and the shadows coalesce. They fly into my open mouth and spread, crawling down my throat and into my writhing, blackened veins. Ice lances my body. Squirmy dark energy vibrates my bones. I'm so accustomed to the sensations that it barely phases me, but Ezrah's eyes are wide as she takes me in. Perhaps she's realizing now that the shadows aren't just magic; they're extensions of me. When they aren't in the room, they're festering in my body, poisoning it.

"Does it hurt?" Ezrah asks.

Golden light shines down on her, and fuck if she isn't the prettiest damn creature I've ever seen. In the dark, Ezrah is beautiful. In the light, she's fucking devastating—more so than any of the other Varrens combined. Spinning on me, she touches my forearm and traces a featherlight path up my veins. The feel of her soft skin against mine is fucking euphoric.

No one touches me like this. Not anymore.

"It's only a problem when I hold the magic in for too long," I say.

She keeps stroking. Goosebumps spread across my forearms, and the slithering veins still.

With great restraint, I place my hand over Ezrah's to stop her. No matter how much I might crave it, her touch is just as poisonous as Enen's. Like every Varren, it's calculated, cunning, and fake. Lyenna and Arrovin placed her here for a reason, and unlike Avum, I haven't forgotten that.

My wife is a duplicitous snake.

"Can you feel them?" she asks. "Not when they're in your body, but when . . ." Her cheeks flush rose quartz, and I smirk.

A duplicitous, horny snake, it would seem.

"When they're what?" I ask, wrapping my arms around her waist. I pull her flush against my body, bending to whisper in her ear. "When they're in your pussy? Down your throat?"

Her pathetic moan sends blood straight to my

cock. Like a well-behaved slut, Ezrah parts her legs for easy access and loops her arms around my neck, tempting me to double back to the playroom after all.

"Of course, I can feel it," I say. My hands rove her backside, squeezing two fistfuls of ass as she molds to me. "Every twitch. Every spasm. I fucking love it when you come on my shadows."

She bites her bottom lip and grinds herself against my pelvis, but I can see the dark bags forming beneath her eyes. My slutty little wife is exhausted and sore. If she fucks me now, it'll be for my benefit, because she thinks she can get something out of it. I'm through with her manipulation games for the night.

I let her go and point to the top of the stairs, smacking her pert ass. "Off to bed. I trust you can find your way back."

"I . . ." Through heavy-lidded eyes, Ezrah glances at me then at the exit. Her golden eyelashes flutter, casting shadows over her sparkling cheeks. "I hate sleeping alone."

"And I care why?" This is too desperate even for her. As if some sad puppy-dog eyes could convince me to sleep next to a trained assassin. "Get the fuck out of here, Ezrah, or I'll reanimate Ranin and make you suck him next.

The look of horror on her face is absolutely delicious. It's so easy to scare her, embarrass her, fuck with that deceitful, clever brain. The fact that she believes the worst of me only makes it that much more fun.

Without another word, Ezrah pads up the rickety staircase, fumbles with the trap door, and disappears.

Like every night, I wait until my wife is asleep to open her bedroom door. The latch clicks shut behind me, and shadows pour from my throat, consuming me in inky blackness. Like mist, my darkness fills the air, pushing up against the walls and pooling over the floors. It stops around the perimeter of Ezrah's bed—*I* stop it there, wanting to watch her for a bit before wrapping myself around her skin.

I prefer Ezrah this way; it's more honest. My wife can't lie to me when she's asleep. She can't manipulate or placate or *pretend.*

Leaning against the wall, I take in her still form. Besides her face, it's hidden by blankets and furs—all bundled up to escape the winter chill. That simply won't do.

My shadows move like any other limb; they take form when I want them to, bending and flexing to perform whatever task I require. Right now, I mold them into spindly fingers that tug at the soft blankets near the corner of the bed, sliding them down my wife's body just low enough to display her breasts. She shudders, her brows pinching together, but doesn't rise. Sometimes, she wakes and returns the covers to her skin. Most nights, she doesn't.

I wait until the crease lines in her forehead smooth before ghosting those fingers over a peaked nipple, then around her glittering, glowing throat. Ezrah whimpers and my cock jumps in response. I unbutton my pants and pull myself out, slowly stroking myself from base to tip as those shadows glide between her parted lips, into her warm, wet mouth. It feels as good as if my cock were inside her—sensitive and slick. I can control how much sensation I want my shadows to feel, and right now, I want them to feel it all.

Or at least, I did until I hear her moan *his* name.

My consciousness brushes against Ezrah's, pressing against her mental walls just long enough to catch her life in glimpses. A deeper dive would be risky as exhausted as I am, but I have to know what she's thinking about when I touch her.

Tristan's words hit me in chunks.

"You said you love me, now get on your knees and prove it."

"I'm going to make your daddy watch the next time so he can see just how much I've ruined you."

"Baby, I need you to fuck him for me. When you're finished, take this gun and put a bullet through his brain."

I'm soft in an instant. My shadows retreat, though my mind lingers, unable to stop.

"Does it hurt, baby?"

"You look so beautiful when you bleed for me."

Tristan-fucking-Fontaine is the bane of my existence, and despite everything he's done to her and everything he's made her do, she still loves him. There's a special place in the ninth hell for masters who manipulate their pleasure slaves into believing that they actually love them. One day, I'll send him there myself.

Tears leak past Ezrah's closed eyelids—the real kind, not the fake ones I'm used to—and my chest fucking aches for her. I button myself up, fighting the craving to wrap my arms around her and promise vengeance. She's a Varren sent to ruin me. I should want to break her, too, not kiss away the pain from every man who's tried.

Swallowing, I reach for the door handle, but I can't fucking do it. I can't leave her like this.

I take a deep breath and cross the space between Ezrah and myself, sinking onto the foot of the bed.

It's fucking ridiculous to play comforter to a creature like her, but I suppose it's no more ridiculous than marrying her in the first place.

I clear my throat, but a soft tap on the door interrupts me before I can wake her.

"It's Rayne." Bron's thoughts are frantic in my head. *"We need you. Now."*

PRINCESS EZRAH VARREN

FORTRESS HEDRA, CENTRAL CARTHINIA

Blankets pool around my middle, exposing me to the morning chill. Shivering, I curl my fingers around the soft animal furs and yank them over my shoulders, recocooning myself in warmth. It's so hard to drag myself out of bed most days. Between the icy tiles and melancholy sky, it hardly seems worth the effort—especially now.

Twenty-eight days and I have nothing to show for it short of a sore pussy and bruised ass. My research is gone, my ally is no longer interested in helping me, and Malin is furious.

I close my eyes, remembering the sting of his palm against my ass, the way his hands fisted in my hair as he forced me to swallow Avum's cock. I should be sickened by the things Malin did to me last night, but I'm not. I crave his punishments, his cruelty. They're an aphrodisiac stronger and more addicting than any of the drugs I've been given to perform.

My thighs are slick with need as I imagine him finger-fucking me on Kyree's pedestal, coming around his cock as his dead father watches. This should not turn me on, but my fingers have a mind of their own, slipping over my piercing to rub my swollen clit.

My brows furrow.

I tug on the metal loop but nothing happens. I can't feel it. I can't *feel* anything.

"No. No, no, no, no, no."

Somehow, he made the spell worse.

I fling the blankets off and leap out of bed, rushing toward my bathroom door. Leaning over the sink, I turn the metal levers until hot water pours out. Humid steam climbs over the bathroom mirrors, fogging them until my face is a glittery blob. I snag a washcloth from the countertop and wet it under the sink, wincing as the hot water grazes my fingers. Once it's soaked, I spread my legs and press the burning cloth to my pussy.

Hot water drips down my thighs, scalding them the color of rubies, but I can't feel anything where I want it most.

I try again. Cold water this time.

Sobs bubble up my chest when the result is the

same. The rag slips between my fingertips and splats to the obsidian floor. For years, I've been poked and prodded. I've been trained to fuck on command with the only reprieve coming in the pleasure allotted to me. Being unable to orgasm was brutal, but this . . .

Hiccupping, I grip the edges of the cool countertop and stare at my hideous, splotchy face in the mirror's fogged reflection. An amalgamation of pale and rhodonite skin stares back, my gold eyes set above swollen, aching bags. I look as dead as I feel.

Being here is too much. Wanting Malin is too much.

I reel my fist back and slam it into the mirror. Glass shatters. It crunches beneath my knuckles and plinks to the floor, scattering to the cabinet and the sink below. Golden blood mixes with the glass shards and splashing water, swirling as it runs down the drain.

Pain comes next.

Knuckles burning, I sink to the floor into a pile of broken glass. Then, I bury my face in my hands and cry—for the little girl who wanted to be a sailor and for the lieutenant who stole my heart. In another life, we were happy. In another life, I wasn't Malin Varuz's whore.

I CAN BARELY HOLD my eyes open by the time the tears run dry. My legs wobble as I rise from the floor, stroking the matted hair from my face. Jagged glass crunches underfoot and sharp splinters stab my heels until they leak blood onto the stonework, turning it into a messy compilation of dark obsidian and flashy, gaudy gold. That mess is someone else's problem, though I'd like to see them scrape hardened metal off the floor.

Destroying Malin's things is at least a small consolation prize.

Gold flakes cake my knuckles but I ignore it, falling into my morning rituals so I can ignore the hollowness in my chest. I sink onto the vanity's bench, grab my hairbrush, and run it through my tangled hair, pushing glass shards into my scalp, ripping out golden threads. I brush until my fingers grow stiff around the handle. Then, I brush some more, staring out the balcony to the snowy pines and gloomy gray sky. Somewhere beyond that forest lies a freedom I'll never know.

Dressing comes next, but only after my scalp radiates pain and blood leaks down the sides of my face.

Malin usually sets my dresses on the ottoman by the bed; today is no different. My newest slutty outfit is a shiny emerald gown with a plunging neckline that will likely expose my navel.

I step into it, shimmying the tight, clingy fabric over my body, forcing it over glass-embedded skin, then stop. It's halfway to my hips when I realize, what's the fucking point? Why bother dressing at all if my only purpose here is to service Malin and his friends? What's the point of going through all this effort? Pride? Civility? Neither of those things matters in this wretched kingdom.

I peel the dress down my sides and drag it to the vanity, opening a drawer where my shears are located. The bronze blades *shink* when I open them, snipping and cutting messy lines through the cloth. Scraps fall at my feet. Beadwork scatters beneath the furniture and bed.

When the dress is nothing but a pile of ribbons, I open my closet doors and move on to the others—all twenty-seven ridiculous, impractical, embarrassing gowns he's made me don. I run the shears over each of them, sweating by the time I finish.

It feels good. It feels . . . honest. Putting clothing on a whore is the equivalent of painting windows on walls—useless and ineffective.

Wiping the sweat from my brow, I dust off my hands and straighten my spine. Then, I do what I do every day; I march out the door to revisit the library. My notebook is gone, but the books should still be where I left them. Maybe I can salvage something out of this disaster. The spell might be impossible to break, but that doesn't mean I can't poison Malin's food—not enough to kill him, but enough to make him hug the restroom for an evening.

What my husband—my *master*—doesn't know about me is that I can be quite the vindictive bitch.

I swing the door open and am met with a faceful of plate mail as one of my goonish undead guards barricades the entrance. Its black, spiky armor doesn't terrify me like it used to. Malin's skeletons can't do anything to me that hasn't been done to me before.

"Out of my way," I hiss.

It doesn't speak; they never do.

It doesn't move either.

"Are you deaf as well as dead? I'm headed to the library. I'm *allowed* there, remember?" The word rankles me. It tastes like acid on my tongue. I'm a goddess; I go where I desire.

The creature doesn't budge. Its plate mail rattles as it raises its armored hand, clenching a folded sheet of parchment. I snatch the letter and turn it over, breaking a black wax seal with a crescent insignia on it.

Gone until week's end. ~M

P.S. I never realized your cunt could instill such loyalty in others. I'm certain we can find a way to thank General Avum upon my return.

When I glance up, the guard is holding a pair of small but rugged boots lined with wolf's fur and fleece. I briefly wonder what I'll have to do for them and if Avum knew that giving them to me would be contingent on my whoring. He doesn't strike me as the type to make that exchange, but I'm still bitter about it.

Not bitter enough to go another day with cold and blistered feet.

I snatch the boots from my guard, lean against the doorway, then pluck glass shards from my feet, wincing when they finally come free. Gold drips from my soles into the plush inserts as I lace the boots up my ankles. It's euphoric—the warmth, the softness, the small amount of human decency that comes with getting to own something so ordinary. Not strappy sandals or spiky heels, but a shoe that's actually useful.

I rub my blurry eyes.

The guard puts its metal gauntlet on my shoulder like it's trying to comfort me.

I must look so fucking pitiful right now, crying

over a pair of shoes. I push the guard away and stand, brushing past its looming figure. "Don't feel bad for me," I snap. "At least I'm still alive."

It's a low blow. I know that. Guilt twists my insides, but I refuse to apologize to one of Malin's creatures; it's beneath me.

The guard remains several paces away as we walk to the library, its boots clanking against the stone floor. My own feet are silent as I scour Malin's letter, but the sheet is blank. He's left me with no explanation, no tasks to complete, and no rules for roaming the palace grounds. Crumpling the parchment, I hurl it down the hallway into a solid sheet of black mist.

As always, purple torches illuminate the dark corridors, but the light stops where the mist starts. Without passing through it, I can't reach the library.

"Of course, I can feel it." Malin's words are velvet against my ears as I slide my fingers through the darkness. They disappear instantly, though they're barely an inch away.

I take a deep breath and step inside. My chest constricts. Ice weaves through my veins, sucking all the air from my lungs until I'm forced to backpedal.

No library then.

I flip the shadows off and pivot, unsure where to go. My stomach answers for me, grumbling loud enough the guard inclines its head. Eat first. Sabotage Malin later.

My meals typically manifest themselves, appearing outside the doorway of whatever room I'm in. If I wait long enough, I doubt today will be any different. But I still remember where that little kitchen is that Avum took me to, and I still remember where his bedroom is in relation to it. I look like shit, covered in blood and glass and dressed in nothing but boots. I have no idea if he even wants to see me, but I can't be alone. I don't trust myself alone.

My fingers inch over a long, invisible line down the center of my wrist. Already, I've reminded myself three times today that death isn't an option—Malin would only bring me back. Logically, I know the long glass shard in my boot can't save me, but three days of peace seems almost worth it. Maybe I'd be ugly dead and Malin wouldn't want me anymore. Maybe I'd stop wanting him.

My knuckles rasp against Avum's hidden bedroom door.

No response.

"Avum, I need you." My words come out choked. "Please."

I knock again, but the only answer comes from

the grinding of my guard's metal armor. I can't seem to get rid of it today.

I wait for several minutes, hands shaking, tears welling in my heavy-lidded eyes. Maybe he's busy. He could have left with Malin.

Or maybe he decided spending time with me isn't worth the risk.

I can't fault him for not wanting to end up in long-term storage. It's not his job to save me. Sniffling, I shuffle off to the kitchen alone, not hungry anymore but unwilling to return to my chambers.

Toeing at the door, I find the secret groove that opens it. Stones grind together, and a sliver appears in the wall. I heave it open, forcing the door just wide enough for myself to slip through. Unlike last time, no golden lights or sweet smoke bombard my senses. The room is sterile and dark, and the undead woman is nowhere to be found. A single lantern hangs from a post above the sink, the flame inside it little more than a faint wisp.

I open cabinets, rummaging through them for something stronger than food. A year ago, I was so strung out on drugs and liquor, I could hardly remember my name. I preferred it that way back then, and I'd prefer it that way now. If I'm to be Malin's whore from now until the end of time, the least he could do is supply me with the same vices I had before. Something to take the edge off, to rot my brain until I'm nothing more than a slave to pleasure.

I don't want to care anymore. I want to erase every trace of the eighteen-year-old girl who designed the *Midnight Sun* and made grand plans to be something else besides my father's pawn.

Perfect.

My fingers curl around a bottle of wine, then another, scooping them out by the armful from a cabinet underneath the white marble island. As I'm removing them, a mat of tangly magenta moss comes into focus. My mouth twists into a broad smile, unable to conceal the delight.

Tannix. My drug of choice.

I scoop it up, too, rubbing its dry leaves across my cheek, taking big whiffs of its sweet, herbal tang. Hopefully, when Malin returns home, he'll see how amenable I can be with the proper drugs. Maybe he'll like me better this way.

I know I will.

KING MALIN VARUZ

THE CITY OF TARINTH, CARTHINIAN BORDERLANDS

Rayne is a fucking cunt.

Fire ravages my city, climbing up the pointed stakewalls that encompass it. Plumes of thick white smoke billow into the night sky, consuming log cabins and black, stone walkways. Rayne's little tantrum started with the government buildings, but those have burned to cinders. Now the fire has taken on a will of its own. I warned the villagers years ago that using hay as insulation would bite them in the ass, but those idiots never listen to me until they need my help.

I click my tongue, and my sabretooth pinecat sprints left, barreling us through a hazy side street, near the overseer's estate. The heat of the fire nips at us, but Tally doesn't slow. She's a good girl, unlike the women in my life.

Gripping onto her saddle, I maneuver us past a group of sooty villagers who wander the streets like zombies. They hold in their arms whatever they could salvage—clothing, trinkets, toys. A little girl in a torn pink cloak clutches a crocheted doll in her fist. My throat bobs when I see the long gash splitting her forearm.

"Get to the gates," I say, coughing up a lungful of bitter smoke. "My general will help you."

"Fuck you." The girl throws her doll at me. It bounces off my shoulder, landing in a pile of dirty snow.

Tally lurches to a halt. Her hackles rise, a low growl forming in the center of her chest, vibrating my saddle.

"It's alright, Tal," I whisper, pinching the scruff on the back of her neck. "I'm fine."

The growling stops, but she hunches lower to the ground like she's preparing to pounce.

I glance between Tally and the girl's parents, waiting for the groveling to commence. Perhaps a hasty apology or a blubbering excuse for their child's poor manners. They meet my gaze instead with raised chins and tight lips. One of the villagers—a boy barely older than the girl—flips me off, flashing his index and middle finger over a soot-covered face.

What fuck did I do? It's Rayne who set the fires.

This isn't worth my time. If they want to be assholes, they can die here for all I care.

I click my tongue and Tally whips past them, bounding over an upturned carriage through a wall of flames. Before the fires graze me, icy wind whips across the path, carrying ash and cinders with it. I shield my eyes against the debris, angling Tally toward the wreckage of City Hall, where a mob gathers around a twenty-foot effigy of . . .

My stomach drops. The shadows in my veins writhe, begging for retribution, for slaughter. It can't be her. Rayne wouldn't fucking dare.

I wait for the effigy to morph into someone else, but it doesn't. Dressed in a sparkling yellow dress is a woman made from hay, wearing a clay mask covered in glitter. A crown of thorns presses into her mop-like, yellow hair, and even though the colors are all wrong, I know exactly who she's meant to be. *My Varren wife.*

This fucker told them where she was, what I did. He put her entire life in jeopardy. If this news spreads, the moontouched will slaughter her, Fontaine's men will come, and my marriage contract will be null and void in the eyes of Arrovin Hade. He could start a war. *He could take her back.*

I clench my jaw so fucking hard, it might shatter a molar. The things I'll do to Rayne when I wrap my hands around his traitorous neck—

"Mal." Bron's voice comes from inside my head. Now that my father is dead, he's the only other psion in Carthinia. *"Pull back. If they see you, you're fucked."*

"I'm not afraid of peasants."

"It's daytime. The sun is out."

Shit.

I grab the scruff on Tally's neck and we lurch to a halt, observing the black sky from the cover of an abandoned food cart. I no longer appear moon-touched, but I still suffer the wretched curse. In Varren, it's easy to navigate. I can see the sun's glare off the water or the added brightness of the plants, but in Carthinia, our skies are overcast. Besides a slight change in temperature, night and day are indistinguishable to me.

None of that would be a problem if shadows didn't need darkness to survive.

I'm all but powerless. My undead are occupied with Arrovin's forces and my psionics can only help so much. But if Rayne thinks I will let him or his army of peasants get away with this . . .

"Fuck it. I'm going to squash this insurrection before it has time to spread."

"Mal—"

I tune him out. I hunker low against Tally's back and give two clicks. Like the predator she is, Tally lowers to the ground, sneaking across the pavement, hiding behind rubble and refuse and roaring flames.

We approach the effigy, where my asshole of a brother stands on a podium, surrounded by his pathetic excuse for an army. Pitchforks. Rifles. Kitchenware. It's almost laughable how they think that'll conquer a kingdom.

I put them down before, and I'll do it again.

I'll swim in a pool of their fucking blood if that's what it takes to sink the message home—*this kingdom is mine. Ezrah Varren is mine. And I don't give two fucks what they think about it.*

"We'll make that bastard pay for bringing Varren trash to our doorstep!" Rayne says. One of the insurgents passes him a lit torch. "We'll carve that gilded heart from her fucking chest and ship it back to Arrovin Hade to remind him that Carthinia is not for sale!"

The booming roar of the crowd sets my blood pumping. They raise their weapons in the air, shouting their agreements. If they agree with him, they can die with him.

Tally angles us close enough that I could reach my half-brother in a matter of seconds. I slide off her back and tap my finger to her wet nose. *Playtime.*

Rayne shoves his torch into the effigy. Fire flashes and gunpowder sparks, shooting up the haystack. The crowd disappears in a wave of orange smoke and bright lights as Ezrah's face explodes, the clay mask shattering into small fragments that rain down on us.

I shake chunks of melted, yellow debris from my hair and creep up the podium.

My brother screams to be heard over the cracking flames and clapping crowd. "That Varren whore—"

I grab him from behind, snaking my arm around his throat to press him against my chest. "That Varren whore is my wife," I whisper. "And you'd be wise not to speak of her in that manner."

I can feel his pulse against the inside of my elbow, fluttering like a frightened bird. Someone grabs my arms and pulls. I nearly lose my grip on Rayne and stumble backward into the crowd. More hands. Everyone is touching me. Pulling me. Yanking me as my brother splutters for life.

And then they're not.

Tally's thunderous roar cuts through all other sounds as she sinks her sabreteeth into the insurgent who pulled me down. Swinging her thick neck from side to side, she severs the arm from his body, spraying blood into the crowd. She jumps and dives again, angling for fresh meat, her white jowls soaked in crimson.

The screaming crowd separates, climbing and stumbling over one another to get away from her as I tighten my grip on Rayne, dragging him through the ashy, blood-soaked streets. He struggles. He kicks and slaps, but without magic, it isn't enough. There's a reason our father chose me over him; Rayne is weak. And he's an idiot.

The man becomes deadweight in my arms—unconscious but alive. For now.

"Tell Avum to seal the gates," I say, reaching for Bron's consciousness.

"What did you do?"

"The gates. No one leaves. Is that understood?"

"You can't hold an entire town hostage."

I pull Rayne into an alleyway, where we'll hide until nightfall, when I have my magic back. *"I don't intend to hold this town hostage. I intend to murder them."*

Every man, woman, and child who knows about my wife's presence here must be dealt with. It will be messy and brutal, but that's the only way to protect her. If I fail to keep the information secret, then I fail to keep the treaty intact. If Arrovin or Fontaine come for her—if the moontouched rise against me—then I risk losing her forever. I won't have her dying for Rayne's insolence.

"You can't do this," Bron says.

"You can't stop me."

PRINCESS EZRAH VARREN

FORTRESS HEDRA, CENTRAL CARTHINIA

Groaning, I stretch along the floor, arching my back like a cat freshly woken from slumber. The taste of soured wine lingers on my tongue and my head is still swimming from last night's drink. In front of me, blue fire hisses and crackles in an unfamiliar hearth made from white limestone and crushed seashells. The heat of the flames scorches my naked flesh, turning it a soft shade of morganite. I take a deep breath, inhaling the sweet pink smoke that billows from the wood pile, spreading haze through the equally unfamiliar room.

I don't remember how I got here or how long I've been here for. When Malin didn't return last week, or the week after, I doubled down on the wine and tannix. My coherency comes in flashes. It wouldn't come at all if I could avoid it.

The world spins as I crawl to my knees then fall back down. Laughter pours from my lips.

How much tannix did I add to the hearth?

The magenta moss is gone now, little more than powder on the logs, but I can still smell it everywhere, can feel it lick along my skin like a lover's touch. I'm so fucking wet, so fucking high, and I can't do a damn thing to remedy either. I slip my hand between my thighs and try anyway because what better way is there to pass the time?

"The desk, Ezrah."

"Open it. See what's inside."

The voices of my childhood have returned for the first time in three years—thousands of them whispering in the background. They're the only company I've had, and somewhere, in the back of my mind, I know they're the reason I'm here in this strange room. Memories of lockpicking flit across my mind, but they're ephemeral. Inaccessible.

Ignoring the voices, I picture Tristan's fingers as I trace my swollen, tingly clit. I feel nothing. The nerve endings are oversensitive from hours—no, days—of attempted self-pleasure. I ache so fucking badly from the drugs, from the need to feel something inside of me, but every time I touch myself, it's devoid of sensation. Despite the tannix and alcohol, I'm wound as tightly as ever.

Sweat breaks out along my glistening body,

beading against my forehead, my breasts, my thighs. I lick the salt from my lips and moan my frustration, slipping a finger deep inside my cunt. My body is a ball of fire. Hotter than the hearth, than any of the nine hells.

I add another finger, and the illusion of Tristan snaps. Suddenly, it's Malin and his shadows that are touching me, stroking me, his voice demanding that I come for him. Behind closed lids, his abyssal eyes stare into my soul like they're going to shatter me into a million pieces, and gods, how I want them to.

At least I'd be able to feel it.

What the fuck is wrong with me?

I stop touching myself and roll over. Fluffy white fur tickles my skin—a thousand gentle caresses which I promptly ignore as I reach for a half-empty bottle of wine. Uncorking it with my teeth, I spit the stopper out then tip the bitter liquid down my throat, taking one long draw, then another.

Soon, the bottle is empty, but I'm far too drunk to stand, walk all the way to the pantry, and find a fresh one. Still, the idea of spending another second by the fire, wrapped in Malin's blankets, is equally unappealing.

"The desk, Ezrah."

"Do it."

"You know you want to."

The voices can be so damn insistent sometimes.

On hands and knees, I crawl to the back of the room, bumping into trays of fruit, knocking over piles of precariously stacked nautical textbooks, before I reach a bright purplewood desk that sits far away from everything else, shielded by a purple privacy screen. Behind the desk is a painting of the sunrise. On top is a single human skull and nothing more.

In the back of my mind, I know this must be Malin's office, even if the interior design is all wrong. It's too bright. Too beautiful.

White leather scrapes beneath my nails as I half-scramble, half-claw my way into his office chair. The skull on top of the desk glares at me, its four—no, two—unseeing eyeholes way too judgmental for my taste. I stroke the top of its dome, petting the skull like it's one of my father's hunting dogs.

"Shhhhh," I whisper. Giggling, I press my finger to its mouth. "Let's keep this between us, ok?"

The skull doesn't answer; I'd probably shit myself if it did.

"That's what I thought. Good boy." I give it a final pat then flip it around so it can't watch me work.

Golden tresses spill down my back as I tug the pin free of my tightly wound bun and press my ear against the top drawer of Malin's desk. My pin is bent and sharp at the ends—great for gouging out eyeballs and picking locks. I adjust it in my hand then jam it into the keyhole, or rather, where the keyhole should be. My vision blurs and I miss, scoring the wood instead.

Ooops.

Biting my bottom lip, I run my thumb over the white line that wasn't there before and make a face. Maybe Malin won't notice?

"Maybe he'll punish you if he does?"

I clench my thighs together and try very hard not to imagine my face smushed against the desk, Malin's hand wrapped around my throat as he takes me from behind. The voices murmur their approval and for the millionth time in my life, I wonder who's more fucked up—them or me? Probably me since I'm the only one who can hear them.

I readjust my grip on the pin and, this time, hit my mark. Wiggling my hand, I angle the tip sideways, sinking it deeper into the keyhole.

Click.

Click.

The tumbler shifts. The bolt gives way. Even drunk, it takes me all of seven seconds to break past the best lock money can buy, which is why Malin should have never trusted me alone with his things. But men rarely think with their brains, just their cocks, and they have a habit of grossly underestimating women.

Tristan never underestimated me.

"Yes, he did."

I tune the voices out and pry open the drawer, exposing a giant stack of paperwork, a bottle of very expensive brandy, and two glass snifters. Scooping up the sheets of paper, I throw them onto the table then use my arm to fan them across the work surface. Some scatter onto the floor. It's too much work to pick them up so I don't.

My brain pounds against my skull as I scan the pages in front of me, trying to make sense of them. The text shifts and doubles, rolling out of focus the longer I try. I clutch the sides of my head and curse —this is what happens when you snoop while drunk.

It's pointless.

Grabbing my hairpin, I wedge it into the next lock, hoping the contents will be less intensive to read through. The first spring clicks into place when a sheet on the ground catches my eye.

A date. A list of names. An itemized account of everything aboard the *Valiant*.

I reach for it and tumble face-first from Malin's chair, thudding as I hit the ground. I barely feel it. My fingers crumple around the note as my eyes drink it in. It's a full account of my father's sea battle —a battle that occurred on my wedding day, which I knew nothing about.

Sour saliva floods my mouth when I see Captain Andrews' name among the list of mortalities. Then, Arri, Rikon, Torvald, plus a dozen other sailors who once treated me like family. I press a fist to my lips and hold back a hiccupping sob.

"Shhhh, Ezrah. This isn't your fault."

"I should have been there." I ball the paper up and hurl it across the room. "I could have saved them, dammit!"

I slam my fist into the desk, and white-hot pain sears my knuckles. The sensation grounds me and stills my tears, but it isn't enough. I do it again and again, imagining my father's face cracking beneath me. This is his doing. If he hadn't sold me to Malin . . . If he hadn't . . .

The wood splinters and groans.

Golden blood breaks the surface of my cracked skin.

"We'll make them pay," the voices promise.

"How?"

I'm stuck here, languishing away as Malin's whore.

They don't answer. Instead, they hum, soothing me with one of my mother's favorite songs. Dark and deep, an ancient lullaby with no words. As it ends, the tension fades from my body, and the anger cools to a dull simmer.

I wipe my eyes on the back of my hand and retrieve the hairpin. Within thirty seconds, I've broken past the remaining locks and am scouring the desk for more information. The wood thrums beneath my fingertips as I reach the bottom drawer.

Strange.

I crack it open. My brows furrow when I see what's inside. "How in the nine hells did Malin manage to steal you?"

PRINCESS EZRAH VARREN

FORTRESS HEDRA, CENTRAL CARTHINIA

Aressa va Anish Tae—The Book of Desires.

The text is primordial, sacred to the Varren, and written in a language spoken only by monsters and gods. It's spent the past two thousand years in my family's archives, passed along from mother to daughter since the dawn of time—or at least that's what they say. The book was meant to be mine, but instead, my father claimed it for himself, putting it on public display behind a lock even I couldn't pick.

My hands shake at the sight of it—my birthright, my mother's final gift to me. The tome is bound in black velvet, with the words *Aressa va Anish Tae* stitched into the cover with silver thread. The pages are darker than charcoal, abyssal like Malin's eyes, and the title glistens in the moonlight as if it's been slicked with mercury.

"Beautiful," the voices whisper.

Impossible is more like it.

I heft it from the drawer and set it on my lap. My vision swims as I crack open the spine, my thoughts swirling from wine and tannix. Inside, the book is empty—no images, or maps, or text of any kind. The silken pages ripple where I touch them like raindrops in a puddle, though my skin remains perfectly dry. As the ripples expand, the color changes from black to a near-transparent blue, mimicking the texture of the ocean.

The water moves around my finger, forming a current as I trace nonsensical lines through it. The pages are no thicker than a strand of my hair, but the depths appear endless. Tiny fishes swim beneath the waves, and flashes of iridescent pink and emerald green splash along the surface before disappearing.

I ball my hands into fists and rub my blurry eyes, convinced I'm hallucinating. When I'm finished, the cover is no longer smooth velvet but coarse and gritty sand. It's as pale as the beaches in the Laithe Isles, as hot as the Karmaskus sun. Seagulls squawk in the distance, and briny wind tangles in my hair, caressing my cheeks, my neck.

My breathing catches as sapphire fishtails splash

near the book's edge, and black dolphins jump into the center bindings then disappear.

"It's yours to command."

"To control."

"Say something."

I lick my lips and swallow. Nerves twist my stomach, souring the wine inside it. Suddenly, I feel more sober than I have in days.

"Tranna vorex," I whisper.

Reveal yourself.

The pages rear up at me, consuming my hand in icy water. Something sharp pricks the tip of my index finger and I rock back, wincing as my blood splatters the book, flooding it in glittering gold. I shove my finger into my mouth and suck down on the pad. The puncture is already gone, the blood absent. The book absorbs the rest, spitting it back out in the form of gilded, handwritten scrawl.

Before I can blink, every page fills with pictures and maps, spells and ingredients—a list of everything I've ever wanted and how to acquire them. Everything except...

Behind me, Tristan sinks to his knees and his fingers curl over mine. He rests his chin in the crook of my neck and peers over my shoulder, nosey as always. *"I miss you, Ezzy."*

Something between a sob and a whimper crawls its way up my throat. "You're not real."

"No, but I could be."

I can taste the tobacco on Tristan's breath, can smell the familiar spice of his cologne. His hands are blistered, his tunic stained by gunpowder and dried blood. *This* is the Tristan I fell in love with, in his white and gold lieutenant's uniform, before time and circumstances made us what we are. It's a Tristan I'll never get back.

"Come find me," he says. *"I miss you. I love you. I want to see you again."*

His lips ghost over mine, and I blink to keep from crying.

"You did this to me," I hiss. "You're the reason I'm broken."

For the first time in months, it isn't sorrow that bores its way into my chest; it's rage. Everything that I am, he's responsible for. I could have been happy with Remi or Corvin. I could have lived a normal fucking life before he . . .

I slam the book shut and shove it beneath Malin's desk, slicing the illusion in half. It doesn't matter anymore. It's finished—*we're* finished—and wallowing won't change anything.

The world tilts as I clamber to my feet then fumble through Malin's desk in search of a glass snifter. I can barely tell my ups from my downs, but still, I need more. More alcohol. More tannix. Really, anything that'll help me forget the crack of my father's whip or the sting of Tristan's absence.

My head lolls as I grab the snifter, then the brandy, and slam them both on the desk. Leaning on my elbows, I unstopper the bottle then pour, spilling an indecent amount in the process. The paperwork is soaked, the wood slick. Already, my golden blood has hardened into a solid sheet of metal, ruining any chance at clean up.

Fuck it. I down the drink in a single, fluid motion, hissing as it ravages my throat. The relief is instantaneous.

Pouring another, I fall into the chair, sipping on sweetened paint thinner as I stare at the illegible paperwork. My blinks grow longer, my breaths heavier. Snifter in hand, my cheek hits the sticky desk with a resounding thunk and the spilled brandy soaks into my tangled hair. Groaning, I shut my eyes. The sound of the ocean waves greets me—my dream of the *Midnight Sun*.

"Join us, Ezrah. Come home."

Glass shatters against tile. Boots thud across the chamber, and someone curses under their breath as a metal platter clangs to the floor.

I snap my head toward the sound, my stomach lurching at the resulting kaleidoscope of colors. When the room finally settles, a towering silhouette darkens the other side of the privacy screen, their pale fingers curling around the purple edges.

"I see you've made yourself at home," Malin says. His voice is icy as he folds the divider in half then pushes it against the wall, appraising the wreckage of his office. Frowning, he sets his sights on me.

"You're back," I croak.

Black veins twine down Malin's cheeks, his neck, sinking into the collar of a dark cape. His hands are gloved, his curly hair wet with freshly fallen snow. I stare at those hands, swallowing as I imagine all the ways they might punish me—bent over his knee, fisted in my hair, splayed wide on the desk. The tannix has me squirming in his chair—hot, terrified, and nauseated all at the same time.

Clit throbbing, I cross my ankles and bite my bottom lip.

"It smells like a whorehouse in here," Malin says, peeling off the leather gloves. He tosses them to the floor then unhooks the clasp to his cape and shrugs it off. "Do you have anything to say for yourself?"

"Um . . ."

"Um?" Malin arches an eyebrow. "Is that it?"

"You're out of wine."

Stepping toward me, he pries the snifter from my hand and knocks back the contents. "Out of tannix too, I presume."

My cheeks heat. I lick my lips and scoot infinitesimally closer, as if I have some kind of death wish—which I guess I do.

"I was bored," I say, slurring the words.

"Obviously." Malin rolls up his shirtsleeves, revealing strong forearms. Dark veins writhe at the surface, struggling to break free. "Tell me something, Ezrah, do you normally rifle through locked drawers when you're bored?"

I meet his gaze despite every instinct begging me not to. "Yes."

Actually, I do a lot worse.

A smile creases the edges of his lips. Malin pats the top of my head, and I flinch then purr the second his fingers stroke my aching scalp. I know he's petting me like I'm a dog—that I should be grossly offended by it—but the fucked-up parts of me enjoy this. The praise. The attention. The power he so brazenly wields against a rumored goddess.

"Arrovin trained you well, didn't he?" Malin asks. "Not too well, though, otherwise you wouldn't have been caught."

I open my mouth to protest, but he interrupts.

"Find anything of worth?"

My gaze flickers to *The Book of Desires* lying shut beneath the desk. The cover is black velvet again, the pages charcoal.

"Ah. What did it show you?"

When I don't answer, Malin yanks me to my feet

and the world sways. I throw my arms around him to keep from tumbling to the floor.

"You smell like a winery," he says.

"And you smell like peppermint." I playfully poke the tip of Malin's nose then peel free the top button of his tunic. He puts a hand over mine, stopping me from unhooking the next.

"You're drunk."

"And you care, why?" I tangle my hands through his hair and grind my hips against his.

"Because," Malin says, pulling my hands away. "When I punish you, I want you sober enough to learn a lesson from it."

A shiver and a thrill runs through me. I fumble with his belt buckle, but he grabs me by the waist and tosses me over his shoulder. My stomach lurches at the sudden movement. My skin turns clammy, and goosebumps spread along my arms and back.

"I think I'm going to—" Before I can finish the sentence, I'm vomiting on him, the floor, my hair. And then a dizzying darkness overtakes me.

"Ezrah, I need you to cooperate here." Strong arms wrap around my waist. A hard chest presses into my back. I moan at the pounding in my skull and the stinging pain in my right hand.

"Tristan?"

Steamy water surrounds us. I'm weightless, standing on something gritty and pointy like sandpaper.

"There's a wall in front of you," the voice whispers. He guides me to it then helps me grab the ledge. "Lean on it so I can clean you up."

I do as he asks, folding my arms across the cold tile, laying my whirling head on top of it. The air tastes like peppermint—not tobacco, not cologne—and for a brief moment, panic bubbles up my chest, though I can't remember why. And then nimble fingers are running a sponge over my back, cleaning my flesh with a gentleness I haven't experienced in what feels like forever.

I lose myself to the sensation, to the scent of lavender soaps and humidity. My eyes hurt too much to open them, and the light around me is far too bright. So I keep them shut.

"There are scars on your back," he says. "I can't see them, but I can feel the lines. They're deep."

I bite the inside of my cheek. Why would Tristan bring them up when he knows how much I hate them? "Varren glamor," I mumble. "Not so pretty once you look close enough."

His fingers trace the lines, and warm tears spill down my cheeks, mingling with my wet locks of golden hair. Once he realizes they don't stop at my back, his hand dips lower, curving over my ass, then my thighs.

"Who did this to you?"

"You know who." I swallow back a mouthful of sticky saliva.

The room is quiet save for the long draw of his breath and the echoing splash of water as he dunks the sponge into the pool. He washes my neck, then my arms, then pours water over my sudsy skin. It's a peaceful kind of quiet. Safe.

Sighing, I let the warmth of his touch lull me into a stupor—not quite awake but not asleep either. His fingers delve into my hair, and something vibrates the inside of my skull. It's not unpleasant, but it makes my tongue feel heavy, my teeth itchy.

I groan, wiggling as much as I can with my body pinned between his and the wall.

"Shhh. Stay still."

My brain is slushy—too drunk to formulate the words that'll make him stop, too tired to fight back. I force my tense muscles to relax, whimpering when his fingers massage my temples.

"Good girl. Now take a deep breath."

I obey.

Dark shadows crawl over my eyelids and penetrate my mind, consuming everything, leaving in their wake an impossibly tall wall made from crushed seashells and glittering, golden blood—my consciousness, or rather, the wall defending it. I've never seen it before and yet its presence is so familiar, so . . . *me.*

A bright, amethyst light flares in front of the wall. Seashells crunch and shatter, crumbling into a black void of nothingness, revealing a jagged rip in the center. Sunlight and seagulls wait on the other side of it—memories better left buried.

In the living world, I thrash against the man who holds me.

He kisses my forehead and a tingly numbness takes hold. "Let me see. I won't hurt you."

An invisible force nudges past me through the narrow opening, and the shadows follow, slipping through it just seconds before the seashells mend themselves and the rift closes. The last thing I see is myself ten years ago, standing on the beach beside my father. My eyes are pitch black, my skin covered in dark web-like veins. And then, there's nothing.

VARREN

EARLIER...

PRINCESS EZRAH VARREN

THE GOLDEN COAST, CAPITAL OF VARREN

Blue sky stretches for as far as the eye can see—not a cloud in sight. The wind is still, the surroundings silent, as Daddy's galleon sits motionless in the harbor. Its crew lounges on the upper deck, their feet dangling off the sides of the hull as they pass around liquor bottles. No wind means no sailing, means another day trapped here.

I can relate.

Beads of perspiration gather at my nape as the golden sun bores down on me. The sand is sweltering against my bare feet and so bright, I have to squint my eyes against it. Twisting my hair into a bun, I walk along the coast, kicking up seaweed, collecting hidden seashells underneath the masses of tangled greens.

The cool water makes my skin prickle—my

bones hum—and it's all I can do to keep from rushing in, swimming straight up to that galleon, and demanding they take me with them. It would probably give Captain Andrews a heart attack.

"Little bird, you're starting to burn," Daddy says, appearing beside me.

I jump, my heart skipping at the sight of him. Unlike me, Daddy doesn't glimmer in the sunlight. His olive skin and white hair blend almost seamlessly into the sandy beaches, which is probably why he can still take me by surprise.

Forcing myself to relax, I continue onward. Daddy matches my pace as I near the edge of the palace grounds.

"Won't you please come inside?" he asks.

"I want to go to Orista with my sisters," I say. "It's not fair. Why do they get to be on that ship and I don't?"

Daddy steps in front of me, blocking my view of the *Valiant* and casting a shadow over my blistering skin. He's so much bigger than I am—more like a mountain than a man.

"Little bird," he says, bending so we're at eye level. "We've talked about this."

My eyes burn. Blinking back tears, I swallow the lump in my throat and fidget with the seashells in my hand.

"You are the most precious thing I own," Daddy

whispers. He cups my cheek, staring down at me with storm gray eyes. Lighting crackles inside them—a reminder of the raw power lurking underneath.

"I have big plans for you," he says. "Someday, you're going to make me the most powerful king in all of Ranada."

"But Daddy—"

He tucks a flyaway hair behind my ear. "You're not like your sisters, which is why they get to leave and you don't. This isn't a punishment, little bird. I'm only trying to protect you."

A tear leaks past my eyelids. Daddy wipes it away with the pad of his thumb then strokes my stinging cheek.

"Gods, you remind me so much of your mother," he says.

Slowly, Daddy's eyes appraise me, scanning me from head to toe. I twist my fingers in my skirts, worried he won't like what he sees, that I'll be different somehow. Being nervous is silly. I look the same way I looked yesterday, which is the same way Queen Ariella looked her entire life. Everyone says so.

After a while, Daddy offers me his arm and I relax—inspection passed.

"You've definitely inherited her free spirit," he adds, guiding me back to the palace walls.

"And her voice," I say.

A smile creases Daddy's lips. "That too."

Reaching into his trouser pocket, he offers me a prickly orange seashell and presses it into the heel of my palm. "I found this yesterday and thought of you."

My heart swells as I turn it over. It's perfect. Throwing my arms around him, I bury my face into his massive chest. "Thank you for thinking of me."

"I always think of you," Daddy says. He strokes my back in a way he hasn't done since I was a little girl. "Now I need you to pay attention in lessons today, alright? Auntie Lye and I still have so much to teach you before your first Oksas."

"I don't want to go to the Oksas," I say, frowning up at him.

The Oksas is where women go to get married and dreams go to die.

"Little bird." Daddy's voice takes on a dangerous edge, a warning as he squeezes my shoulders and glares at me. "When the time comes, you will go. And you will behave yourself. Do you understand?"

I shrink inside myself, wishing I could disappear. Again, tears form, and again, I blink them away. "Yes, Daddy," I croak.

"Good. Because if I can't marry you off, then you're of no use to me."

He pushes me inside the palace and our lessons begin anew.

A CYCLONE of darkness swirls in front of me. Amethyst light blinks inside it like dots of starlight blipping into and out of existence. When the shadows clear and the light fades, my arms are wrapped around my sister, my face buried into her neck.

"Grow up, Ezrah. We all have to do things we don't like."

Aliyah shimmies out of my embrace, smoothing down the front of her golden bodice, checking her braided coronet for flyaway hairs. Gilded butterfly clips weave throughout the strands, blending almost seamlessly into the metallic locks. My sister's skin is a solid wall of gold, slicked with avendessa that gives it the same luster as her clips and hair. Standing still, she looks more like a regal statue than a person made from skin and bone.

"You're not listening to me," I hiss, wiping my oily, painted hands on the front of my red dress. I'm stained where I've touched her—stained where I haven't—but she can't see the layer of crimson soaked into the hem of my skirts; that's why Daddy and Lyenna made me wear them.

I step between Aliyah and her stupid, full-length

mirror, blocking her view. "My lessons with him aren't the same as yours. Daddy makes me . . . He . . ."

Tears spill down my cheeks.

"Oh, for the love of—" My sister rolls her eyes. It's the first time I've ever seen her break her regal composure. As if noticing the mistake, she works her face back into a neutral expression. "You're eighteen, not eight. It's unbecoming of you to behave this way."

I quickly wipe the tears away, but more come to replace them. My hands won't stop shaking. The scent of rust and decay stings my nose, clings to my outfit, but she either doesn't notice or doesn't care.

Pushing me aside, Aliyah fluffs her puffy, golden skirt then admires her reflection in the mirror. She's everything I'm not—thin and elegant, tall with high cheekbones and a straight nose that gives her this wise, bookish appearance. They say I'm the prettiest of Daddy's children, but what they mean is I look the most like a show horse—something for men to gawk at and parade around. Aliyah, on the other hand, is every bit a leader. Or at least, I thought she was.

"You have to help me," I say. "Please."

She twists her body into a pretzel to make sure the oil isn't smeared then applies more where my fingerprints have smudged into her arms. "Our father wouldn't treat you like a baby if you didn't act like one," Aliyah says. "If you want to sail with us next time, stop throwing tantrums every time he speaks about the Oksas. I became eligible at fourteen, you know?"

"That's not what this is about," I whisper, fisting skirts in my palms. "Why won't you listen?"

"Children collect seashells, Ezrah. Children call their fathers Daddy. You're a spoiled, petulant brat and—"

"I'm sorry I bothered you." Eyes stinging, I rush from her bedroom and into my own across the hall, then I slam the door behind me.

I rip the dress from my body, yanking at corset loops, pulling down sleeves. At some point, my lady's maid appears behind me, though I don't remember passing her in the hall or hearing her come in. Her gloved hands reach for my skirt and I jerk away.

"Don't fucking touch me!"

"Your Highness?" Her voice quivers. Her brown eyes widen with fear. "Are you alright?"

"Get out," I hiss.

She hesitates.

"I said get the fuck out of my room!"

The minute she's gone, I collapse to the floor and strip off what remains of my gown. Crimson stains the bottoms of my bare feet and the tips of my toes. When I close my eyes, I see the man's greasy, unwashed hair, his rotten prison garb, and a bloodied heart in the palm of my hand. I feel the organ pulse and squirm against my fingertips, watch the light leave his eyes as I—

No. Don't think about it.

Shaking my head, I swallow back mouthfuls of sticky saliva and wait for the nausea to pass. Then, I crawl toward the veranda.

My bedroom floor is filthy, covered in puddles of saltwater and layers of slushy sand. Hundreds of seashells lay scattered across it, hidden in the water and muck. I wince when they dig into my knees, curse when the bumpy-textured tiles turn my skin a glistening shade of rubies. I crawl anyway, using the pain to ground me.

At the far side of the room, humid air blows through an open pair of glass doors. It tangles in my hair, carrying with it the sweet scents of hibiscus and jasmine. I force myself to my feet and weave through the garden that hides my room from prying eyes, past the guards who stand watch outside it. Neither men speak to me, though I can feel a thousand questions on their tongues as I tiptoe naked into the chilly ocean and sink to my knees.

Normally, the water soothes me, but not today. Though the blood washes away, the ache inside my chest remains, and as I swim farther from shore, hiccupping sobs claw their way up my throat. Why was I made like this? Why not Aliyah, or Meera, or

Talyanna? What did I do to deserve this power—this curse?

I dive below the surface and scream. Bubbles pour from my lips, and tiny reef fishes swim far away from me, darting into mounds of purple coral, weaving through porous holes. I scream again, and hairline fractures appear in the reef. One of those fishes floats to the surface—dead. Scooping up fistfuls of sand, I squeeze my frustration; it's the man's heart that bursts.

"Come home, Ezrah."

"Be with us instead."

The waves swell around me, and something emerald green splashes to the surface. Giggles fill my ears. I swim toward the shimmery thing, but it's gone by the time I reach it, and the beach is nothing but a speck on the horizon.

Farther out, where the sand disappears and the coast becomes deep ocean, a pearly iridescence shines in the sunlight. More giggles.

"Join us."

Something brushes against my ankle. My stomach drops into my butt and it's all I can do not to panic—because panic is how sailors die. I scan the horizon, searching for someone close enough to help should I need it, but Daddy's ships are too far away, and I'm not dumb enough to chase down a fishing vessel. Whatever monsters lurk within the ocean are still safer to be around than a desperate man around a Varren girl.

Something sharp slides across my back, like a serrated blade or jagged fingernail. Goosebumps break out along every inch of my body.

A sapphire tentacle wraps around my wrist, tugging me below the waves. I inhale a lungful of saltwater, pulling at the creature, kicking my feet toward the surface. Their grip tightens. Another tentacle winds around my ankles, my thighs, pinning them together.

No, no, no.

I scream. I cough. Lungs burning, I scan the sand for a sharp seashell to stab the creature with.

Nothing.

I'm going to die here.

"Your Highness?"

The concerned voice comes out of nowhere. When I blink, I'm on the beach again, sitting in water up to my waist, clutching fistfuls of sand. My breaths come in ragged gasps. I look for the tentacles and find Asix instead. Asix—the youngest of my guards with skin as dark as widow lilies, long braided hair, and the kind of smile that could make a priestess blush.

He stands beside me in water up to his knees, his white uniform soaked, his saber switched for a plush golden towel.

"Are you alright?" he asks.

"I . . . I don't know."

My brows furrow. I drop the sand and peer up at him. Usually, Asix isn't afraid to meet my gaze, but today his face is downcast, his expression bashful. My cheeks flame when I realize why.

"Could you . . ." I swallow and cover my breasts with my arm. "Could you close your eyes for me?"

He obeys and turns his head toward the palace.

Grunting, I heft myself from the water then snatch the fuzzy towel out of his hands. Twisting it around myself, I tie a knot between my breasts before tapping him on the shoulder. To Asix's credit, his eyes remain on the sand as I loop my arm through his and allow him to escort me back to my chambers.

My guard's hands are gloved like all our servants are, and he's dressed in heavy layers to prevent our skin from accidentally touching. What I wouldn't give to peel off his justaucorps and hug skin that doesn't belong to Daddy or Aliyah. It's been months since another person held me in their arms, months since Tristan—

"It's getting late," Asix says, gesturing toward the sky. The sun is gone, the horizon a beautiful shade of cobalt. Silver moonlight turns the sand as white as snowfall, and the constellations glow overhead.

"You'll miss your rendezvous if you don't hurry,"

he adds, grinning at me. His teeth are bright against the backdrop, his dark eyes crinkled near the edges.

"My rendezvous?"

Asix grabs my shoulders and spins me toward the harbor. "She made port while you were swimming."

"What are you talking about?"

Near the docks, there's a dozen merchant vessels hoisting flags that bear the Kamaran and Laithe sigils and a pink carrack owned by Aliyah's most recent suitor. None of them hold even the slightest bit of interest to me.

Asix points deeper into the bay, and then I see it —the faint outline of the *Black Death.*

"Tristan!"

Squealing, I rush inside, dragging my guard along with me. In a matter of seconds, I'm in the closet, rummaging through outfits, shoving past row upon row of ornate gowns. The hangers clink together as I slide them down the racks.

Gold.

Gold.

Gold.

Gold again.

Green.

Pulling the dress free, I hold it up to my body and twirl. "What do you think, Asix?"

"I think if His Majesty catches you in that, your

ass will be bruised sapphire for a week. What in the nine hells did you do to it?"

"Cut off the sleeves. Ripped out the corseted bodice. Do you like it?"

He grunts.

I slide my fingers over the soft cashmere, admiring the handiwork anyway. Despite what he and Daddy might think, there's nothing immodest about it. Most of our commoners wear scorzy—thin cotton dresses with high slits, plunging necklines, and hand embroidered belts. They bind their breasts in simple tubes of cloth rather than corsets, leaving their figures unhidden. I'm not doing anything they wouldn't do.

"You can stop looking at me like that," I say. "It's too hot to dress in those stupid layers and I need to be able to breathe."

"You're Varren, Your Highness. There are expectations—"

"No one's going to see me."

"Besides Tristan," he grumbles.

"Besides Tristan."

Smiling, I withdraw a black woolen cape and matching headscarf then pilfer through my shoe collection for a pair of strappy sandals that go up to my knees. I'd prefer boots—Tristan made me do sprints the last time he came here—but Daddy controls all my purchases, all my clothes, and he'd never see me in something so unladylike.

"Let the record show," Asix says. He leans against the wall, facing the veranda as I dress. "I still think this is a horrible idea. If you get caught—"

"We won't get caught."

"If you get caught, gods know what Arrovin will do to him."

"You worry too much," I say, pulling the cape over my outfit, hiding as much glittering skin as possible. "Daddy is busy this week with Aliyah and Corvin. And even if he wasn't, he never checks on me."

Emerging from the closet, I clip my hair into a makeshift bun then wrap the scarf around my head and neck, giving myself a once-over in the reflection of my vanity. Good enough.

"He never checks on you because you're not allowed to leave, princess."

"I don't appreciate that tone," I say, crinkling my nose at him.

Asix levels his gaze. "I don't appreciate how cavalier you're being right now. Tristan is like family to me and—"

I wave him off and return to the garden, still dripping saltwater, still covered in sand. Asix follows me through vines of jasmine, past the other guard who gives us both scathing looks. To say Penna doesn't approve of our secret, late-night escapades would be a gross understatement, but my guards are far more loyal to each other than to any king.

As we reach the edge of the palace grounds, the rocky cove comes into view. "You can go now," I say. "I don't need a chaperone. I've made it here and back hundreds of times with you and Penna none the wiser."

"Yes, but—"

"Go. I'll see you in a few hours."

He mutters something under his breath but does as he's told, kicking up sand in the process.

I'm lucky Asix is the one who caught me with Tristan last time. Luckily, he found us before my father sent the entire army in search of me. Still, I miss the privacy of having the cove to myself. Now, when Tristan isn't here, Asix fights me till my lungs are blue about going this far unescorted, but the more my magic develops, the more I wonder who my escorts are protecting by keeping me on a leash —me or the Varronians.

A pair of arms wrap around my waist, interrupting my thoughts as they pull me close. All the tension drains from my body at the familiar scent of tobacco and spicy cologne, and despite everything— Daddy and Lyenna's lessons, the voices, my increasing loss of sanity—I can't fight back a smile.

"Did you miss me?" Tristan asks.

"More than you know."

AMETHYST LIGHT PULSES around me and suddenly, I'm lying in Tristan's arms, laughing while he feeds me moongrapes.

It pulses again.

He's balancing on a rock, singing a folk song from Laithe as I throw shells into the water.

A third pulse.

When the light clears, the neon tones have softened into morning sky. Yawning, I stumble back to the palace, wiping crust from my eyes, blinking away the heavy fog of sleep. Mist clouds the beach, turning my surroundings hazy gray. Besides the whooshing ocean and the gentle wind, the world is quiet. Dreamlike.

Cold sand squishes between my toes. I make footprints in it, only to watch the tides take them away.

> I know a lass,
> A maiden fair,
> Who took my dreams
> When I left her there

Along the coast.

Shoes in hand, I swing them as I sing. My words hitch when Daddy's palace appears in front of me. It's enormous, made from gold and white spires, lined by moonstone pathways, and filled with tropical plants from every island nation: red ginger, purple coneflower, orange elephant ears. It's the most beautiful palace in Ranada, but that doesn't make it any less of a prison.

I close my eyes and take a deep breath, ignoring the heaviness in my chest. One day, I won't return; I'll walk the other direction and never look back.

> She cursed my wife
> And sank my ship,
> Marooned me here
> Where I'm still adrift,
> Along the coast.

I've barely made it to the edge of the gardens when Asix pulls me behind a row of plants and pushes me against the wall.

"It's too early for this," I mumble, dropping my shoes. "Scold me later."

"The King is looking for you," he says, tone urgent. "I told him you left for the palace library. If you run and take the servants' route, you might beat him there."

Crap!

My eyes widen. No longer tired, I glance down at my dress and bite the inside of my cheek. Asix was right about Daddy; he'll spank me if he sees me in this. He'll do much worse if he doesn't see me at all.

I hesitate for only a second then bolt, sprinting around the palace to the kitchen entrances. The guards ignore me as I pass. They always do unless told otherwise. I'm not sure if it's the mythos that leaves them so afraid of my sisters and me—that as descendants of Eliah we could moontouch them, so they never see sunlight again—or if it's the fact that Daddy would hang them from the gallows if we claimed they so much as touched us. I guess it doesn't matter since it serves my purposes regardless.

The servants' area buzzes with chaos. Hot steam wafts from open ovens. Pots and pans clang against each other as the head chef barks orders to his crowd of waitstaff. In front of me, a small boy pours lumps of banana mash into muffin tins while his mother kneads dough into bread. Unable to touch me, they both bow their heads and clear a passage as I walk by.

"What's she doing in here?" the boy asks.

"Mind your business," his mother hisses. "It's not our place to question the motives of gods."

Gods.

Because that's what we are to these people. Yet I'm trapped here, forced to hide my body, to live separately from everyone else, including my sisters. It isn't fair.

"You could live with us instead."

Ignoring the voices, I make my way through the kitchen and down the hallway. As I pass, servants smoosh their bodies against the narrow corridors and offer up apologies when I brush into them. Daddy would have them hung if he learned of their closeness. Or worse.

My mind drifts to the bloody heart and bile rises up my gut again. I shove it down, ducking into the library just as Daddy's white suit appears in my peripheral vision. Hands shaking, I grab the first book I see and plop down onto a leather sofa, straightening my cloak as best I can.

The door whooshes open, and Daddy strolls inside, his pleated suit freshly pressed, his white hair combed into a fishtail. The heels of his golden loafers click across the marble tile as he approaches me, holding his hands behind his back. I do my best not to squirm but fail miserably.

"Do you know why I'm here, little bird?" he asks.

I swallow and shake my head.

"I'll give you a hint. The number is eleven."

Daddy drops his hands to his sides, revealing a leather whip with nine knotted tails protruding from the end. Serrated copper coils weave throughout the tails, and blue electricity fizzles down them.

Tears fill my eyes. "Daddy, please—"

He peers around the room, his gaze meeting each of the librarians, guards, and waitstaff. The main floor is nearly empty, but nobles linger on the second and third, their bodies leaned over the gilded railing, their expressions amused. Aliyah is among them, giving me her best saccharine smile. The little bitch.

"Leave us. Now," Daddy says. He doesn't yell, but he doesn't need to—his voice carries all the same, echoing between the frames of ancient bookshelves and gilded walls.

As they shuffle out, Daddy bends over me and strokes my cheek. "Have you thought about that number yet?"

I'm so scared, I can't talk, so I shake my head instead.

"Eleven is the number of men you exposed yourself to yesterday afternoon, when you left the palace naked."

"Oh." I bite my bottom lip and look anywhere but at him.

"Care to explain yourself?"

Sweat breaks out along my palms. I wipe them on the front of my cloak as I try to conjure up an explanation that will appease him—not the truth. Never the truth. Admitting how the lessons affected me would only make things worse. I'd disappoint Daddy, disgust him perhaps, and there'd be another lashing.

"Ezrah?" Lightning crackles in his irises and it takes all my willpower not to curl into a ball and cry.

"I wasn't thinking, Daddy."

"I know you weren't, but our actions have consequences, little bird."

Sighing, he lifts a lock of my hair and rubs it between his thumb and forefinger, sniffing it before letting it drop. "Eleven strikes and I guarantee next time, you'll think before you act."

He tightens his hold on the whip.

"No, Daddy. Please, I'll do anything." I grab the whip and a bolt of electricity travels down my spine. My muscles twitch and I convulse in pain, unable to release my grip.

"Two additional strikes for insubordination."

He yanks the tail from my hand. The serrated metal sticks to flesh, ripping it out in chunks. I yelp as golden blood pools onto my lap, as the electric current makes my muscles twitch. Even though his magic is gone, I can still feel it zapping through my chest, constricting it. I can't breathe. Can't think. Gasping, I cradle my injured hand, clutching it over my jittering heart.

"Now, undress."

I glance up at him through blurry eyes. "What?"

"You heard me. Undress and bend over the chair. If you didn't want me to see you naked then you shouldn't have let everybody else."

My cheeks flame. I can't expose myself to him. He can't be serious. "Daddy—"

He grabs my injured hand and drags me from the seat, grinding his thumb into the lump of raised flesh. I fall to my knees. Starbursts cloud my vision and chunks of acrid bile bubble up my throat, spewing onto white tile.

"Undress and bend over the chair."

With shaking hands, I wipe the sickness from my lips and unclasp the cape. It falls into a pile on the floor, revealing my sleeveless, layerless dress.

The lighting in Daddy's whip buzzes. His face twists into a deep frown. "Why do you insist on disobeying me? Do you think I enjoy these reprimands? Do you?!"

"No, Daddy." Tears spill down my cheeks. I don't know what's worse, his anger or his disappointment.

"It's alright," he says, lifting my chin. "After today, things will get easier for you, I promise. I should have used the whip a long time ago. I won't make this mistake again."

Daddy wraps his arms around me and I shake my head, begging—no, screaming—for him to stop when the sound of ripping fabric echoes in my ears. My tattered dress pools around my body, leaving me completely and utterly exposed. No underlace. No chemise.

My shame burns white-hot, worse than the pain in my hand. I try to shield my breasts with the ruined fabric, but Daddy rips it away.

"What will I do with you, walking around like that?" he tuts. "Bend over the chair. You won't like it if I have to put you there myself."

Resisting the urge to retrieve the fabric, I do as I'm told. Snot and tears stream down my face as I take up the position and close my eyes. His heels click against the floor. The tails of his whip graze my back as he puts his foot between my legs and knocks them apart.

"Daddy?"

"Eleven lashes for yesterday," he whispers, his breath moist against my skin. "Two for talking back. And fifteen for what you've done to that dress."

"Twenty-eight?" My voice quivers. "That'll kill me."

"I want you to count them out. If you stop, I stop. And then we start over. Understood?"

The whip cracks against my spine. I gasp, my fingernails clawing into velvet cushions as a wave of lightning pierces my heart. The smell of burnt flesh permeates the air. Heat licks across my body and my bladder empties itself, leaking down my thighs onto my bare feet. I try to clasp my legs together, to hide what I've done, but Daddy nudges them apart again.

"One," he says. He yanks his hand back and the serrated metal pulls skin.

"One."

Speaking is agony. Standing is worse. Blood spills from my back, turning the floor golden and sticky, and my legs twitch with the electrical current. I try to catch my breath when the next blow strikes.

Pain.

Blackness.

Daddy's voice.

"Two."

"Two," I squeak.

Another strike, this one between my legs, over my most intimate parts. I collapse into a puddle of my own blood and urine, unable to speak, unable to move as Daddy returns me to my feet and drapes me over the recliner.

It takes another three strikes before I get my voice back—one to my butt, another to my thighs, and the last to my feet. It takes another forty-seven before the punishment is complete.

CARTHINIA

PRESENT DAY

PRINCESS EZRAH VARREN

FORTRESS HEDRA, CENTRAL CARTHINIA

My eyes snap open at the sharp and sudden pain consuming my right hand. Yanking back, I find my wrist pinned under Malin's unforgiving grip.

"Hold still. I'm almost finished." The stool at my bedside creaks as he readjusts in it. Gauze in hand, Malin unwinds the spool around my cracked and bleeding knuckles, his brows furrowed in concentration. The soft glow of the lantern light gives his face an almost boyish appearance, even if it burns my eyes to hold them open.

"Are you . . ." My voice is hoarse. I cough to clear it and my whole head pounds as if it's been struck by a hammer. "Are you being nice to me?"

"No."

The gentleness in his touch says otherwise.

"Your hand looks like shit." Malin ties the gauze into a knot then checks its tightness. Satisfied, he sets my hand on the mattress and yawns.

Yellow light bounces off my skin. Sapphire and amethyst blotches peek out from beneath the bandages, glittering brighter than the rest of me. It's beautiful, if not a little bit morose.

I tilt my head to the side. "You don't like the way I bruise?"

"What?" Midstretch, a deep frown crosses his features, like I've said something offensive.

My brain is foggy. I replay the words but still can't make sense of his soured expression. Raising my hand, I hold it closer to the lantern and turn it over, examining the damage. "I bleed gold and bruise sapphire," I remind him. "My father demonstrated this for other suitors when they asked. I figured you . . ."

"You figured I what? Love mutilating women?" Malin's nose crinkles and he crosses his arms. "Pain can be pleasurable, Ezrah, but this . . . the lines on your back . . . What the fuck was Arrovin doing to you? What was he letting other people do to you?"

I don't answer.

"Where the fuck was your captain during all this? If he loved you so much, why wasn't he there?"

"He couldn't help me. My father would have—"

Malin's stool screeches as he rises from it. "He

chose not to help you, Ezrah. Just like he chose to turn you into a pleasure slave. The man never has and never will love you."

Tears leak past my eyelids, soaking into my pillowcase. Every insecurity I've ever had about him, about *us*, has finally been laid bare. But if Tristan didn't love me, then all of this—the past ten years of my life—has been for nothing.

Turning his back to me, Malin hunches over the bookshelf and grabs at items I can't see. Glasses clink together. Metal slides across polished white marble. When he returns, he's carrying a porcelain teacup filled with teal liquid. Fog swirls menacingly across the top of it.

"Drink," he says, pressing the cup into the palm of my hand, curling my fingers around it.

"Why?"

"Does it matter?"

I sniff it. The drink smells like nothing. It feels like nothing. For a second, my whole body turns tingly and numb. "If I drink it, what happens to me?"

"Not *if* you drink it, Ezrah. That implies you have a choice in the matter." He grabs my hand, lifting both it and the cup to my lips. "Drink."

I open my mouth. The liquid tastes like air. There's no form to it. No texture or temperature. Still, I shudder when the fog slides down my throat.

Sighing, Malin takes the cup from me then sets it on the bedside table.

"It's for your headache and your hand," he says. "Before I became what I am, I used to be a gifted healer. I've preserved some of that magic in potions and trinkets."

My brows pinch together. "Used to be? You're not a healer anymore?"

"Necromancy is the corrupted form of life and light magic. When I made my pact with Enen, it darkened my soul in an irrevocable way. I no longer have access to that part of me."

"Then why did you do it?" I know better than anyone what it feels like to lose access to magic. I can't imagine choosing that fate willingly.

"Because I stole your father's book and it showed me that Enen was the only way to get what I desired. To get you." He rakes his hands through his glossy curls, staring down at the mattress. The way the moonlight hits him, Malin doesn't look corrupted; he looks ethereal, like a phantom or a god. Pale white light bends around his naked body like his skin is made of starlight.

My tongue sticks to the roof of my too dry mouth. "You became a necromancer for me? I don't understand. I barely know you."

"I'll explain later," he says, walking to the other side of the mattress. "Not tonight."

I open my mouth to protest and his eyes darken.

"Not tonight, Ezrah."

My hands have a mind of their own. Rolling closer to him, my fingers trace along Malin's abdomen, feeling the thick grooves of his muscles. The man might be a king, but he's built like a soldier.

I don't know if it's the tannix or if it's me—I don't know which would be worse—but even after everything he's done to me, I still want him. The darkness calls to me almost as strongly as the ocean. It always has.

Before I can overthink it, I trace lower, like a good whore.

"Do you regret it?" I ask. "Corrupting your soul?"

"No."

When I reach Malin's cock, he puts his hand over mine, squeezing firmly but gently. "Not tonight. You're drunk and I'm exhausted. If it's alright with you, I'd rather sleep."

I open my mouth to protest—I'm not drunk, or at least, I'm not *that* drunk—but then I see the dark bags beneath his eyes, the way his shoulders slump. Nodding, I clasp Malin's hands in mine then guide him to the bed, pulling the sheets over our naked bodies, pressing my face into the warmth of his chest.

"You're not a spy, are you?" he asks.

Malin kisses my hair and pulls me closer, gently tracing the invisible lines on my back.

I take a deep, shuddering breath, suffocating under the weight of the blankets, the heat of my tears. "I want them dead as much as you do."

"I can arrange that. We'll kill them together—not just Arrovin and Lyenna, but everyone who's ever hurt you."

And what about you?

I don't voice the question aloud, but he answers anyway.

"I know I fucked up. I let my prejudice and anger get in the way, but I can be better."

I'm not sure that he can. I'm not sure that I want him to. I never asked Malin to treat me like a princess; I just didn't want to be treated like a whore. I wanted a chance to say yes and a choice to say no.

A thick ball of emotion wedges in my throat but I swallow it back down. I don't know if I can ever love a man like Malin Varuz, but I don't know that I can't either. So, I settle for the diplomatic answer.

"We'll see."

THE KARMASKUS SEA

PRESENT DAY

PRINCE LOWEN HADE

LOCATION UNKNOWN

My ankles are cuffed.
My hands are chained behind my back.
I'm standing, teetering really, a half foot away from the bow of Captain Tristan Fontaine's brigantine, *Daycrawler*.

My eyes adjust to the blinding brightness, assessing my surroundings as the skull-faced pirates remove the bag from my head. A crowd of armed men and women encircle me—that bitch *Livi* amongst them. Their uniforms blend into the oceany backdrop, the same shade of sky blue as the ship and its sails.

Camouflage. That's why their ships have been so difficult to detect and impossible to fight.

In my periphery, something moves across the skyline, then something else—another brigantine and a frigate. Wherever I am, I'm in the thick of Fontaine's armada, surrounded by equally invisible warships. Eyes weeping, I blink into the sunny sky and shoot off a quick prayer to Eliah. I've never been the religious type, but now seems as good a time as any to start. It doesn't take a genius to know Fontaine wouldn't let me see all of this if he had any plans on facilitating my release.

I'm as good as dead—a living ghost.

"Tell us where she is and we'll make it quick," promises a deep, booming voice. A familiar voice.

The crowd snickers. They part for a man who isn't Fontaine, though he's dressed in a captain's justaucorps and matching tricorn. Dark skin peeks through the top of his collar, exposing gilded tattoo ink that gleams in the sunlight—ink that was undoubtedly bled from my twin sister at Fontaine's command.

I bite back a snarl. Years of military training have taught me when it's best to talk or remain silent.

Heavy footfalls shake the deck as the captain—the *traitor*—grabs me by the back of my hair and yanks. "Tell us where she is, Lowen."

My Adam's apple bobs.

It can't be him. I'd rather it be anyone else.

The man's fingers have done this to me a hundred times before. They've pulled on my hair, dug purple bruises into my skin, fucked me hard and hot and messy with abandon. They know my body more intimately than anyone else, which makes his betrayal cut all the worse.

"Fuck you," I spit.

His other hand curls around my throat but doesn't press. Lowering his voice, he whispers something only I can hear. "Tell me where she is and I'll get you out of this mess. You have my word."

"Your word means shit, Asix. What the fuck are you doing here, slumming it with pirates?"

"Don't make me do this." Behind the gallon of face paint, I see a glint of something almost genuine, like he doesn't want to trample on my heart or pass my sister back to her rapist. Still, it's not enough to make me second-guess my loyalty to Arrovin or to double-cross Ezzy.

"I would rather die than let you assholes take her."

His lips draw into a thin line. That glimmer turns to darkness, his brown eyes hardening. Asix clamps down on my windpipe, sucking the air from my lungs.

"Pretty boy says we can go fuck ourselves," he shouts, turning to the others.

Blackness creases at the edges of my vision as he lifts me into the air. Feet flailing, lungs burning, I claw at his arms. I thrash and kick and choke, the chains jingling as my movements become frantic.

"Any suggestions for how to draw it out of him?"

The crowd bellows their responses, but I can't hear them over the blood rushing to my ears. My thrashes become jerks. My sweat-slick palms slide over Asix's fingers, pulling, prying, but they won't fucking budge.

"Don't do . . . thi—" My vision goes dark. My fingers slip from his, arms falling like deadweight to my sides. I smack the deck seconds before unconsciousness takes me.

"Wake up, pretty boy." Asix grips my face, squishing my cheeks between his oily hand. "That's it."

His long snake-like hair drags over my chest, tracing painful lines in my sunburnt skin. I'd rip it from his scalp if my hands weren't chained.

"One more chance," he says. "Tell me where Ezzy is."

I spit in his face.

Sighing, Asix wipes the thick glob of saliva from his eyes, smudging the skull paint in the process. "You did this to yourself. Remember that."

He yanks me to my feet, where a thick hemp rope

wraps around my ankles, connecting them to a pulley system at the other side of the deck. My arms are similarly tied, looped to a rusted mechanism that swings on a support beam near my face. Curling his arms beneath my biceps, Asix drags me to the side of the ship. The backs of my heels knock against the wood with each step.

"Allow me to explain what's about to happen," Asix says, stopping in front of the railing. "I'm going to toss you into the ocean, and Pen here is going to pull you back in."

He gestures to the man at the farthest pulley system. A crowd has gathered around him, their skull faces twisted into wicked sneers.

"You're going to dunk me." I roll my eyes. "I'm shaking in my boots."

Asix doesn't smile. "We're going to keelhaul you, Lowen. Pen and I will drag you under the ship from port to starboard. Then, you'll be given a second opportunity to comply. Should you refuse, it'll be from forward to stern next."

I thrash in my bindings. "Are you fucking insane? You'll kill me."

He lifts me over his shoulder, voice lowering again. "You'll want to turn your head to the side. Don't. If you do, it'll cost you an ear. Throw your head back and it'll save your nose."

"Asix, please, don't do this."

"Take a deep breath."

For a second, I'm weightless, freefalling, and then the rope on my legs goes taut, smashing me upside down against the hull. I groan, twisting in time to see the macabre display that Fontaine's ships are famous for. Hanging upside down, bound by their ankles, are the rest of my crew . . . or what remains of them.

My throat constricts.

Jace. Cameron. Samel. Kyde.

A dozen of my friends and half-brothers swing with the waves, slapping against the hull so hard their bones crack. Brain matter leaks from broken skulls. Missing eyes and half-eaten faces stare back at me, their lips frozen in pain. Nine years on conscription, and they're the only family I've ever known outside of Pria and Tarin.

Now they're bird food.

"I'll fucking gut them for this," I snarl, balling my hands into fists.

Jace's blank eyes stare back. A fly buzzes between us and lands on his pupil, rubbing its front legs together. It's the last thing I see before the ropes on either side of my body tighten, stretching me until I'm flush against the hull. Then, I'm moving, rubbing against smooth, wooden planks, lower and lower, until my head hits icy water. I instinctively draw breath, closing my eyes against the stinging salt.

Sharp barnacles slice into my cheek, cutting deep. I fight the urge to scream as the water consumes me, soaking into my white trousers.

The shells grow closer together, forming a solid, bumpy mat that's sharp enough to kill. They sink into my ear, tugging, ripping, as Pen drags me deeper beneath the ship.

Fuck.

FUCK!

I scream so hard, my lungs might burst, but the sound gets lost beneath the waves. Bitter water floods my mouth, choking me as the barnacles cut at my chest and legs, ribboning the fabric as well as my flesh.

Everything burns. Everything bleeds.

I open my eyes and through the hazy, stinging saltwater, and see nothing but crimson.

The rope keeps pulling, scraping, dragging me along the bottom of the ship. I swallow lungfuls of water as I tug on the bonds that hold me. They don't budge.

I'm going to die here.

By the time they're finished, I'm going to be nothing but a mangled lump of flesh. Like Jace. Like Cameron. Like Tarin.

They're gone.

My girls are gone. My crew is dead. What reason do I have to keep going?

I lose myself to the pain, letting my body go lax. This is what I deserve. I couldn't protect them, and the gods are making me suffer for it. Drifting in and out of consciousness, I barely register when I clear the bottom of the ship and start crawling up it toward the faint, rippling sunlight. Warm air hits my body as the water falls away, pouring back into the sea.

Coughing, I'm lifted onto the deck and thrown onto my belly at Asix's feet. Blood gushes from my wounds. Tears leak down the sides of my cheeks as I spit up ocean water. I don't have the strength to move.

"Kill me," I beg. The pain is so intense it feels like my innards are falling out—they very well might be.

"Tell me where Ezzy is," he says.

I shake my head. She's the only person I haven't failed yet.

"Tell me or it's port to stern. I will keelhaul you over and over again until you give me what I want. I'll stitch you up and send you back between runs if I have to."

My body trembles. The cutting. The slicing. It's too much. Tangy blood gushes down my nose and into my swollen mouth and raw throat. "Asix, please. She's my sister."

His expression is merciless, his arms crossed over

a thickly muscled chest. "Move him to the forecastle."

Pen forces me to my feet. A sharp, shrill noise exits my mouth as he digs his grubby fingers into my bleeding side. "Please! I can't!"

Bending, Asix takes my face between his hands and strokes his thumbs along my cheeks. "You have five seconds to tell me where she is or I toss you over."

I shake my head, tears dripping onto the baby-blue deck. I can't go back. I just can't . . . not even for Ezzy.

"She's in Carthinia with Malin Varuz."

EPILOGUE

CAPTAIN TRISTAN FONTAINE

> I'm coming for you, Ezzy.
> I'm bringing you home. —T

CONNECT

If you liked this story, please consider reviewing it on Amazon or Goodreads.

For updates on new stories, you can sign up for Loren Huxley's newsletter at lorenhuxley.com or follow her on Instagram @lorenhuxleybooks.

Thank you so much for reading!

ACKNOWLEDGMENTS

I would like to give a big thank you to all my critique partners who made this novel possible. I couldn't have done it without you Ali Breshears, Billie Grey, Kaela Woodruff, P.C. Nottingham, Nic Scrim, Ashley G., Jenni Tayla, Megan M., and Wes Ellis. I'd also like to give a big shout out to my mom, who knows exactly what kind of novels I write and still asks about them. I'd also like to thank my husband who has spent many late nights helping me plot and scheme with my characters.

I am truly blessed to have such an amazing support group!

NEXT IN THE SERIES: SEAS OF MALICE

SNEAK PEEK

1. ASIX

PORT ELIERA, NORTHERN KAMARAN

TRISTAN DRAPES HIS HEAVY COAT over my shoulders, then breathes warmth into his palms. No one in the city notices us—two boys hiding in the piss-soaked alleyway, huddled together for warmth. They never notice us, even when we beg.

Teeth chattering, I try to return the coat to Tristan, but he refuses. "You need it more than I do."

It isn't true. We're both in rags, both rail thin and swollen and on the verge of frostbite. The pins and needles streaking through my fingertips are the first thing they've felt in hours. I should put up a bigger fight, demand he take the coat back, but I don't. I pull it tighter instead, basking in the delicious warmth.

Just a few more minutes, then I'll insist.

It sounds like a lie, even to my own ears.

1. ASIX

Tristan's reefer jacket is made of dark, luxurious wool with golden buttons down the front that shine brighter than anything I've ever owned. He doesn't speak about how he got it, and I know better than to ask. Kids like us only acquire finery in three ways— murder, theft, or prostitution— and there's a suspicious rust-stained blob on the inside.

"Nabbed this in the mines today," Tristan says. He reaches into his dusty trouser pockets and procures a jagged blue crystal the size of my fist—*kamaran gypsis*, the country's namesake. Our nobles use it to dye their fabrics, and export is forbidden. He tosses the piece to me, and I catch it in trembling palms.

"Are you crazy? If they catch you with this—"

"Then what? They kill me? I'm dead anyway." Tristan coughs, and flecks of blood spray the gray cobble. Pneumonia or miner's lung, I can't tell— either one's a death sentence without the proper medicine, which we'll never be able to afford. "That stone's your ticket out of here."

I flip the kamaran gypsis in my hands. When the sunlight catches it, it'll turn sky blue, but the sun hasn't shown for weeks now. Underneath the cloudy gray sky, the crystal is as foggy as smoke. "How much do you think it's worth?" I ask, passing it back to him.

"If you can get it out of port? Enough to buy one of those boats." He points down the alleyway, past the main road where fishing vessels bob in the harbor. Sheets of ice blanket the gray ocean, but an icebreaker ship powers through them, creating large enough fissures for the smaller boats to travel through. Black smoke billows from the top of the icebreaker, polluting the sky.

Tristan shoves the kamaran gypsis into his coat pocket, then sinks onto the ground beside me. When our stomachs growl, I fish through my knapsack and procure a loaf of stale bread that I stole from the pigpens earlier this morning. Mud and mold darken the edges, but the pit in my stomach doesn't care. I rip the bread in half, offering the bigger portion to Tristan, but he refuses, shoving it back into my palm.

"You need your strength," he says. His voice is scratchy from puberty, wheezy from the mines.

"What about you?"

Tristan doesn't look at me. And then I realize what he said—the stone's *my* ticket out of here, not his, not ours. His skin is as pale as the icy waters and dark circles rim his sea-green eyes. The winter's lasted too long, the food's too scarce, and he's already given up.

"When spring comes, you sell everything I own. It should be enough to buy you passage south if you volunteer as a shiphand. Then, find a buyer for that

1. ASIX

stone." He coughs until I think his lungs might fall out.

"Tristan—"

"I'm not going to survive the winter, Asix. But you can still get out of here."

My eyes blur. Wiping them, I force myself to chew the stale bread. It's mostly tasteless, except for the dirty parts, but I've had worse. Slowly, the gnawing hunger fades to a dull ache. I push it from my mind as we sit in silence.

It's been Tristan and me for as long as I can remember. Greenpox took my parents before I could walk, and he's cared for me ever since. Even if I were old enough to be a shiphand—which I'm not—I couldn't leave him. Not after everything he's done for me.

Near the docks, the buzzing crowds disperse, fishermen and shoppers heading home for the night. Footsteps fade to a trickle as the gray skies give way to black. It's too cloudy to see the moonlight, too cold for even the jacket to insulate. Our breaths come in white puffs, my lungs aching with the air's icy sharpness. Tristan rubs his hands over his shirt sleeves, trying to generate friction.

Bracing myself, I pull the coat off, spreading it across us like a blanket before he has a chance to say no. The temperature of his skin jolts me, but I force my body closer until we're the same level of barely warm.

Howling wind rushes through the alleyway, and Tristan blows out a shaky breath. The air changes course, striking the buildings instead. *Wind magic.*

"We could go to the palace," I suggest. "They're always looking for mages."

"It's barely a parlor trick," he mumbles.

"You could train it."

Closing his eyes, Tristan leans his head against the stonework and greasy blond hair falls over his face. "I don't want to train it. None of the kings let their mages leave. If it's all the same, I'd rather live and die a free man on my own terms."

End of discussion.

I'll have to try again later, but for now, I let it drop. Talking takes too much energy, which neither of us has. Curling into him, I close my eyes and fall asleep, dreaming of a better tomorrow.

I wake to the sound of a flintlock pistol cocking and Tristan's shoulders tensing beside mine.

"Don't shoot," Tristan says, raising his hands. The

1. ASIX

jacket slips off us, and the icy wind slaps my skin, jolting me to alertness.

Standing in front of us is an armed guard dressed in a royal-blue military uniform. His curly hair is cropped short, and his skin—like mine—is so dark he blends into the night. A brass pistol gleams in his hand. "Hand it over, you little shit."

Tristan's jaw flexes. "I don't know what you're talking about."

The guard bends, pressing his gun to Tristan's temple. Their eyes lock. "Don't play games with me, *boy*. The foreman watched you take it."

Strange images flicker in my mind, like I'm watching them through a stereoscope in fast motion.

Tristan retrieves the kamaran gypsis from his coat pocket and passes it to the guard. The guard shoots anyway.

The vision changes.

Tristan spits in the guard's face. Grabbing my hand, he pulls me down the alleyway and the gun explodes, hitting Tristan in the knee.

Another set of images.

I slap the gun away from the guard. We scramble to break free, and ... nothing.

Before I can see what happens next, the world returns to normal and time resumes. In my periphery, Tristan slips his hand into his coat pocket—that

1. ASIX

black stone shining like obsidian. He's about to hand it over, and now I know what'll happen if he does. *How* I know is the confusing part. But I can think about that later, when our lives aren't on the line.

On reflex, I smack the guard's hand, and the pistol flies from it, skidding down the darkened corridor. Adrenaline sends my heart pumping like a piston. "Run!"

Tristan and I scrabble to our feet, taking off into a sprint down the slippery ice. My worn soles threaten to send me toppling. The coat nearly slips from my fist. But I hold on and keep running until each breath splinters my lungs. The guard's footfalls land heavy behind us as we weave through the port, jumping over cargo crates, ducking between shipping containers and sailors' brothels. Slowing down means getting caught, and getting caught means dying.

As the guard nears us—so close his hot breath grazes my neck—Tristan peers over his shoulder and blows. The winter wind coalesces behind him, shooting toward the guard as if it were a physical weapon. He slides, collapsing into the side of a brick building.

"Hey—you there!" Up ahead, another guard overhears the commotion and leaves his post at the dock's end. The first guard groans, limping back to

1. ASIX

his feet, and within moments they're coming after us from both directions.

"This way." Palm sweaty, Tristan pulls me past the dockyards into the noblemen's district. I grimace, my head swiveling as I take in the large, columned houses, the blue bricked road tiles dyed with *kamaran gypsis*, and the kerosene lanterns that brightly illuminate the street. I know as well as he that they post guards here at the end of every block —that we need papers and pedigrees to even step foot in this place.

"Tristan, we can't be here," I say through heaving breaths.

But he ignores me, squeezing us between gated houses and manicured gardens that are green even in the winter. Red spiceberries and winter hedges fill the air with heat, like cinnamon and chili powder. And it makes my nose itch. We duck between a row of hedges, toward a wrought-iron fence covered in ice and snow.

In front of us stands the most beautiful house I've ever seen—a wooden palace, painted a vibrant Kamaran blue to match the road tiles, with white shutters accented in gold. A garden surrounds the building from all sides, filled with winter hedges and spiceberries like the others, but also with lilac tear-reeds, red and yellow cross-flowers, and ice-blue sedges. Golden light spills from several lanterns

1. ASIX

around it, but especially along the blue-tiled path leading from the front gate to the entryway.

Tristan unhooks the gate—unlocked because who would be dumb enough to trespass here—and pads onto the bricks.

"Tristan, what are you doing?" I hiss, pulling my hand from his.

He gestures for me to follow, and I peer over my shoulder, but the guards—at least for now—aren't tailing us. There's stealing from the mines, but then there's this. Getting caught here is the type of thing that lands people in the king's prison—wherever *here* is.

But he seems to know exactly where he's going. Tristan turns off the pathway, disappearing behind a wall of plants, and I groan, following behind him because that's better than being stuck out here alone. At the darkest part of the estate, crowded in by yard tools and empty animal cages, sits a small white shed with a little bronze key strung up around the door handle.

Unfurling it, Tristan unlocks the door and pulls me in.

There's nothing inside—no tools, no gardening equipment, no animal feed, nothing that would belong inside a shed. Groaning, he thuds to the floor and pats the space beside him.

"Where are we, Tristan?"

1. ASIX

"My mother's house," he says, wiping the sweat from his brow.

"I thought she was dead. I thought you were an orphan like me." *To think we've been living on the streets all this time, when we could have been—*

"I know what you're thinking. And you're wrong." Tristan leans his head against the wall and exhales. *But I need more than that for an explanation.*

I tug the jacket back on and fold my arms over my chest. "So, you're not a runaway nobleman?"

He snorts. "Do you think anyone would voluntarily *choose* to live on the streets? When we met, I told you my parents were gone, and that's the truth. My father is a criminal, serving out a life sentence for stealing from a baron. And my mother—if you can call her that—is remarried to *this* prick. Sometimes when I'm desperate enough, I come here and beg for scraps. When he's not home, sometimes she helps me. But the last time . . ." Tristan shudders. "The last time Duke Ryndell beat me bloody and said if I ever returned, he'd kill me."

I remember that night—tending to his wounds. I had always assumed it was a mugging.

"Why are we here then?"

He shrugs. "Because we have nowhere else to go. We'll leave in the morning once the guards are done searching."

I. ASIX

"You'll leave now," a man's voice booms from outside the shed, and Tristan stiffens, his face turning ghost white. A moment later, the shed's door swings open and a nobleman comes through—broad shoulders, long black hair, and a sparrow-like nose. His reefer jacket is identical to the one I'm wearing. Behind him, a woman pads barefoot in the snow, a baby on her hip. A knitted coral shawl covers her poor excuse for a nightgown, slipping off her shoulders as she walks.

She tugs at the man's jacket, the wind blowing long blonde hair into her face. Her eyes are the same shade of green as Tristan's. "Please, Ryn. Don't do this."

Duke Ryndell jerks free of her touch, glaring down at Tristan and me like we're subhuman. "I warned you never to come back," he spits. And then he turns that venom on the woman. "Did you give that bastard my coat?"

The woman flinches. I notice now, the dark circles beneath her eyes, the split in her lip. "He's my son," she whispers.

"He's nothing." Ryndell yanks the coat off me faster than I can blink, and the winter wind stabs at my flesh. I watch the way the fabric dips in his arms —weighted down by the *kamaran gypsis*—and my entire body goes rigid. His meaty fingers delve into those pockets and a moment later, the glittering stone rests in his hand. "You filthy little thieves. You're no better than your peasant father. Perhaps it's time you joined him."

The door slams shut.

A hammer and nails pound against the shed outside, trapping us in. "You can wait here until the guards arrive, and then you can answer to the king."

ALSO BY LOREN HUXLEY

THE SEAS OF PARADISE SERIES

Paradise Entombed (Seas of Paradise Book One)

Seas of Malice (Seas of Paradise Book Two)

THEY CALL ME BLUE TRILOGY

They Call Me Blue (Book One)

ABOUT THE AUTHOR

Loren Huxley is a full-time author who loves all things dark—dark fantasy, dark romance, dark chocolate (you get the point!). By seventh grade, she was listening to heavy metal, playing RPGs with her older siblings, and writing horror-themed short stories. By high school, she was sneaking dark romances from her aunt's favorite bookshelves. When Loren isn't writing something brutal, she's playing tabletop games with her husband or cuddling with her two giant dogs.

www.ingramcontent.com/pod-product-compliance
Lightning Source LLC
LaVergne TN
LVHW040131080526
838202LV00042B/2867